THE GIRL IN KELLERS WAY

Megan Goldin worked as a foreign correspondent for the ABC and Reuters in Asia and the Middle East where she covered war zones and wrote about war, peace and international terrorism.

After she had her third child, she returned to her hometown of Melbourne to raise her three sons and write fiction, often while waiting for her children at their sports training sessions. *The Girl in Kellers Way* is Megan Goldin's debut novel.

THE GIRL IN KELLERS WAY

MEGAN GOLDIN

MICHAEL JOSEPH
an imprint of
PENGUIN BOOKS

MICHAEL JOSEPH

UK | USA | Canada | Ireland | Australia
India | New Zealand | South Africa | China

Penguin Books is part of the Penguin Random House group of companies
whose addresses can be found at global.penguinrandomhouse.com.

 Penguin
Random House
Australia

First published by Penguin Random House Australia Pty Ltd, 2017

1 3 5 7 9 10 8 6 4 2

Text copyright © Megan Goldin, 2017

The moral right of the author has been asserted.

Cover design by Adam Laszczuk © Penguin Random House Australia Pty Ltd
Text design by Samantha Jayaweera © Penguin Random House Australia Pty Ltd
Cover photographs courtesy Shutterstock.com
Typeset in Adobe Garamond by Samantha Jayaweera, Penguin Random House Australia Pty Ltd
Colour separation by Splitting Image Colour Studio, Clayton, Victoria
Printed and bound in Australia by Griffin Press, an accredited ISO AS/NZS 14001
Environmental Management Systems printer.

National Library of Australia
Cataloguing-in-Publication data:

Goldin, Megan, author
The girl in Kellers Way / Megan Goldin
9780143785446 (paperback)

Detective and mystery stories.
Noir fiction.
Suspense fiction.

penguin.com.au

MIX
Paper from
responsible sources
FSC
www.fsc.org   FSC® C009448

For my sons, whose boundless enthusiasm for my whimsical bedtime stories encouraged me to venture into the world of imagination.

The truth is rarely pure and never simple.

OSCAR WILDE

CHAPTER ONE

Julie

If you go by the calendar, it's already spring. Yet winter hovers over us in a perpetual chill. They say it was the coldest winter in years. To be honest I don't remember much of it. The season went by in a haze of pills and numbness.

I'm afraid to think what would have become of me if I hadn't stumbled across my running shoes packed away in a shoebox in the back shelf of my closet. They reminded me that I'm better than this; that I'm a survivor. I put them on and went running for the first time in months. I've jogged every day since.

Even this morning I run, though it's drizzling and I'm exhausted. Running is the only way I know to ease the dread that has gnawed at me ever since Matt and I argued last night. It was a vicious, barb-filled fight that made me feel our marriage was teetering on the edge of a precipice. When I finally fell asleep my dreams were strange and unsettling, permeated by lashing wind and rain crackling on the slate driveway. I woke feeling bereft.

The morning routine began the moment I opened my eyes.

It was typically frantic. Alice threw a minor tantrum because we were out of her favourite cereal. Matt hastily cooked scrambled eggs with toast to placate her. I plaited her dark hair while she wriggled restlessly in front of the hall mirror. We both ransacked the house looking for the seashell Alice insisted on taking to show-and-tell. Despite the chaos, the atmosphere was icy. Matt and I didn't exchange a single word.

When I finally got Alice in the car to drive her to school, the storm from overnight returned. Rain flicked onto the windshield in an endless stream, taunting me as I drove the familiar route, past our local shopping strip lined with cafes and stores selling useless designer novelties. I watched our plastic toy-land town pass by through the whir of windshield wipers and thought to myself: if only the blemishes in my life could be erased so easily. I turned on the radio. The music didn't help. I couldn't stop thinking about last night's argument.

It began over dinner. Matt told me over the main course, in the same expressionless tone he uses when he asks me to pass the salt, that I'm not invited to Laura's memorial dinner. He tried to let me off gently by making it sound as if he was doing me a favour. How boring it would be to sit through all those longwinded speeches. How the evening would run late, and how my medication would make me drowsy. And then he pulled the Alice card. 'Darling,' he said. 'Someone needs to stay with Alice. She isn't comfortable yet with the new babysitter.'

I couldn't believe it. I still can't. Does he have so little regard for my intelligence that he thinks I don't know why I'm banished? Oh, I know alright. Matt can hardly play the grieving widower when I'm sitting next to him at the head table, clapping politely as scholarships are awarded in honour of his first wife. Dear Laura, who was in his bed and in his heart first. And there she will remain for eternity. Laura will never age, never get fat, never grow wrinkles, never disappoint him in the ways that I have done. They talk about her in superlatives, even after all these years. Me, they barely notice.

'That's just great, Matt,' I said, trying to make a joke of it. 'I never realised that I was your skeleton in a closet. The inconvenient second wife. Hidden from public view.'

'Don't be crass, Julie,' he fired back. 'You hate these functions. If I'd asked you to come then you'd have made up an excuse to get out of it. Isn't that how it works with you, Julie? One excuse after the next.'

'You could have asked me before you made a decision on my behalf. I have the right to make a choice.' I ran upstairs and buried my tears in the quilt covering our bed. Deep down I knew that Matt was right. I wouldn't have gone. I rarely socialise these days.

They say running is a loner's sport. I'm a natural long-distance runner in both build and temperament. I'm at my happiest when I'm running alone into wind that roars into my ears and drowns out everything.

Of all the routes I take, Kellers Way is my favourite, with its steep hills and deep silences. I don't care what anyone says, no gym equipment can replicate the sense of freedom you get from running through a forest. Not even the top-of-the-range treadmill that Matt gave me two birthdays ago. It sits in the downstairs spare room collecting dust. I've only used the treadmill twice, both times when blizzards hit and we were housebound.

Matt doesn't like me running on the streets. He doesn't say why, but I know well enough. We live in the shadow of Laura's tragedy. He wants me to exercise at home, or to use the platinum membership he bought me at the fitness club.

Why can't he see that it's all fake? The effervescent step instructor who can't possibly be that happy; the personal trainer flirting shamelessly with his clients for bigger tips; the stay-at-home moms surreptitiously measuring thigh gap while they exercise. Those women judge and covet at the same time.

After class, they sip vegetable juice through clear straws at the health-club bar with the giggly excitement of schoolgirls getting drunk on homemade cocktails. I can't believe I used to join them, drinking my own vitamin shake like some pathetic sorority pledge desperately trying to fit in. And failing miserably.

These days, I prefer running alone, with the cold air slapping my cheeks until they sting and rain hitting me until I'm soaked through. Today the morning air is so frosty that my breath leaves loops of mist hanging before me like strange apparitions. They shatter as I run through them.

I peel off the main road and descend into Kellers Way. The rain has eased to a light drizzle. I run until a deafening hum blocks out everything, even the excruciating pain that runs through me. I hear nothing for the longest time until loud gasps rip through the daze that has enveloped me. It takes a moment for me to realise the wheezing is coming from me. I'm struggling to breathe. I clumsily remove my asthma spray from my pocket and inhale until the tightness in my chest recedes.

Behind me, twigs snap sharply. I whirl around. I am surrounded by trees as far as the eye can see, most still stripped of leaves. Then I see it. The soft eyes of a deer stare into mine until a flash of terror passes across them. The doe looks at me almost accusingly before running off.

When I get to the university, Matt's lecture is in full swing. Everyone listens with rapt attention. I've always admired the way

Matt effortlessly controls a room. The navy shirt he wears with the sleeves rolled up to his elbows, and the hint of dark stubble on his jaw, makes him look more like a revolutionary plotting insurrection than a psychology professor.

I sit anonymously in the shadows and watch his fangirl students cross and uncross their legs as they move restlessly in their seats, listening to the rich tones of his voice. I see the hunger in their mascaraed eyes.

I've read comments about Matt on online college forums that made me blush. The things these girls have said and thought about my husband. He pretends not to notice the array of pastel panties that tease him from under their skirts.

'Impulse.' Matt writes the word on the whiteboard with a red marker pen. He underlines it twice.

'We all have urges. Some urges we share with other animals. Hunger, for example. One of our most primitive urges. Other urges are more sophisticated. They reflect the human condition. The urge for power. The urge for ownership, or success. Or for recognition.' He pauses.

'If everyone in this room were to give in to their urges right now there would be chaos. Mayhem.' He pauses until the uncomfortable laughter subsides. 'Resisting urges, resisting desires is what sets us apart from our primate cousins. It's what makes us human. It's what, in fact, makes us civilised.' Matt waits with his arms crossed until the crackle of anticipation is the only sound in the auditorium. His students strain to hear his next sentence.

'The ability to resist the temptation of an immediate reward and instead wait for a better reward later has been shown to result in greater success. Higher SAT scores. Better professions. Higher income. The question is why people who are able to delay gratifying their urges are more successful. Anyone?'

Someone sitting near the back puts up his hand. 'It's a sign of self-control,' he says.

'That's right. Self-control. We exercise it all the time.' Matt pauses. 'We resist desires every waking hour of our lives. Chocolate, cigarettes, coffee.' He pauses. 'Sex.'

He lingers on the word as he looks directly at a girl with long black hair swept behind her shoulders. I inhale sharply. The resemblance is uncanny. No wonder Matt can't keep his eyes off her. Of all the students he's decided to fuck this term, it has to be the one who looks like Laura.

CHAPTER TWO

Mel

We get a noticeable spike in murder cases in early spring. In winter the killings drop off suddenly and then rise again slowly to reach a peak in high summer when the heat is at its most stifling and tempers are explosive.

Some say the annual rise in homicides in the spring is caused by the changes to sleep patterns from the switch to Daylight Saving Time. The truth is more mundane. Melting snow reveals secrets buried over winter. Old bones mainly. Pale and brittle. They peek through muddy soil to be found by hikers, who inevitably assume the remains are human. Occasionally they're right. Mostly the finds are animal bones, often roadkill swept to the side and buried in winter snow. We spend an awful lot of time chasing old bones in the spring.

The Kellers Way victim would never have been found if it hadn't been for the worst springtime storms in two decades. We'd had three days of rain so bad there was minor flooding in the low-lying parts of town. Several forest roads were closed due to damaged trees in danger of toppling. One of those roads was Kellers Way.

'We need you to head over to the national park, Mel.' The dispatcher's voice echoed through the kitchen from my cellphone's speaker, drowning out the sizzling of the eggs I was frying for my kids before they headed to school. 'We've found a body in a clearing near the road there.'

When I reached the entrance of Kellers Way I skirted my car around a 'road closed' sign. Loose gravel crunched as I steered through a series of hairpin bends, making my way towards the strobed lights of emergency vehicles somewhere on the road ahead.

Our forensics specialist had preceded me. Carl's all too familiar grey head was bent over the crime scene, which was cordoned off by yellow tape. On the far side was a shovel and a neat pile of topsoil that had been dug from a hole in the ground that Carl had lined with white plastic sheets.

'Hey Carl.' My voice cut through the quiet. Carl's head immediately shot up.

'Sorry,' he said, standing up. 'I started without you.' His silver moustache drooped, mimicking the bleak set of his mouth.

'What have you found?'

'Suit up and I'll show you.' He tossed me a crime scene pack and waited with his arms folded as I pulled on a disposable set of plastic overalls. I slipped my shoes into plastic covers and worked my hands into blue rubber gloves.

The sickly smell of death wafted towards me. I put on the paper mask and pulled the white hood over my head so that I was a pale face in a mass of white plastic. I scooted under the crime scene tape.

I walked in Carl's footsteps as he slowly moved towards the body. There's nothing worse than having to rule out dozens of tread marks from cops and medics who have polluted a crime scene by strolling all over the place like they're on a family picnic.

The beam of Carl's torch hit a body lying under a tree, partly covered by soil. I looked at the gnarled branches and the imposing trunk and thought, If only trees could talk.

'The forestry folk were cutting down the trees along the road that were damaged in the storms. One of the branches they cut landed near here. When the crew came to remove it they found the victim's leg, partially exposed by rain.'

'What do you know so far?' I squatted next to Carl.

'The victim is most likely an adult female,' he said. 'Whoever buried her here did not expect her to be found.'

I ran my torch along the uneven bark of the thick tree trunk looking for initials or any other mark the killer might have cut into the tree.

'Carl, I'd like impressions of the tree trunk. The killer might have left a carving in the bark to mark the burial site.'

I returned my attention to the body. Disintegrating pieces of fabric indicated the victim had worn black pants. There was a thick black leather boot on the exposed foot.

'Have a look at this,' said Carl, dusting off dirt with a brush until a hand emerged with polished nails. It was a sophisticated shade, classy. Not the sort of garish nail polish shade you'd see on street girls or strippers. On the wrist was a watch with a stylish, razor-thin face. It was misted over, though not enough to prevent me from seeing that it had stopped working at 2.44.

The victim had money and taste. The two don't always go together. This wasn't a runaway or a callgirl whose disappearance might not have been reported to police. This victim was somebody whose absence would quickly be noticed.

'How much longer until we can get the body out of here and start working on identification?' I asked.

Carl shrugged. 'We'll probably get the body out by nightfall. Otherwise we'll bring in spotlights and work the scene into the night. If we run out of time we'll come back tomorrow to bag the topsoil around the grave and bring it to the lab.'

That was standard in these cases. The killer might have dropped something while he was burying the victim. Back when I worked cases up in New York we once found a hotel room key near a body found in a dumpster. It led us straight to the killer. He was fast asleep in his hotel bed, oblivious to the fact that he'd dropped his spare key card at the murder scene.

'Let me know when the body is at the morgue,' I told Carl as I bent under the crime scene tape. 'There's not much I can do until the autopsy.'

That's the thing about autopsies. They can make or break a case. When I first moved here four years ago I was called to a murder scene at a house on the outskirts of town. The victim lay on the ground under her backyard laundry line with her head bashed in. Blood splatter stained a white bedsheet she'd been pegging out when she was killed. We thought her ex-husband was good for it. He'd been drinking the night she died. Couldn't remember a damn thing about what he'd done or where he'd been.

Then the lab results came in. Microscopic fibres removed from the victim's wound turned out to be from the talon feathers of a horned owl. The victim was killed by blunt force trauma alright, but not the type we'd thought. An owl hit her from behind and knocked her to the ground, where she died of a brain haemorrhage. The owl was probably protecting its young, as they do in the spring.

The case would have been forgettable except as a dinner party anecdote if there hadn't been a life lesson in that investigation.

The crystal owl paperweight that glints on my desk as I walk into the squad room each morning is a reminder of the one lesson no cop should ever forget: sometimes you have to look beyond the obvious to get to the truth.

That was never more true than with the Kellers Way case.

CHAPTER THREE

Julie

No matter how much I try, I can't stop thinking of the smug expression on that bitch's flawless face as Matt flirted with her during yesterday's lecture. Every detail runs through my mind in an endless loop: the way she self-consciously flicked her dark hair as Matt looked in her direction, the secret, self-satisfied smile on her pretty lips as she took notes, the faint blush on her fresh, young cheeks as she walked past him after the lecture. Most of all, I remember the thinly veiled hunger in Matt's eyes as he turned to watch her leave. I knew that look well. It was the same look he once gave me.

As if to rub salt into my wounds, he came home late last night. No explanation. I was in bed with the lights out when he slid in next to me. I could swear he smelled faintly of another woman. I pretended to be asleep when he pulled me to him, and when he ran his fingers over my breasts, and even when he slid his hand between my thighs. I held out for as long as I could. I am tired of sharing him. But Matt is nothing if not persistent when he wants something. I gave up the pretence of sleep and turned to him.

I wipe away a tear and pull my jacket hood over my dark-blond hair as I run downhill. The drone of a mower on an anonymous lawn is the only sign that I'm not alone in this pretentious street of ours where the neighbours don't even know one another's names. Where each morning driveway gates are locked and burglar alarms set, and bored, neglected dogs bark to each other across backyard fences. Where children pedal bikes up and down the street after school in a desperate bid to escape their regimented suburban lives.

I've lived in this leafy neighbourhood of lavish homes and manicured lawns for almost five years and I can say with confidence that it's all spun sugar. It's perfect from a distance. When you finally taste it, it's cloying and unsatisfying.

I turn a corner into an arterial road. Cars pass in blurs of washed out metallic hues. Their engines soothe and frighten. I count to myself as I turn another corner. When I reach twenty, I start again. I focus on my breathing, my stride, the pump of my arms. I inhale and exhale in audible bursts.

Two blocks later, a courier van pulls over right in front of me. The driver jumps out and opens the sliding door as I pass. Further down, a woman leading three yapping mixed-breed dogs walks as if in slow motion. She smiles, I nod. And then she's gone.

When I've passed all the houses and I'm on the edge of the forest, I turn down Kellers Way. It's rare to see cars along this narrow, mountainous stretch. There are faster roads. More convenient routes. As it happens, a car passes me on the road today. Its tyres grate against the asphalt. Its engine whines as it overtakes me.

I sprint until my throat burns and my legs feel like they're about to buckle. When I reach the bottom of the steepest hill, I drink from my water bottle at my usual stopping point, under the branches of a poplar tree. It's the only one of its kind along this strip of forest.

I tighten my shoelaces with fingers stiff from cold. I'm about to run up the last hill, to the road leading to the university, when I hear a rumble. Like rolling thunder. It's loud enough to scare a flock of blue jays out of a tree. I look up to see the birds flap their wings to escape.

A car emerges from around the bend. It's driving too fast for such a narrow, winding road. I wait for it to brake. It doesn't slow down. It accelerates and veers towards me.

———————

Is this what it feels like to be dead? I lie on the ground and watch the sun's rays creep around the clouds in an ungodly halo. I vaguely remember the crack of my skull after I dived over an embankment to escape the path of the car hurtling towards me.

My whole body aches when I get up. My head throbs. Yet I don't care about the pain. Adrenalin surges through me as I climb the muddy slope, using plant roots to pull myself up. I smell the wreckage before I see the cloud of smoke pouring out of the bent hood. The windshield is shattered into a spiderweb of cracks.

With a shaking hand I pull open the front passenger door. The driver lies slumped over. He moans faintly, like a wounded animal before the kill shot. Blood drips from a gash on his forehead, down his chin onto his shirt.

My voice is tight from fear. I try to speak. No words come out. I swallow and try again. 'Are you alright?'

The only response is a movement so faint I might have imagined it.

'You're going to be fine,' I reassure him. I try to sound convincing but it falls flat.

He opens his eyes. Very suddenly. His pale irises strike a chord in the deepest recesses of my memory. His hair is wavy, shot with auburn.

'Julie?' he says in a cracked voice. 'My God. I didn't know —' His words cut off abruptly as he is hit by a spasm of pain.

'Didn't know what? Who are you?' I ask through tears. He is a faceless man with a scrappy beard and covered in blood. He almost killed me. So why am I crying?

'I would never have done it if I'd known it was you.' His words are barely more than a whisper.

'Done what?'

He doesn't answer. He's bleeding badly. I tell him that I will run for help. That it won't take long for an ambulance to come. That he will be alright.

'No,' he rasps. He coughs blood. It sprays onto the dashboard. 'I'm sorry.' He squeezes my arm hard, smearing blood across my sleeve.

'It's not your fault. It was an accident,' I tell him. 'The brakes probably snapped.'

'No.' He shakes his head. 'You're wrong. It wasn't an accident.'

He whispers something. I can't make out the words. My face must register confusion for he lifts his head and, mustering all his strength, he rasps: 'You're not safe, Julie. You need to get away.'

Those words reverberate as I limp into Matt's unlocked office half an hour later. I have a splitting headache and a bruised shoulder from the fall. I am still trying to process what happened. He died so quickly, that man in the torn-up car. His breathing became thin and shallow. And then it stopped abruptly and his head slumped against the window with a thud.

'You need to get away,' he'd told me before he died. So I ran. I ran through the forest, slaloming around trees and up the hill, cutting through wild brush towards the university campus. I came directly here to look for Matt. He'll know what to do. Except he isn't in his office. I stand by his office window and watch students moving like ants across the rectangular lawn between the faculty buildings. Classes are over. Matt should be here soon.

I try to rub the blood off my clothes but it has set into the fabric. A permanent stain. The last time I'd seen that much blood was the night I woke with the feeling that something was wrong. I went to the bathroom to pee and instead watched with morbid fascination as my white satin pyjama pants turned bright red.

Matt called an ambulance. The paramedics strapped me to a stretcher and shoved maxi-pads between my legs. They'd soaked through twice over by the time we reached the ER. I was half-conscious by then, but I knew it was bad in every way. Even a D&C wasn't enough to stem the bleeding. The surgeon performed a radical hysterectomy. Matt gave permission as my next of kin. I had no say. I wasn't conscious.

Damn it, Julie. Stop thinking about the haemorrhage.

I move a pile of books off Matt's office couch and rest my head on a velvet cushion. I'm overcome with exhaustion. The click of a woman's stilettos in the corridor lulls me to sleep.

When I wake it's to the smell of Matt's distinct citrus scent. He leans over me, concern etched on his face.

'Honey,' he says softly. 'What's happened? Julie, you're hurt.'

'There was an accident. I fell and hit my head.'

He checks my skull. I wince when he rubs his thumb over the bump.

'You might have a concussion. I should take you to a doctor.'

'No, I'm fine,' I protest. 'Matt, a man almost hit me with his car. He said something strange about me being in danger. And then he died. Matt, he actually died.' I burst into tears, all that pent-up fear and shock pour out in great gulping sobs. Matt pulls me towards him to comfort me. 'We need to go to the police and tell them what happened,' I tell him as I rest my head against his chest, relieved that I am safe.

'Julie.' Matt kisses the crown of my head and gently caresses my hair. He talks to me patiently, like I'm a child. 'You had a fall. You probably have a mild concussion, which can often cause confusion. I want to take you home and make sure you're alright. After that, I'll speak with the police.'

At home, Matt gently undresses me while he runs a hot bath. He sits on the ledge and lathers my hair with shampoo. His fingers gently rub against my scalp. He runs the bar of soap over my abrasions and the bruises that discolour my shoulder and thigh.

Neither of us speaks as he rinses me clean with the shower nozzle and wraps me in a towel. In the bedroom he dresses me in fresh pyjamas and helps me into bed.

'I forgot. I need to get Alice from school.' I sit up with sudden urgency.

'I'll get Alice today,' he reassures me. 'I've taken the afternoon off from work to take care of you.'

'There's nothing wrong with me,' I say. 'It's just a bump.'

'It's more than a bump, Julie, honey,' he says. 'You may have a concussion from the fall. And you're badly bruised. We should get you looked at.'

Matt goes downstairs. He talks softly on the telephone. He must be speaking to the police. I'm relieved. The stairs creak as he returns upstairs. He sits on the bed next to me, holding a glass of orange juice and two capsules in his palm.

'For your headache and to help you sleep,' he says firmly. My heart sinks.

I've been off my meds for weeks. I don't want to go back on them. I want to say this to Matt but I don't have the strength to resist as he lifts the tumbler to my lips. He puts the capsules in my mouth, one by one, as if I'm an invalid. All I need to do is swallow.

'You'll be fine.' Matt takes the glass away and lowers my head onto the pillow. 'You'll be just fine.' He repeats it like a mantra until my body is floating and my mind is disconnected from the rest of me.

CHAPTER FOUR

Mel

Don't judge a town by the size of its morgue. Our morgue was huge. It had two dozen fridges. I couldn't remember a time when it'd been even close to capacity.

But never say never. Over the past year or so there'd been a marked rise in murders induced by methamphetamine and chemical cocktails with equally unpronounceable names. It was bad enough for our department to request funding to hire two more detectives. It's never a good sign for a town to be expanding its homicide unit.

The morgue was located in a white building with protruding windows of smoked black glass. It was a failed eighties design style more reminiscent of a rundown casino than a government facility housing the regional forensics institute.

I swiped my access card and entered a passcode on a keypad at the reinforced door near the rear vehicle bay. The door opened with an abrupt click. I walked down an empty tiled corridor that smelled of disinfectant.

I'd spent most of that morning going over the Wilson case with the assistant district attorney. He told me he wanted to reach a plea bargain so he could clear the case from his load. He gave me some line about not having the bandwidth to take the case to trial. He motioned towards a pile of files on the floor heaped so high they were on the verge of toppling over.

Mary Wilson had been bashed by her boyfriend at a trailer park south of town. She was twenty when she died, a mother of three children by two men, one of whom shoved her head through their bedroom wall during a bust-up over the television remote control. She died three days later of a blood clot that the pathologist said was likely caused by the head injury.

The assistant DA told me the defence attorney could claim the clot was unrelated to the head injury. That she would have died anyway. I couldn't argue about the medical stuff, but I had pulled together enough evidence to prove the boyfriend had been abusive for months. And that more than once he'd threatened to kill Mary Wilson.

There was no way this guy should be walking the streets until he was old enough to need a walking stick. That's what I told the prosecutor. I could tell he was torn between doing what was right and what was expedient. I hoped to God that I'd convinced him to go the distance.

While we were wrapping up, I received a text message from the chief pathologist saying the autopsy on the body from Kellers Way would begin shortly. He'd done an initial examination on Friday, when they had brought the body into the morgue late in the evening. It mostly involved taking tissue samples and collecting maggots and other insects to help the forensic entomologist date the death and figure out if the burial site had changed.

There was no rushed weekend autopsy. I didn't request one. To tell you the truth, I'm not sure the overtime would have been approved even if I had. It was hardly an urgent job. The victim had been dead for a while.

At the antechamber to the autopsy room, I pulled scrubs over my clothes. I put on a disposable hat, mask and rubber gloves, and dipped my finger in a jar of extra-strength vapour rub that I keep in my purse to mask the smell of autopsies. Death has a sickly scent, but the decomp cases are the worst.

We're vigilant about preventing even the shadow of a doubt of cross-contamination, ever since we lost an open-and-shut murder case a few years back. The defence attorney, a high-priced lawyer from Charlotte, claimed cross-contamination on forensic findings that were so damning that under normal circumstances, hell, under any circumstances, his client would have been found guilty.

His client was likeable. White, a church pastor. He had a pretty wife with a heart-shaped face and four blond, slightly hyperactive sons who sat behind him in court during the final summation. They wore matching cream suits and light blue ties that matched their eyes.

When the prosecutor spoke I heard one of the kids whisper to the other, 'What is rape?' It was inappropriate for them to be in court. But protecting children wasn't exactly a priority for the defence team. Those kids were props. They were there so the jurors could look into their precocious blue eyes before going into the jury room to determine their father's fate.

Their daddy, the pastor, had raped a teenage prostitute and then strangled her to death. We'd found traces of his semen on her clothes. He'd worn a rubber but it dripped. We were lucky that his DNA records were on file from a rape case that never made it to trial when he was at college. That information was inadmissible to the jury, but it helped us find him.

He had a good lawyer who did what all good criminal attorneys do: he threw dust into everyone's eyes. He obtained the forensic facility records and found that while the evidence from the victim and the accused were examined in two different labs within the building, a low-level technician was present in both laboratories that afternoon.

He had the nerve to claim cross-contamination. The jury was looking for an excuse to acquit. The defence attorney gave them one on a platter. Reasonable doubt. He knew the jurors would rather believe his client's claims of innocence than deprive four flaxen-haired boys of their daddy, and face the reality that even church pastors are capable of bestial acts.

I've heard prosecutors say that juries place too much emphasis on forensic evidence because of TV shows that have them believing forensics has an almost god-like power. This trial was a case in point. There was even a witness – a gas station attendant – who had seen the victim in the pastor's car on the night she disappeared. The defence used the witness's past as a drug addict to tear his testimony to shreds. It should have been a slam dunk case. Instead the defendant walked out of court with his name cleared, despite the detailed testimony of a witness and damning DNA evidence.

The internal inquiry set up after that case established strict protocols around handling evidence. None of us wanted to lose another case over some bullshit defence tactic. That's why I was covered in plastic protective gear as I walked through the antechamber into the autopsy room where the Kellers Way body lay on a slab covered by a white sheet.

Mike looked up briefly from the computer screen where he

was examining scans to acknowledge my presence. Mike and I had worked together long enough for me to know that he didn't want to lose his train of thought while he looked at the X-rays.

I used the time to examine the victim's belongings. They were set out on the counter in a long row of plastic evidence bags. Each had its own number and description written in indelible black ink.

The first bag contained a left black boot, a zip-up, the type that came to just below the knee. The right boot was in a separate bag alongside it. They were both partly caked in mud, though there was enough leather exposed to see it was well-made footwear, possibly hand-stitched. Boots like these did not come cheap. The heels were thick. Sturdy. Not stilettos. These were not fashion boots.

There was a pair of women's underwear in another evidence bag; black, bikini. Nothing fancy. I held the bag to a strip of fluorescent light in the ceiling to get a better look at the underwear.

'There are no deliberate rips or tears.' Mike spoke without taking his eyes off his computer screen. 'We'll check it for semen traces in the lab.'

The bra was taupe and flecked with dirt. There was a white shirt that looked grey through the plastic of the bag. Another bag contained a red jacket, single-breasted with brass buttons down the lapel and, from what I could see, no label. It had a tailored quality you can't buy in stores. I guessed it was custom-made.

Two gold stud earrings with diamond insets were packed in a small evidence bag and a gold chain necklace with a semiprecious pendant was in a separate clear bag. There was also the wristwatch I'd seen at the crime scene, sleek and stylish. I jotted down notes so I could cross-reference the victim's belongings with missing persons lists.

'No wallet, I gather. No ID?' I turned to Mike. It was a super-
fluous question. He would have called me straight away if he'd
found any identification. He shook his head.

'Have you done the dental scans?'

'Sure have,' he said. 'There wasn't much dental work done
except braces as a kid. A couple of minor fillings. Wisdom teeth
were removed when she was a teenager. Bring me the dental records
of possible victims and we'll be able to confirm identity.'

That was the problem with dental records. They were only useful when you had potential victims to identify. The reverse didn't
work so well.

'Any identifying marks on the body?'

'Nothing that stands out,' Mike answered as he stood up and
pushed back his stool. 'There is a surprising amount of tissue left
on the body given the estimated passage of time. But we've found
nothing so far that can help ID her. No tattoos or anything like
that. We'll get to work on facial recognition later in the week.'

He unrolled the autopsy kit as he spoke and fixed his metal
probes in a neat line on a table next to the body.

'What about the clothes? Is there anything that might identify
her?'

'The labels were too faded to read,' he said. 'Dennis will examine them in the lab. The gold earrings are eighteen carat, by the
way.'

'Was she wearing a wedding ring?' I asked.

'No rings,' he said without looking up. 'The lab will sift through
the soil this week. They have thirty-four bags of soil to go through,'
he said. 'You still have search parties at the scene?'

I nodded. We had cadaver dogs out over the weekend and again
this morning. The crime scene team was using metal detectors and

ground probes to examine a wider area around the burial site in case there was additional evidence, or bodies.

'Any idea when she died?'

'I don't have a definitive timeframe,' Mike responded. 'I doubt that it was less than five years ago. It's unlikely to be more than ten years ago. So that gives you a five-year window to work with for now. I'll get you something more concrete when we get the tests back.'

'What about her age?'

'Her age,' he said, as if contemplating it for the first time. 'Judging by her teeth, I'd say mid-thirties. Early forties, maybe. She's white, or possibly Hispanic.'

'Do you have any idea of the cause of death, Mike?' I asked the question even though I knew his answer before he gave it.

'There's nothing obvious,' he shrugged. 'Once I've done the autopsy and I've gone through the scans thoroughly, I'll give you a working theory.' It was the standard answer.

'Damn,' I said under my breath.

'Sorry Mel,' Mike said without looking up. 'With the body this badly decomposed, I'd be grappling in the dark if I told you any-thing else.'

Mike lifted the sheet. The victim was lying with her legs pulled up to her chest. Her right hand was over her face.

'From the position of the body, it looks as if she was trying to protect herself when she was killed,' Mike said.

Whoever she was, she knew she was about to die.

CHAPTER FIVE

Julie

It's almost 6 p.m. when Matt's car pulls into the driveway and the wrought-iron gates close automatically behind it. He's an hour late. The effect of the gin and tonic I drank earlier for Dutch courage has dissipated. I half wish I could pour another, but then I'd be in no fit state for the evening ahead.

I watch through the curtains of the upstairs bedroom as Matt walks towards the front door carrying a leather briefcase. It bulges with what I guess are student papers to mark over the weekend. He looks preoccupied. I tie my satin robe loosely so that it gapes open and I knot my hair above my head the way Matt likes.

When we first dated, Matt would press his thumb along my cheekbones and tell me that he'd like to have my face cast in bronze so that my beauty would last forever. He said my face was the epitome of ancient Greek beauty, with perfect symmetry and features so delicate that he was afraid of crushing them. These days, when I look in the mirror, I see threads of age forming in the corners of my eyes; a portent of my eventual decay. Matt notices as well.

Despite all my efforts, Matt doesn't so much as glance in my direction when I come down the stairs in my half-open robe. Instead, he checks a pile of mail on the hall table with an inordinate amount of fascination, given that he knows without looking that it's mostly junk from car dealerships and the like. My cheeks burn with humiliation from acting like a dog in heat, from trying to seduce my own husband. And from failing miserably.

Ever since my fall, he treats me like fragile glass. He talks to me like I'm a child. He doesn't ever touch me. We're like characters in a stuffy fifties movie, sleeping on separate sides of the bed and platonically kissing the other on the temple before we go to sleep. I'll lose him if things stay this way.

Matt eventually acknowledges my presence. He mutters some sort of greeting and then absent-mindedly leans over to give me a rote kiss on the forehead. He's been doing that all week. He treats me like I'm an unwanted house guest whom he must grudgingly tolerate out of sheer good manners.

To hell with that. I move my face at the last second so that his kiss lands on my mouth. I deepen the kiss, putting my arms around his neck. I press myself against him until I know for certain that he wants me.

'Where's Alice?' he asks in a husky voice.

'Sleepover,' I mumble. 'We're all alone.'

Pretty soon we're sliding up the stairs in each other's arms. I untuck his shirt. He runs his fingers up my thigh and wraps them around the elastic of my lace panties. By the time we reach the landing my panties are hanging off the balustrade. Matt is unzipped and his shirt is lying somewhere in the hall.

Later, when we're showering together, Matt touches the bruise on my shoulder.

'Does it still hurt?' he asks.

'A bit.' I try to pretend I don't care, but tears well in my eyes.

'What's bothering you, Julie?' he asks as he helps me out of the shower, wrapping me in a soft towel. He lifts my wet hair off my shoulder and kisses the back of my neck. 'You've been down lately.'

'I can't stop thinking about the man in the car. I should have done something to help him.' I wipe away an errant tear.

'Julie,' sighs Matt. His expression is grave. 'How much do you really remember about that day?'

I shrug. 'Bits and pieces. Not a whole lot.'

'I took you to the hospital. You were diagnosed as having a grade three concussion. The symptoms of which include confusion and memory loss.' He talks to me slowly so that each word sinks in. 'I know it's hard to process, but you're imagining the incident with the car. It didn't happen. You had a fall when you went running. You hit your head. When you came to, you ran the rest of the way to the university. It wasn't the smartest thing to do with a concussion, but you'd left your phone at home and you panicked.'

'Matt, I'm not making it up,' I snap. 'The driver was covered in blood. It got on my clothes. I remember that clearly. Before he died, he said something that terrified me. Something about me being in danger.'

'If that's the case,' says Matt, his eyes steadily on mine, 'then why is there no record of a car accident?'

'No record?' My voice cracks in surprise.

'Nothing,' Matt says definitively. His blue eyes are serious as he meets mine. 'I spoke to the police right after we arrived home that day. They sent a patrol car to check and called me back later to say there was no car crash anywhere in that vicinity.'

'How can that be?' I say almost to myself. 'I don't understand.'

'It's a false memory,' Matt explains patiently, as if I am one of his students. 'You've superimposed the trauma of your fall at Kellers Way with memories from Roxy's death,' says Matt. 'It wasn't a dead man in a car, it's Roxy that you're remembering. You were covered in her blood after she was hit by that car. You held her in your arms until she died. You're using this phantom driver as a substitute for Roxy. It's a coping mechanism.'

My heart broke when our labrador Roxy was killed a week before Christmas. Roxy lunged ahead on her leash and was knocked over by a car that came out of nowhere. The driver didn't even stop to help. Roxy died in my arms. Things were rough afterwards. I was put on a higher dosage of meds. To tell you the truth, I don't really remember much about the weeks that followed.

'It seemed so real, Matt. The car, the smoke. I can almost smell the blood. It got all over me. Don't you remember, when I came to your office my clothes were covered in blood?'

'Julie, there was no driver. There was no car accident. There was no blood,' Matt says. 'Your running clothes are still in the laundry. Take a look at them yourself.' Matt goes downstairs and comes back with my running gear. I put the clothes to my face. They smell of sweat. They're grimy. But when I look closely, there's not a single bloodstain. Not even a drop.

'The sooner you accept this car accident didn't happen, the sooner you can move on. Darling,' he says, lifting up my chin, 'I don't want it to drag you back to the way you were after Roxy died. You need to accept what really happened. You slipped and fell while you were jogging. That's it. Stop eating yourself up!'

Everything about the day of my fall is hazy and surreal. Trauma plays tricks on memory. Matt has authored psychology journal articles on this exact topic. He pulls me against his chest and runs his hand reassuringly down my back. His gentleness overwhelms me. It makes me think for a fraction of a second that maybe everything will work out.

'You should have reminded me this morning that Alice is out tonight,' he teases me. 'I would have come home earlier.'

'I asked Lucy's mom if Alice could stay over for the night because we have that dinner with Stephen and Chelsea,' I remind him.

'Let's make an excuse,' he says, kissing the nape of my neck. 'We can stay in bed and order takeout. I promise we'll have more fun than talking shop with Stephen.'

'You know we can't.' I reluctantly wriggle out of his grip. 'Anyway, it's too late to cancel.' I look at my watch. 'Oh, my God, Matt, we have to be there in forty minutes. The Marshals are punctuality freaks.'

I stand in my lace panties and bra, applying lipstick in the bathroom mirror, while Matt puts on a freshly laundered shirt. I see his expression in the reflection. There's no lust or tenderness as he runs his eyes over my half-naked body. There's something clinical about the way that he watches me that leaves me feeling unsettled.

CHAPTER SIX

Mel

Time covers up a multitude of sins. None more so than murder. I left the morgue before the whirring screech of electric saw on bone, well aware that chances were slim I'd ever catch the Kellers Way killer.

The likelihood of finding a killer erodes over time, just like the body of the victim. Decomp cases defy the cardinal rule of homicide investigation: if you know your victim then nine times out of ten you will find your killer. I knew nothing about my victim. The odds were against me.

I walked back to headquarters past squat office buildings of pristine mirrored glass to put whatever scant information I had through the missing persons database. I needed to give a name to that woman lying on the slab in the morgue. Once I had her name, the rest would follow.

The cobbled pedestrian mall of converted tobacco warehouses was filled with the lunchtime office crowd eating at outdoor cafes in the early-afternoon sun. As I walked past, I wondered what little secrets they were hiding as they ate their burgers and fries. What vices, passions and lies were hidden beneath the surface of their seemingly mundane lives. Most people's secrets die with them. In a homicide investigation, no secret is safe. Every transgression is pored over and documented in detectives' notebooks, and case files, and court transcripts.

By the time I'm done with a case, I know more about the victim than his or her closest relative; a fondness for fetish porn, a penchant for stealing hotel bathrobes, an addiction to Vicodin or slot machines, a predilection for cross-dressing or callgirls. I know what the victim last ate, what the victim last wore and what the victim last searched for on the internet. I am privy to the most intimate details of the victim's sex life, no matter how mundane, or kinky. What, when and, most importantly, with whom. I wondered what secrets the girl from Kellers Way was hiding before she died.

The squad room was empty when I arrived, holding my lunch in a brown paper carrier bag and sipping from an oversized disposable coffee cup. I turned on my computer and drank the rest of my coffee while I contemplated how I should run the search.

On any given day there are 80 000 to 90 000 people listed as missing in the United States. Of these, 50 000 are adults. Roughly half that number are female adults. I had a potential pool of 25 000 victims to sort through on the national database of missing people.

The pitfall with running these searches is that if you narrow a search too much, you risk excluding the victim. If you keep it too broad, you get a list so long and unwieldy that it's of little value.

I opted to start broad and then narrow the search in subsequent rounds. I inputted the gender – female – and a broad age range of thirty to forty-five. Then I narrowed the search by focusing on those who went missing between five to ten years ago. It gave me

71 376 profiles. Of these, most would be women who'd disappeared of their own accord. Women who didn't want to be found for whatever reason; escaping an abusive partner, debt collectors, mental illness. There were plenty of reasons why a person might disappear and change their identity. Less than five per cent would be missing because they were dead.

I unwrapped my cheese and pickle sandwich and took a bite. I had to find a way to narrow the results further. I decided to look for women missing within a six-state area. Now I had 4131 potential victims. That would take me a week to go through. I ran another search with descriptions of the red jacket and other clothes and jewellery found on the body. Zero hits.

I pulled the desk phone over and called the forensics lab. Dennis answered on the second ring.

'It's Mel. I'm working through the NamUs database. Do you have a shoe size for the victim? Also, any idea of the victim's height?'

'Let me check,' Dennis said, putting the phone down with a clatter. I took another bite of the sandwich while I waited with the phone pressed to my ear.

'I just measured the victim's boot. I'd say her foot size is a nine, nine-and-a-half,' said Dennis a couple of minutes later. 'With a foot that large it's unlikely the victim would be shorter than five foot five.'

'Do you have anything else that might help with a missing-persons data search?'

'Maybe.' I heard the rustle of papers as Dennis flicked through the file. 'The pendant the victim was wearing,' he said finally.

'What about it?'

'We believe it's morganite.'

'That's a semiprecious stone. It's quite common, isn't it?'

'This one isn't at all common. It's a bright pink variety only found in Madagascar,' Dennis responded. 'It's called Zambezia morganite. They're rare and expensive. They're sometimes called pink emeralds.'

'Thanks,' I said to nobody but myself. Dennis had already hung up.

Once I entered the minimum height and shoe size that Dennis had given me, the list of potential victims immediately dropped to 291. By the time I logged out of the database, I had a thick pile of missing-persons profiles to go through. Bedtime reading. My biggest concern was that the database was only as good as the information that was inputted into it. That's why I don't like relying only on computers.

I looked up to see Casey walking into the squad room for his afternoon shift. He wore the same deadbeat clothes as his drug-dealing perps: torn jeans and a long-sleeve tee under a plaid shirt. Casey worked homicide on and off for years with my partner Will before I moved here. Then he was transferred to the drug squad.

'Hey, Casey. You're just the guy I was looking for.'

'What's up, Mel? Are you missing Will already?' he teased. Will had gone on his honeymoon and left me to run the homicide department alone during the busiest time of the year.

'Will's the only one around here who knows how to make a decent coffee,' I joked. 'Actually, I have a new case from before my time here. Do you recall a missing person, a woman in her thirties who disappeared wearing a red jacket and expensive jewellery? Around five or ten years ago.'

'Nothing jumps out,' he said, rubbing his wispy moustache, which gave him the emaciated air of an addict. 'That could mean nothing. Ever since we had the baby, I'm getting three hours sleep a night. I can barely remember my own name most days. If anyone would know then it would be Lenny. You should speak to him.'

'Lenny? I thought he moved to Florida.'

'He did. Believe it or not he likes it better here. Moved back just after Christmas.'

Lenny Miller handled all missing-persons investigations in this part of the state up until he retired four years ago, not long before I was hired. Lenny was better than any database. Just about every missing-persons case went through Lenny. He was old-school. He knew them each by heart.

'Lenny's a golf nut,' Casey said, jotting down a phone number on the back of an envelope. 'If you can't get hold of him by cell-phone then I'm betting he'll be at Twin Lakes.'

There was no answer on Lenny's phone when I called. I left a message on his voicemail. Then I telephoned the Twin Lakes golf club directly.

'Yeah, Lenny's here. He's on the fourteenth hole, so you'd better get here quick. He's having a lucky day,' drawled a guy called Dave, before the phone went dead.

CHAPTER SEVEN

Julie

It was Matt who insisted on going out with the Marshals. He said something about wanting to make nice with Stephen, who's just been appointed to the university research-funding board. The thing is that Matt doesn't need to brownnose Stephen to secure funding. They're old buddies. They play racquetball every week for goodness sake. This dinner is about Stephen's wife Chelsea. And me.

We take Matt's car. That suits me fine as I can't drive properly in heels. He turns on the radio as we back down the driveway. The car fills with the booming voice of a sports reporter giving a preview of the weekend's baseball games.

Matt is a baseball nut. When we were first married, we'd go to games all the time, doing it the way it should be done, with hotdogs, shelled peanuts and Cracker Jack. The whole nine yards. I find baseball boring but I never let on. Not once.

We're ten minutes late when we walk into the restaurant. It's mostly my fault. I couldn't find my grandmother's diamond necklace. My turquoise wrap dress looked incomplete without something around my neck. Chelsea is always immaculate. Never a hair out of place. I'll be damned if I turn up looking like a poor relative from the wrong side of the tracks. I'm not ashamed of my background, but I don't need to wear it carved into my forehead either.

Matt takes the blame. I knew he would. 'Sorry we're late,' he says smoothly as we reach the table. Chelsea and Stephen are sipping wine and trying not to look pointedly at their watches. 'It's my fault. I was held back at work by a student having a crisis over her final-year paper. Julie was furious with me for making us late.'

He reaches out and squeezes my hand. Chelsea's jaw tightens as her eyes shift to our intertwined hands and Matt's damp hair. She knows exactly why we were late.

We're at a new restaurant that has great reviews. It's not my preference. I'm a vegetarian. Not by taste, by ideology. I actually love the taste of meat, I just can't stand the thought of what happens to get that meat on a plate.

It drives me crazy sitting in a restaurant filled with the aroma of grilled meat and having to dig into greens. I order skewers of roast vegetables and halloumi cheese with a side of Greek salad. Everyone else orders steak. Deep inside I hate them for it, especially when the waiter arrives with three medium-rare steaks that sizzle on hotplates.

'You're looking fit, Julie.' Chelsea's tight smile is filled with insincerity. 'Do you work out?' I'm more than ten years younger than Chelsea. It's obvious that she resents it like hell.

'I jog occasionally,' I respond, hoping someone will change the subject.

'Don't be so modest. I hear you could run a marathon without breaking a sweat,' says Stephen. That comment annoys his wife, though she masks it well.

'I didn't know you're a competitive runner,' Chelsea chimes in.

'It's just a hobby.' I try to play it down. I hate the attention.

'Where do you run?' asks Chelsea.

'Around our neighbourhood. I like running on hills because it's good cardio.'

'You're brave. I'm a treadmill girl myself,' Chelsea says. 'The roads around here are too quiet. I worry about something happening. There are so many crazy people in this world.' Stephen kicks her gently under the table as Matt turns pale.

There's an awkward silence. Chelsea swallows as she registers the faux pas. 'If you're interested I could arrange a visitor pass to our gym. I have the most amazing personal trainer. His name is Emilio. It's hard to get bookings with him but I could pull some strings.' Full marks to Chelsea as she valiantly tries to dig herself out of that hole.

'I'd love that,' I say just as insincerely as she made her offer.

Chelsea has never liked me. She's always been polite, even friendly, in a breezy, officious sort of way. But we've never been friends. There's a decade separating us in age. Her kids are teenagers. One is going to college next year. We don't have much in common.

She disapproves of me. Don't get me wrong, not an unkind word has ever crossed her lips. But still. One gets a feel for these sorts of things.

There is a gaping distance between us that goes beyond age. Chelsea and Laura were best friends. By all accounts, the two couples were inseparable. They went on joint weekends to the Marshals' beach house, ski trips, dinner parties, doubles tennis matches. They did everything together.

That's why we're all here at this awkward dinner, to re-establish those bonds. Except instead of Laura, it's me. And I can't pull it off.

Matt's a psychologist so he notices things that your ordinary, obtuse male might miss. I don't do well in large groups. I find it nearly impossible to establish a rapport with people with whom I have nothing in common. It's become worse since the haemorrhage.

I've done my best to keep up with Matt's social circle. Even when I feel at a low point, I attend cocktail parties and faculty functions. I dress up, smile, and make the requisite small talk. At the end of these evenings I feel deflated, as if I said something inappropriate or acted excruciatingly gauche.

Chelsea fits into Matt's milieu effortlessly. She's around Matt's age. Maybe a year or two younger, with a similar pedigree. They ran with the same crowd as teenagers. They both grew up with more money than they knew what to do with. Her mother plays bridge with my mother-in-law. I'm perfectly aware this dinner may be repeated in blow-by-blow detail at their next game.

Matt's friends are a tight-knit group. I blend in physically. God knows I've done enough to make sure I look and dress the part to neutralise any doubts on that score. My trailer trash origins are buried deep. But I'm the first to admit that I come up short in other ways. I read enough to sound intelligent, but that's only paper-thin. Don't they know it. I can almost hear them wondering why Matt chose me after being married to the vivacious, brilliant Laura, summa cum laude at everything. Even today, all these years after her death, people who knew Laura speak about her with genuine affection and admiration.

Beautiful, brilliant Laura, who could light up a room with her smile and sharp intellect. That's how she was described in an obituary I found in Matt's papers.

So why am I sitting here while Laura's best friend judges me and finds me wanting? Because Chelsea is the apex predator in her group of faculty wives. The real reason we're at this dinner is to help me get accepted by her clique. All these years and I'm still an outsider.

The first time I met the faculty wives was at a Christmas party at the university. That's when Matt and I first came out publicly as a couple. Nothing has changed since that night. The winter draught in the room was nothing compared to the frosty reception that I received from his friends' wives. Cold handshakes. Icepick eyes surreptitiously giving me the once-over with a hint of amusement. A brief burst of small talk before the faculty wives delicately backed away to resume their conversations, abandoning me like an unwanted puppy.

Matt left my side to talk with a colleague recently returned from a sabbatical in England. Leaning against a column with a glass of red wine in his hand, he was oblivious to the toxic atmosphere. There I was in the midst of a room of people I didn't know, overdressed, with eyes boring into me. Watching me. Judging me. Comparing me to Laura. And finding me falling woefully short.

To hell with them. I pasted a confident smile on my face and walked over to the bar for a drink. I wouldn't allow them to grind me down. When in doubt, fake it.

I was on my second drink when Matt found me.

'There you are, darling,' Matt said, taking my empty wine glass and putting it on the bar. He kissed me, a long lingering kiss to let everyone know this was not an ill-advised flirtation. He was in love. With me. A woman more than a decade younger. That was another reason why they disliked me. They disliked me because Matt couldn't keep his hands off me. They disliked me because I tarnished Laura's memory. They disliked me because I was a poor substitute.

Sometimes I think Matt chose me in a last-gasp bid for normality. Matt's embarrassed by his family's wealth. It's not something that anyone outside the family might notice, but I see it. His mother, Anne, does too. It irritates her no end. She thinks his marriage to me is just another example of Matt slumming it.

Matt likes to pretend he's living a normal middle-class life. Take his car: he drives a Lincoln. It's top of the range, but the rest of his family wouldn't be seen dead driving anything other than an Audi, BMW or Porsche.

Matt's younger brother Stuart is an investment banker with the opposite tendency. He likes to flaunt his wealth. Anne must wonder why her sons went to such extremes. One son lives relatively modestly, trying to blend in to his middle-class college town surroundings, the other is tastelessly flashy, with a garish platinum-blond wife who's a former model. Though not the type of model Anne might boast about at her weekly bridge game. High fashion would have been acceptable. Photographs in tawdry magazines are entirely different.

Kelly clearly appealed to Stuart's more carnal instincts; her chest measurement is probably on par with her IQ. I'm not being bitchy. That's what everyone thinks. Nobody realises that Kelly is smarter than they give her credit for. Not the smarts you learn at university. Street smarts. Based on her street IQ, I'd say Kelly is one of the smartest people I've ever met. After all, she snagged Stuart, and she has him wrapped around her manicured little finger.

And then there's Matt, who opted for academia when he could have done anything. His mother's words, not mine.

He's a leader in his field. He has recently published research that has been hailed as a major breakthrough in cognitive psychology. Despite all of Matt's accomplishments, his mother never understood why he'd want to play academic when he could be doing something 'useful' with his life. As the daughter of a state senator, that meant politics. The thought makes Matt shudder. His mother is equally confounded by Matt's decision to marry me.

Chelsea pushes her food across her plate with a fierce determination. Her taut lips are arranged into a smile that does nothing to cover the hardness in her eyes. She too disapproves of me. Of my marriage. She scrapes her cutlery against her plate as she slices through the undercooked steak on her plate. I notice that she eats none of it.

It's obvious she's here because Stephen made her come. She barely hides it. 'You phoney bitch,' I want to tell her. I don't. Instead, I take a sip of Matt's wine. It's a decent French burgundy. Matt gives me a nudge under the table. Alcohol interacts with my medication.

To hell with it, I think, and drink it all down. I let Stephen fill the glass with more wine. I see a flicker of irritation in Matt's eyes as I take another generous sip. Or is it concern? Don't worry, Matt. I'll give you what you want. Don't I always?

The wine warms me. I close my eyes for the briefest moment and then open them with my attention focused just on Chelsea. God, I can be charming when I turn it on. A thousand watts of charm to melt Chelsea's permafrost.

'Chelsea, I've been meaning to tell you just how much I enjoyed the charity brunch two weeks ago.' That was a total lie. It was stuffy and agonisingly boring. I hated every damn second of it. I drone on enthusiastically about the catering, the flowers, the inspiring speeches.

My sycophantic ramblings break through her guarded expression. Her smile expands. This is a woman who craves nothing more than recognition for what she sees as her own accomplishments.

By the end of the evening, Chelsea and I walk arm-in-arm to our car, giggling tipsily as Matt and Stephen shuffle along behind us bemused. When we get to the car, we kiss each other on the cheeks and release each other's arms reluctantly, like best friends at college parting for summer vacation.

'I'll see you Monday afternoon then.' I inject a wistful tone into my voice.

Matt opens the car door. I scramble into my seat and clip on the safety belt.

'It's time to take your meds,' says Matt, looking at his watch. He hands me the capsules and passes me a bottle of mineral water from the car door. I figure I'll slip the capsules under my seat while Matt is driving but he patiently waits for me to swallow them before starting the car engine.

'The evening went well, don't you think?' says Matt as we drive through town. He's pleased. I feel a warm flush of pleasure at his praise. We sit together in a comfortable silence. It feels like the old days.

'What are you doing on Monday with Chelsea?' Matt's voice breaks into my thoughts.

'Lunch at the country club. And then a round of golf before school pick-up.'

'I thought you didn't like golf?' he says.

'I don't. But anything for you, darling. Anything that gets you funding, or whatever it is you wanted from tonight's dinner.' My voice is flat. My elation is gone. The meds have kicked in.

Matt flinches at the change in tone. We say nothing for the longest time. As he turns the car into our street, I unzip his pants and bend my head down into his lap.

CHAPTER EIGHT

Mel

It took me twenty minutes to drive to the tree-fringed golf club north-west of town. The clubhouse was a renovated old plantation house with long balconies where you could sip iced tea in the summer while watching golfers tee off. Not that I had time for that sort of thing in my life. A genteel clubhouse wasn't exactly the place you took two teenage boys on the weekend. And it wasn't like I had a social life outside of work and family.

I found Lenny sitting on the front verandah in a cream hessian chair, drinking a cold beer from a glass covered in condensation.

'Detective,' he said, standing up and reaching out with a tanned hand dotted with age spots. 'I just heard your message. I keep my phone on silent while I'm playing.' He gave an apologetic smile as he shook my hand. 'What's so important that it brings a homicide detective all the way out here?'

I pulled a chair over and sat close to him. I didn't want to be overheard. The case had no media attention at that stage and I liked it that way. 'We have the body of a female, found in a forest just out of town. Kellers Way. I can't find anyone in the missing-persons database who seems to match the vic. I figured that if she was from these parts then you might remember the case.'

'There were a lot of cases over the years,' Lenny said matter-of-factly.

'I'm sure there were,' I agreed. 'Except there is something about this victim that makes me think she would have stood out when she disappeared. That you would have remembered her.'

'What do you have?' he asked, after a sip of beer.

'Female, probably in her thirties. Dark hair, we think, though we're still waiting for hair analysis in case she dyed it. She was found wearing a red jacket with brass buttons. Black boots and black pants. She wore gold and diamond earrings, eighteen-carat gold. Also, she wore a gold chain necklace with a semiprecious pendant. The stone is rare. From Madagascar apparently. Oh, and she was wearing a ladies' watch. It looks expensive. All the personal belongings are tasteful, classy, the jacket might even be custom-made. Her nail polish is, well, I'm pretty sure it's a forty-dollars-a-bottle kind of nail polish.'

Lenny had a pensive expression on his face as he listened, looking out at a golfer hitting a drive.

'These are the missing persons I've pulled out so far.' I handed him a brown envelope filled with face shots I'd printed at the office.

Lenny examined each and every photo as if he was trying to pull out the cases in his mind. It took him a good ten minutes to go through them all. Wordlessly, he put the photos in a pile and slid them back into the envelope. He said nothing, just pursed his lips and looked out at the fairway below.

'You know,' he said, breaking the silence, 'the one thing I'd hoped for when I got old – I'm almost seventy now – was to forget.

The trouble is that half the time I can't remember where I left my car keys, but I still remember these faces, the faces of the missing.'

'I'm sorry, Lenny,' I said. 'Maybe I shouldn't have come to you.'

'Don't you worry about it,' he said, shaking his head. 'You mentioned jewellery. Do you have photographs of the items found on the victim?'

'Yes,' I said, passing him photographs of the necklace, earrings and watch. 'Anything look familiar?'

'I'm not sure,' he shrugged, squinting as he held the photos away from his face. I noticed he kept returning to the photo of the pendant.

'There was a woman who went missing about five or six years ago.' He took a sip of beer. 'She was wearing expensive gold jewellery on the day she disappeared, including a pendant. We thought the motive was theft. I personally went to pawn shops to look for those pieces because we figured the killer fenced them.'

'That's strange,' I said. 'I couldn't find a single missing person in the state who was last seen wearing jewellery that came even close to matching the pieces we found on the Kellers Way victim.'

'That's because it's not a missing-persons case,' Lenny said. 'It wouldn't be in the database anymore. It's a closed case. We caught the killer.'

'I'm sorry, Lenny,' I said. 'I don't quite understand.'

He leaned forward and wrote a name on a golf club membership brochure.

'This is the guy you need to speak with,' he said, handing me the brochure. 'I suggest you go in person, because he'll stonewall you given half a chance. He built his career on this case.'

I slipped the paper into my bag. I'd follow that up the next day. I had to rush to a parent–teacher meeting across town at Joe's junior high. That's what I liked about living in a town this size, it didn't take very long to get anywhere.

Our town is relatively small but the people living here are an eclectic mix of locals and outsiders. We have three universities around town and a fair-sized population of intellectuals and researchers enjoying the trappings of a middle-class lifestyle without the hassle of big-city living.

Once you get away from the affluent neighbourhoods on the hills you hit long stretches of houses on the fringes that belong to blue-collar stiffs. People who resent their meagre slice of the American dream, which for them died when the tobacco industry keeled over in the nineties. They live in run-down neighbourhoods that once had aspirations and in trailer parks littered with used syringes. A few of them escape, but they're a rarity. By the time they turn twenty-five, most have had every trace of hope squeezed out of them.

I never thought I'd end up in a place like this after spending all my adult life in the city. We arrived here four years ago after a long drive in pouring rain, towing a trailer loaded with all our possessions assembled like a three-dimensional jigsaw puzzle. The boys fell asleep somewhere in Virginia. They woke when I pulled into the driveway of the house I'd rented over the internet.

Even through the misty windshield it was obvious the photos I'd seen before signing the lease were heavily photoshopped. I had a sudden urge to turn the car around and drive home, but I'd promised myself I'd give it three months.

I came here because it's where my father lived after retiring from the military. I guess I was looking for somewhere safe to hide after Danny was killed. What better place than near the Colonel. When I was a girl, my father had seemed invincible. A lot has changed since then.

My father has early-onset Alzheimer's. He deteriorated quickly and now spends his days staring vacantly through the smudged windows of an old-age facility on the edge of town. I visit twice a week. Never longer than twenty minutes. It's the longest I can be in that place filled with the sour odour of incontinence and desiccation. Even in the thralls of dementia, my father seems to revel in my discomfort.

Joe was ten and Sammy just eight when we moved to North Carolina. Living in a small town seemed the only way I could manage to raise them as a single mom. Their father was killed in a shooting near Clinton Hill in Brooklyn. Danny and I had been together all our adult lives. I never imagined a future without him. We had no plan B. Kind of stupid, I guess, us both being cops and all.

Danny was shot in the head by a gangbanger during a routine drug arrest. He never had a chance. He lay in a coma for two days until I gave the doctors permission to turn off the machines. I don't regret having Danny's life support turned off, what I regret is that I had to make that decision in the first place.

After Danny died, I did the unimaginable. I handed in my shield and became a full-time mom. I figured I'd find an office job when the boys were older. I didn't want my kids to lose their mother as well.

I thought the life insurance money would stretch further outside New York City. Then, out of the blue, the markets plummeted and our savings halved. To cut a long story short, my retirement was brief. I heard a homicide job was opening up, I applied, and I've been working murder scenes around here ever since.

The pay is decent and I pretty much always get home in time to eat dinner with my kids. That's almost unheard of for a city cop. Being a sole parent, I constantly have to juggle work, parenting and attending school events like this parent–teacher interview, which I'd already had to cancel twice before.

When I arrived at the school for the meeting with Joe's teacher, there was one parent inside the classroom with the teacher and another waiting on a plastic bucket chair in the hall. I kept walking down the empty corridor flanked by drab rows of lockers. A janitor was mopping the floor.

In the girls' toilet block I washed my hands with the intensity of a surgeon scrubbing up. The liquid soap's cheap scent was floral in a sort of industrial way that made my lungs burn. I fixed my unruly chestnut hair with my fingers so that it was pushed back behind my ears. My makeup had faded over the course of the day and my freckles were exposed. They made me look much younger than a mother of two boys who were growing up faster than I cared to admit. Soon they would be towering over me. Not that I was ever noted for my height. I am five foot five and slim in build, mostly because of the energy that I burn working full time and keeping my household on track.

When I returned, the classroom door was open, and the teacher was waiting inside. The last time I'd met Mr Stratton he was clean-shaven. In the intervening months, he'd grown a thick beard that seemed incongruous for someone who'd grown up at a time when the only men with beards were our grandfathers.

'Thanks for coming.' He shuffled through papers without look-ing at me as I sat down by his desk. 'There are a few issues I'd like to discuss with regard to Joe.'

'He's not doing well at school?' I asked, perplexed. I'd thought this meeting would be pro forma. He'd tell me how great Joe is doing. I'd thank him for his guidance and encouraging words. That's how it'd always been with Joe. Ever since he first started school, Joe had always been a top student. I'd never had to worry about his grades. Truth be told, I'd kind of hoped he might get a college scholarship. He'd been a straight-A student since kindergarten.

'Well.' He cleared his throat. 'I don't need to tell you that Joe's a smart kid. He's doing well enough at school without much effort. If he tried then he would undoubtedly be on the honor roll. That's something we can work towards.'

'But?' From the way his eyes shifted around uncomfortably, I could just tell there was a 'but' coming up.

'He's been skipping afternoon classes. One of the teachers saw him on her day off down at the mall when school was in session. He was hanging out with a group of older kids. Known troublemakers. We sent you a note. Didn't you receive it?'

My handbag felt heavy on my lap. Two days before I had shoved a pile of mail into my purse with the intention of opening it at work over lunch. In the end, there had been no time for lunch, and I'd completely forgotten the letters were there.

CHAPTER NINE

Julie

It's just after eight on Sunday morning when Matt slides out of bed. I watch him disappear into the bathroom and am lulled back to sleep by the spray of the shower. I wake to the loud finality of the front door shutting.

Through the bedroom window, I watch Matt backing the car down the driveway. This sudden, unexplained change of routine unsettles me. We always spend Sundays together.

I watch his car disappear, helpless in my satin pyjamas, which I hate and only wear to make Matt happy. They were a gift from his mother, who conveniently forgot to cut off the discount store price tag. I bet the only reason Anne bought them was to deliver another subtle message. That woman enjoys putting me in my place.

Matt has left a note on the bedside table. He has some urgent work at the university and will be back in time for lunch. So he says. Matt never, and I mean never, goes to work on a Sunday.

He signed the note with the words 'love you' above his name. That should reassure me. When I look closely it's obvious he squeezed in those words as an afterthought.

What work could he possibly have at the university when he's
already brought home a briefcase filled with student papers to mark
over the weekend? Plus we had plans. We'd talked about going
antiquing later in the morning at an open-air market out of town.

I dress and fix my hair and makeup. It's important that I look
my best even on a lazy Sunday morning. I am well aware that my
husband is surrounded by temptation. A few years back, a student
turned up to a lecture with a heart drawn in lipstick on her crotch.
Sans panties, of course. She made sure he saw it too, if you get what
I mean. He told me all about it. I laughed at the time. Today, just
thinking of it scares the hell out of me.

Alice is sleeping on the princess bed we bought when she
turned six. Her dark hair is fanned across the pillow. The bed is a
genuine four-poster that I found at an antique shop and decorated
with gossamer curtains. It's the bed I dreamed of having when I was
a girl, sharing a tiny bedroom with two rickety bunk beds so close to
each other you could jump across them without any risk of falling.

Downstairs I make pancakes. It's a family tradition on Sunday
mornings. That's the other reason I'm annoyed about Matt's
disappearance: he never misses Sunday morning breakfast. We sit
around the table eating pancakes and giggling at silly jokes that
Alice makes up for our amusement. It's my favourite time of the
week. His too. Or so I thought.

I spoon some mixture into the griddle pan and get to work on
making a stack of pancakes. When I'm done I wrap them in a sheet
of foil to keep them warm and put them in the picnic basket along
with a bottle of blueberry sauce. Matt prefers maple syrup. He's
a purist, he always jokes. His damn problem. He should have been
home this morning.

I hate waking Alice, but we need to get moving.

'Hey sleepyhead.' I kiss her forehead. She's a heavy sleeper like her daddy. Alice barely responds. I tickle her softly under her chin. Her blue eyes open and look straight into mine.

'We've got a busy day today, hon,' I tell her. 'Let's get you up and dressed.'

'Mommy,' her voice is hoarse from sleep. 'I thought we were making cupcakes this morning. You promised.'

'We'll bake the cupcakes later.' I put her clothes on her bed. 'Time to get dressed and clean your teeth.'

Alice comes downstairs five minutes later carrying a hairbrush and pastel bands to tie her hair. I brush her hair out as I do every morning. Usually I make little plaits or braids. Today we're in a rush, so I tie a simple ponytail.

'Done,' I tell her. 'Let's get going.'

'But mommy,' she shrieks in dismay, 'we haven't eaten breakfast!'

'I've made a picnic breakfast. We're going to share it with Daddy.'

We arrive at the campus not long after. The place is dead. A typical Sunday morning. Most of the students are sleeping off hangovers. The faculty car park is empty. As is Matt's assigned parking spot. That really rattles me.

I give him the benefit of the doubt. Alice rides her scooter as we head towards his office building. It has a view of a mock-Tudor chapel with a brass bell that rings daily, a hollow ritual designed to give the university a veneer of tradition. I tug the handles of the glass lobby doors. They don't budge. The building is locked.

'He's not here,' says Alice. It takes a six-year-old to point out the obvious.

'Let's try the side entrance,' I suggest. Alice follows behind me on her scooter.

'I told you he's not here,' says Alice, rolling her eyes dramatically when the side door doesn't open either. 'Can I play now, Mommy?'

'You know what? That's a great idea.' My voice lifts in a cheerful falsetto that sounds unconvincing even to my own ears. Alice looks at me oddly.

She loops around the quadrangle twice on her scooter. Her cheeks are pink and her eyes shine. I'm pleased to see how confidently she rides. I let her have a few more turns and then I guide her to the library.

'Let's see the beautiful books,' I whisper as I push open the library door to the hush within. Sunshine from the glass dome illuminates the rotunda with the blinding light of morning.

'Wow, look at the roof, Mommy.' Alice's voice is filled with awe as she cranes her head towards the gold-tipped ceiling. The librarian turns her chair to glare at us.

'Mommy, does it rain through the hole into the library?'

'No, honey. There's glass covering the hole. It doesn't rain inside at all,' I tell her as we take the stairs to the second floor.

I scan every row of bookshelves. There's no sign of Matt working in the library. Not even in the alcoves where the reserve books are kept.

The librarian's eyes bore into my back as we walk out of the swinging doors. Alice takes her scooter from the lobby where I left it and skates around the quadrangle again. After a single loop, we return to the car.

'I'm so hungry,' Alice pronounces as she clambers into her seat. 'Can we have our picnic now? We can save pancakes for Daddy to eat later.'

'Good idea. That's exactly what we're going to do,' I tell her. 'I just need to check one last thing.'

I drive to the faculty club on the outskirts of the campus, where Matt plays racquetball. I see the front fender of a Lincoln parked near the entrance. It's the same model as Matt's car and the same midnight blue colour. Except the licence plate is different. Matt is not at the university.

'Mommy, I'm starving.' Alice gets super irritable when she's hungry. She sings the sentence to the tune of 'Frère Jacques': 'I am hungry. I am hungry.' Usually I find her made-up songs super cute, but today it grates on my nerves. I pull to a stop near the campus's lake.

'You know what Alice, sweetheart. Change of plan. Today, we're going to have our own special picnic by the pond. Just me and you.'

'And the ducks,' she adds, pointing to a family of ducks swimming in the pond. 'They can be in our picnic too.'

'Of course they can.' I help her out of the car.

We eat lukewarm pancakes off plastic plates on a bench overlooking the lake. When we're done eating, I pull apart a pancake and give Alice pieces to throw to the ducks. Alice laughs with delight as a duckling outwits its siblings by snatching the largest piece and swallowing it in one go. I check my phone in case Matt has sent me a text. He hasn't. It dawns on me where Matt might be.

'We have to go now, Alice.' My tone is inadvertently hard, which is always a mistake with Alice. Suddenly she wants to stay. The more I tell her we need to go, the more she insists on staying. 'Just five more minutes, Mommy,' she says. She picks up a stick and pokes it into the water, splashing it over her clean sparkle shoes. I take the stick out of her hand and throw it across the pond.

She's crying now on account of her wet shoes, and the stick, which she says she wanted to show Daddy. I hug her and tell her that I'll clean her shoes at home. I carry her to the car and take off her shoes and socks. She's still crying so I give her a stray mini Hershey's bar lying in the glove box.

I drive at the maximum speed down the highway, heading south, out of town. I take the third exit and drive for ten minutes. When I see the sign I've been looking for I pull off the road into an unpaved parking area. There are three other cars. Matt's isn't one of them.

I park the car facing an adjacent paddock so that Alice can watch mottled cows graze while I'm gone.

'Where are we, Mommy?' she asks.

'In the country. Can't you tell from all the cows!' I give Alice a green lollipop, which I keep in my bag for emergencies such as waiting in cars and temper tantrums in the mall. We get those too, sometimes. Alice does not like shopping.

'I'll be back in a minute,' I say as I pass her my phone so she has something to play with.

She peels off the plastic lollipop wrapper noisily. I get out of the car and lock it.

There's not many people around. Off to the side, a grey-haired man and a younger woman who I assume is his daughter stand with bent heads in front of a gravestone. I walk down the main path until I see a simple white-marble gravestone at odds with the garish monuments on either side.

There's nobody here. My tension eases. I was wrong. I should go back to the car. Yet I'm drawn to the tombstone by an invisible thread. The words 'beloved wife' engraved below Laura's name shimmer in the morning light. A bouquet of fresh white roses lies across the marble slab.

I pick up the roses and open the attached handwritten card. It says simply, 'I miss you. I love you. Forever.'

I received a note with that same handwriting this very morning.

CHAPTER TEN

Mel

Captain Lawrence Howard got up from behind his desk as I entered his office. 'Detective,' he said, gesturing for me to take a seat on a grey upholstered couch that faced a window with a view of the Richmond skyline. An oak bookshelf took up one wall of his office, the other was covered with certificates of merit and framed photographs of him shaking hands with public officials and local sporting celebrities.

Captain Howard looked slick for a cop. His hair was gelled back like a stock trader and he wore an immaculately pressed charcoal suit with a light blue tie and cufflinks. It was the first time I'd ever seen a cop wearing cufflinks to work.

If I'd met him on the street I would have figured him for a realtor, or some other hard-boiled salesman type. But when I looked closely at his face, he was all cop. His eyes were hard and he had a cynical slant to his lips that told you he'd seen it all and nothing surprised him anymore.

'How can I help you?' he said, pulling over a desk chair. It gave

him a height advantage over my seat on the sunken couch. I had no
doubt that was intentional.

'We found a body on Friday, buried in a forest just out of town,'
I said, opening my case file and sliding a photograph along the coffee table. It showed the Kellers Way victim's decomposed remains
in the grave. He examined it without expression. He'd seen images
as bad or worse over his career.

'A woman,' I said. 'She was expensively dressed. Gold jewellery
and a pendant. We don't know her identity. Forensics still hasn't
come in.'

'So if you have nothing to go on, why have you come all the
way to Richmond?' Captain Howard watched me thoughtfully.
There was a tension in his body as he waited for my response. I was
pretty sure he already knew the answer to his question.

'The pendant she wore was unusual. I am wondering whether
it may be connected to the case of Edward Pitt,' I said. Lenny had
warned me to tread carefully with this subject.

'Edward Pitt.' He said it as if he'd forgotten all about his career-
making collar. 'It's a closed case. It has nothing to do with your
victim.' His voice was firm. It brooked no argument.

'Still,' I said, 'could you talk me through the case? At the
moment, we have no ID and no leads. It's possible there might be
a link between the two cases. Perhaps Edward Pitt was the perp
in this new case? He would have been active around the time my
victim was killed.'

'I doubt it,' he said, looking at his watch, 'but we have twenty
minutes until my next meeting so I might as well give you a run-
down.' No cop, least of all a guy with a monumental ego like
Captain Howard, likes it when questions are asked about a closed
case, especially a case he's built his reputation on.

He removed a hardcover book from his shelf and passed it to me. On the cover was a photograph of a man with a weak chin and thinning hair looking blankly into the camera. The book was a distraction. Captain Howard wanted to gather his thoughts. Figure out how he'd play me.

'You've heard about the Edward Pitt case I assume?' he asked.

'Not in detail,' I lied, flicking through the pages of the book. It was a true-crime book written by a journalist from the *Richmond Chronicle*. The inside cover bore a handwritten inscription by the author made out to Captain Howard of the Richmond Police Department for his 'invaluable insights'.

'Edward Pitt was a railway engineer.' He began in a tone that suggested he'd told this story many times before. 'For thirty years of his life, Pitt worked on the railways. Then he lost his job as part of general lay-offs and became an itinerant worker. He worked mostly in rural areas doing day labour, mechanical type of work when he could get it. Odd jobs. He didn't have a record. Nothing. He hadn't so much as racked up a speeding fine in all the fifty-eight years he'd walked this earth.' He paused. 'Pitt was for all purposes an exemplary citizen.'

I nodded like the wide-eyed small-town cop he took me for so that he would get to the point. Fast. I wanted time for questions.

'All his life Pitt's been in the best of health,' he said, 'then he starts wheezing. Night sweats. Loses weight. He's working in Richmond at the time and he comes into our local hospital, which is just three blocks from here.' I gave a firm nod. Cut to the chase, I thought.

'The doctors tell Pitt that he has oesophageal cancer. He has a year to live, maybe less. They tell him to get his affairs in order. He asks if there is any treatment. The doctors say there's a new drug that targets the vascular development of the tumour and slows the spread of the cancer. It's not a cure, they say, but it could buy him a few years. Trouble is it's a non-standard treatment and very expensive. Pitt doesn't have health insurance. He lost it when he lost his job. So what does Edward Pitt do?' He looked at me as if waiting for an answer.

'He comes over here into this building,' Captain Howard paused for effect, 'and says he wants to confess to the murder of fourteen women.'

He watched my face for a reaction. I gave a slight nod to keep him talking.

'Well, we didn't know if this guy was messing with us. You've no doubt worked homicide long enough to know there are plenty of lunatics out there who want to get famous by pretending to be killers. So I asked him for details. He fed me a few scraps to whet my appetite,' said Captain Howard.

'Like what?' I asked.

'He gave me a couple of names and details of women abducted in this area over the previous decade. I looked them up while he sat in a holding cell. He knew stuff that hadn't been released to the public. His story rang true.' I tried to look suitably impressed.

'I get the prosecutor involved,' he continued. 'He thinks it's a ruse by Pitt to get medical treatment. But I've done enough digging by then to know that this guy is not bullshitting us. In the end, we cut a deal. He'll tell us the locations of the bodies and the details of each victim and he gets prioritised for cancer treatment at the prison hospital. We figured it was worth it for the closure it would give the families. And, worst case scenario, he goes into remission and the state executes him before the cancer gets to him.'

'He gave you all his victims' names?'

'He sure did,' said Captain Howard. He took a sip of water. 'We found all the bodies buried right where he said they would be, on an abandoned farm in West Virginia that once belonged to his family, as well as one body that had been burned. He claimed it was his most recent kill.'

'Were you able to identify the burnt body that you found?' I asked.

'Pitt put the body in an oil drum and poured accelerant over it,' Captain Howard said. 'The body was almost incinerated in the flames.'

He opened the true-crime book and showed me a photograph of a woman with an angular face and a wide mouth. In isolation her features seemed irregular. Together they worked perfectly. She was beautiful. Around her neck was a pendant that seemed awfully similar to the pendant we'd found on the Kellers Way victim. Not that I shared that observation with Captain Howard.

'Pitt confessed to her murder. Told us how he abducted her down in your neck of the woods while on a deer-hunting trip. He said he drove across state lines with her alive in his trunk before eventually killing her. He said he incinerated her body because the case had become high profile and he was worried about getting caught. When he gave himself up, the bastard demanded the reward the victim's family was offering for information on her disappearance. He said it was to pay for experimental cancer drugs not covered by the treatment he was going to receive in prison. He was mighty upset to find out that the killer can't claim the reward.'

'Is there a chance he lied to get the reward money?' I asked.

'Absolutely not,' said Howard vehemently. 'He gave us enough information to confirm she was his victim. Even the coroner agreed.'

'Where is Pitt now?'

'Pitt was supposed to plead guilty to the murders as part of the deal. The night before his court appearance, he went to sleep in a holding cell and never woke up.'

'Suicide?'

Captain Howard shook his head. 'The bastard died in his sleep from a heart attack.'

CHAPTER ELEVEN

Julie

Matt returns home in time for lunch, ostensibly from the university. Of course, I know the truth. He was at the cemetery this morning. To leave flowers for Laura. On their wedding anniversary no less.

I know that I should be fine with the idea of Matt visiting Laura's grave. Part of me, the part that feels bad for Laura, gets it. But another part of me resents it like hell, especially when he does it behind my back. The truth is that I'm jealous of what they had together. Nothing we have could ever measure up. Our relationship is weak and uncertain by comparison.

He opens the Sunday newspaper at the table as if he wants to create a barrier between us. I clear my throat and clatter the cutlery loudly as I serve up lunch. Matt gets the hint. He tosses the newspaper onto an empty chair and butters a bread roll still warm from the oven.

'How did it go this morning?' I keep my voice as normal as possible as I ladle pasta sauce on his spaghetti.

'Very productive,' he answers vaguely and then changes the subject abruptly. 'So, what did my beautiful girls get up to today?' He picks up his cutlery and curls the spaghetti around his fork as he waits for an answer.

'We went to feed the ducks,' Alice pipes up excitedly. She has a tendency to give an exhaustive account of absolutely everything that happens to her on any given day. 'And then Mommy drove —'

I quickly cut her off. 'Mommy drove Alice to a picnic breakfast by a pond,' I complete her sentence, 'and then we did some riding on your scooter. Right honey?' I give Alice a sharp look. She is noticeably silent for the rest of lunch.

Afterwards, Matt and Alice plant herbs in clay pots Alice decorated at school. When I bring them a plate of freshly baked cookies, Matt mumbles something about needing to do work and disappears into his study.

He obviously milked Alice for information while they were planting. He must suspect that I went to the campus to check up on him this morning. I have a perfectly reasonable explanation, but he doesn't ask me. He sits at his mahogany desk and contemplates what exactly? Me? Our marriage? I can't remember ever seeing him so mad at me. It's the first time I truly fear that everything is unravelling. I always knew it would eventually. I just didn't know that it would happen so quickly.

'How about we go to the park?' I ask Alice. She's on the porch eating the last cookie.

'Ok,' she says. 'Is Daddy coming with us?'

'Daddy's working today,' I tell her. I help her into her jacket and woollen hat.

Even though the sky is a cloudless blue, the wind chill kind of makes you wish you were indoors. Still, the playground is crowded with kids and parents standing around watching them play. I stay with Alice until she strikes up a friendship with two other girls around her age.

'You can go now, Mommy,' Alice orders, crossing her arms until I've left.

I find an empty seat on a bench. The woman sitting next to me looks vaguely familiar.

'You're Alice's mum,' she says, pushing a stroller back and forth to get her baby to sleep. 'Our daughters are in dance classes together.'

'Of course,' I say as if I remember her. We chat about the only thing we have in common which is, unsurprisingly, dance class.

'How old is your baby?' I grasp for a new subject when we run out of conversation about the extensive preparations for this year's dance recital.

'Fletcher's four months,' she says, tenderly pulling the stroller towards her to straighten his blanket. The baby sucks his pacifier in his sleep like a blowfish.

'He's gorgeous,' I say, trying to hide the longing in my voice.

Out of nowhere a ball hits me in the left knee. Hard enough to leave a bruise. Two boys approach, both around ten. There is no hint of contrition on their amused faces as they stand there defiantly, waiting for me to pick up the ball and return it to them. I hold the soccer ball until they realise they might not get it back and their smirks disappear.

'Sorry,' says the younger boy grudgingly. He flicks his sandy hair in a gesture that tells me he's not sorry at all.

'Be more careful would you!' I throw the ball back so hard the boy loses his footing catching it. Linda, the other mother, watches this exchange with an uncomfortable expression on her face. I look bad. Harsh. Aggressive. They are only kids after all. I soften my tone. 'There's a baby here,' I call out as they walk off. 'He could have been hurt.'

Linda rocks her baby's stroller frantically. She thinks I over-reacted. I want to tell her she'd have done the same thing if the ball had slammed into her leg. It hurt like hell. I don't say anything. We've run out of conversation.

'I'd better find Alice.' I scramble up and scan the playground. I lost track of Alice during the incident with the boys. It's hard to find her now, in a playground full of girls wearing similar outfits of jeans, pink jacket and a woollen hat.

Alice is not in my line of sight. I walk up the ramp right onto the play equipment to look for her. There is no sign of Alice. I head over to the slide, where I glimpse the back of a little girl wearing a pink parka whose dark hair is tucked behind her ears like Alice's. 'Alice,' I call out. 'Alice.' The girl spins around curiously and then walks off. It's not Alice.

'Alice!' I call in panic. Heads turn in sympathetic concern. 'Alice!' My voice rises into an urgent pitch.

The tune of an approaching ice-cream truck drowns out my frantic efforts to find my daughter. A frenzy of excitement follows as children run to their parents pleading for money.

'Ice-cream?' a father tells his daughter. 'You must be crazy. It's freezing today.' He reluctantly takes out money from his wallet and she joins the throng of kids waiting in an unruly line by the ice-cream truck window. Alice is not among them.

The crowd of kids playing in the playground has thinned out as more of them join the line for ice-cream. The swings are empty. A few girls play jump rope on a path. They are all older and taller than Alice. I head over to a group of girls playing by a hedge. As I approach, Alice emerges from the branches and runs towards me.

'Look, Mommy. We've opened a cafe.' She points to a gap in the hedge. 'Would you like me to make you a milkshake?'

'You were supposed to stay near me,' I whisper into her ear so as not to embarrass her in front of her friends.

'I'm sorry, Mommy,' she says. Her eyes are troubled.

'Let's go home, baby.' I engulf Alice's hand in my own as we walk towards the car.

We stop at the supermarket on the way back. I buy milk, macaroni and cheese; Alice's favourite Sunday night dinner. We always do a light dinner on Sundays. It's inevitably mac and cheese. Matt likes it too, probably because his mother never once gave him macaroni and cheese when he was a kid. It's too bourgeois for Anne. I don't think Anne even knows the term 'comfort food'.

It's late afternoon when I drive my car into the driveway. Alice is fast asleep in the back. She's too heavy for me to carry into the house. Matt's car is gone. He often plays racquetball on Sunday afternoons so I figure that's what he's doing.

I carry the groceries into the house. Once I open the front door, I figure I might as well take the groceries all the way into the kitchen instead of leaving them in the hall.

Then I figure I'll quickly unpack the groceries. When that's done, I realise I haven't had a thing to eat or drink for hours, so I slide a coffee capsule into the machine and froth milk.

The coffee calms my nerves after the incident in the park. I pass our baby grand piano in the living room, off the hall. It's been a long time since I played. Soon my fingers are on the keys and I am lost in the music of Chopin's nocturnes.

'What the hell were you thinking?' Matt's voice breaks through the harmony. I stop playing abruptly and look up at him numbly, my hands frozen on the keys.

I can't hear his words through the buzz that fills my ears. But I know he is angry because his finger keeps poking at me accusingly as his mouth opens and closes in angry bursts.

Alice sobs hoarsely in his arms, her head pressed against his chest. I want to ask what is going on, but all I can do is look blankly at Matt and Alice. The throbbing in my ears gets so loud that I cover them to block out the sound.

How could I have forgotten Alice in the car? I wasn't away very long. Was I? I look out the window. It's dark outside.

'I'm sorry,' I say looking up at Matt in confusion. 'I didn't realise I was gone so long.'

'Aside from the fact that Alice was terrified,' Matt says through gritted teeth, 'anyone could have come and taken her. Anyone.'

'I'm sorry,' I repeat.

It's too late. I'm talking to nobody but myself. Matt has stormed out of the living room with Alice in his arms.

Later that night, Matt and I have the worst argument we've ever had. Matt doesn't do loud and dramatic. He's too well bred. Even when he argues he does it courteously. He's a psychologist so he likes to think he's above getting carried away with base human emotions such as anger.

He argues with clenched teeth, cold and restrained. He never raises his voice. Quite the opposite: I have to strain to hear him. He chooses his words carefully. The psychologist in him asks lots of questions in a super reasonable tone that makes me automatically feel at fault. Why did you do this? How can we overcome this issue? Why are you feeling this way?

I think it's passive aggressive. His questions are never directed at himself.

Then he asks me when I last took my meds. 'Julie, you're not acting responsibly by skipping doses. Do I need to hire a nurse to make sure you take your medication?' He goes on and on about my meds until I block out his drone by imagining that I'm running in a forest. I hear the thump of my feet striking the ground, the hiss of me exhaling. In and out. Hard and fast.

'Go to hell, Matt,' I respond when I see from his pursed mouth that he has stopped talking. To emphasise my point, I pick up an ornament that I happen to love and I hurl it across the room. It hits the wall and shatters into a thousand pieces.

Matt says nothing. He looks at me as if seeing me for the first time. That's when I break down in a flood of tears. I can turn on the waterworks on demand. It's a childhood talent I've perfected over the years. This time, it doesn't work. His expression is only one of disgust.

This horrible argument at the end of the worst day of our marriage concludes with Matt barging out of the house. He slams the front door behind him, which is very out of character because Matt likes to think of himself as incapable of childish gestures. Car tyres screech as he reverses the car down the driveway and tears off in a fury.

After he's gone, I hear Alice sobbing on her bed. She heard the shouting and watched through the balustrades as Matt marched out. I can tell that she blames herself.

Her bottom lip wobbles as I cradle her on the bed. 'Daddy asked me where else we'd been. I told him about how I rode my scooter and our visit to the library. But not a children's library, a library with adult books and with a hole in the roof where sunshine comes in,' she tells me.

'Daddy's just tired. He worked hard today.' I hug Alice until her sobs abate. We lie together on her bed and she falls asleep in my arms. The exhaustion and emotions of the day make me drowsy. I close my eyes and doze off alongside her, our hands intertwined. I wake up close to midnight and go into our bedroom.

The bed is as empty and neatly made up as it was this morning. Matt has not come home. I climb into bed in my bra and panties. I'm too tired to shower or change.

He turns up an hour before dawn. He lies on the edge of the bed, as far from me as he can possibly get without falling out. I smell honeysuckle on his skin. He's seen her again. I'm sure of it.

CHAPTER TWELVE

Mel

Rattling around in the trunk of my car as I drove along I-85 were five boxes of files on loan from the Richmond Police Department. They were all stamped with the words 'closed case'.

Those boxes are why I spent four hours driving to Richmond and back instead of filing request forms through the proper channels. I wanted the files immediately, without having to jump through bureaucratic hoops to get them.

When the meeting with Howard came to a close I handed him a records request form, already filled out. All he had to do was sign.

He was in a bind. He could have stonewalled me. He could easily have delayed things a week or two by making me go through the official procedures, but I would have received the Pitt files in the end. I knew that. He knew that. We had a body lying in the morgue, most likely wearing jewellery that belonged to Pitt's last known victim. Whichever way you looked at it, there was going to be scrutiny of the Pitt case. Temporarily blocking my investigation wasn't going to get Captain Howard off the hook.

In the end, he did what I'd bet on when I decided to drive out to Richmond in the first place. He got ahead of the problem, in true political style, by becoming part of the solution. Captain Howard signed my request form and called ahead to get the boxes ready for me. He also made it crystal clear, off the record, that I owed him big time.

The boxes were waiting at the records department's reception, just as he'd promised. I loaded them into my car and turned straight back home without stopping for lunch, even though my stomach was rumbling something awful.

I needed to get back to the office and work through the files as best I could before picking up Joe from baseball practice. I was determined to keep a close eye on my rebellious oldest son until things settled down for him at school.

The day before, I had told Joe what his teacher said in our meeting. 'Big deal,' he shrugged.

'Who are these kids you're hanging out with at the mall?' I asked. Another shrug.

Then he let loose. After all, attack is the best defence, every teenager knows that. He told me that he hates it here. He wants to return to New York City. He wants his old friends back. The kids in this town are hicks. Why did I ever bring them here?

I barely slept that night, trying to figure things out. Perhaps he was right. Maybe we should go back. But what he really wanted, I knew this deep down in my heart, was his father.

This morning, I drove Joe and Sammy to school. Much to Joe's embarrassment. I usually drop Sammy off in the mornings, but Joe likes to get to school himself.

Kids Joe's age take the bus, ride their bike, or they walk. They never, ever get dropped off at school by their moms. That's what

Joe told me. I told him 'tough luck'. Not only did I drop him off but I waited behind the wheel until he disappeared inside the front entrance of the main school building.

I was pleased to see him joined by two boys, good kids who had been his closest friends until a few months back he started complaining that they were geeky. I should have seen the writing on the wall back then. But if Joe was now back with the nerdy kids that had to be a good sign. Right?

Thanks to a clear run on the interstate on the way back from Richmond I arrived at the office in the early afternoon. It took five trips to haul the boxes from the car to my desk. I kind of wished Will was around to carry some of them. Those boxes were damn heavy. Still, I refused all offers of help on the way to and from the car. Ever since I was a rookie, I've made a point of never showing physical weakness to a male colleague. I carried every last box to my desk myself, even though I felt as if I might keel over by the end. In lieu of lunch I bought a candy bar from the vending machine and poured myself a coffee.

The top of the first box contained a file secured with an elastic band. Inside was a thick pile of photographs of Pitt's victims. I flipped through them quickly. They were mostly personal photos, provided by the victims' families for identification purposes. Among them was a photo of a woman with short strawberry blond hair and an exuberant smile. You could tell from her eyes that she didn't have the faintest premonition of the brutal fate that awaited her. They never do.

It reminded me of a photo of Danny that I'd taken with an old Nikon during a hiking trip three weeks before he was killed. He was watching a goldfinch building a nest in a tree off the hiking trail. For the longest time I couldn't look at that photo. The look of wonder on Danny's face broke my heart. He loved life too much to lose his own.

I put the photographs to the side and opened the murder book. It's a fancy name for a binder that consolidates the key leads in the case. It's always a good starting point when revisiting an old case because it summarises all the information collected by the previous investigators.

'Looks like you'll be working through the night, detective.' I looked up to see Lenny heading over to my desk. He was wearing a blue Hawaiian-print shirt and grass-stained pants that told me he'd come directly from his golf club.

'Hey, Lenny, I didn't expect you for another hour,' I said as I closed the file. He pulled over a chair and sat alongside my desk.

'I see it went well in Richmond,' he said, tapping the files covering my desk.

'Thanks to your advice on handling Howard. He was touchy as hell just like you said he'd be.'

'Guys like that need their egos massaged, or else they shut you out,' he said.

'Well, I don't know about massaging his ego,' I said, 'but I got what I wanted.'

I passed Lenny a black-and-white photograph of a dark-haired woman with a warm smile and restless eyes. It was the same photograph that Captain Howard had shown me in his office.

'What do you remember about Pitt's last victim?' I asked. 'The one whose body was burned.'

'More than I care to.' Lenny sighed. 'She was one of my last cases.'

'Can you get me up to speed on her disappearance? There's not a lot of nuance in the case notes from what I've seen so far,' I said.

'I'll tell you what I remember.' Lenny's chair creaked as he leaned forward to examine the photo.

'She was a professor at the university,' he said. 'Fulbright scholar. A list of awards as long as my arm. It was a big deal when she went missing. The students held candlelight vigils. They gave out fliers all over town. Put up posters. Doorknocking. You name it, they did it,' Lenny said. 'She was popular. Widely respected.'

'It says here she went shopping and never came back,' I said.

'Her disappearance was reported the following day. The car was found a few days later, abandoned about twenty miles out of town. There were no bloodstains. No signs of a struggle. It looked as if she'd been changing a flat tyre when she was taken. We'd probably have never found her killer if Pitt hadn't confessed to her murder along with all the others. He told us where the body was. We found it. And the case was closed.'

'Her jewellery was never recovered? That never troubled you?'

'Pitt claimed he sold her jewellery in Atlantic City to cover gambling debts. I went up there to look, but I couldn't find a trace. It was always an outside chance. Those pawn shops turn over gold jewellery fast, and they're lax with their record keeping.'

'Was forensics able to confirm the identity of the burned body?' I asked the question that had been on my mind for much of the drive back from Richmond.

'The body was practically incinerated,' he answered. 'Pitt doused it with highly flammable liquid and burned it in an oil drum. There wasn't much left. And what *was* there was useless for identification purposes. The fire destroyed the DNA. In the end, it was the coroner who called it.'

'What about the victim's family? Didn't they fight the decision to close the case even though there was no DNA confirmation?'

Usually, families of victims hold on to the smallest scrap of hope until they get indisputable evidence that their loved one is no longer alive.

'We found the charred remains of a woman in a burnt-out oil barrel just like Pitt said. He flat-out confessed to her murder,' Lenny said. 'The coroner ruled that she was murdered by Pitt. The remains, or what was left of them, were handed over to the family for burial. They got their closure.'

'Back up for a second,' I said. 'What do you mean it was clear from the way the car was left that she was abducted?'

'The car had been wiped clean,' Lenny said simply.

'I didn't see that in the file.' I flicked through the pages. 'So you didn't even find the victim's prints in the car?'

'The killer had gone through the car with a bottle of cleaning spray and a rag. He cleaned everything; door handles, seatbelts, dashboard. Best damn car detailing job that I'd ever seen. We found not a scrap of evidence that anyone had been in the car.'

'I don't get it,' I said, standing up and checking through the files littering my desk until I found the one that I wanted. 'Pitt had no criminal record. He wasn't in the system. Why would he go to the trouble of removing all his prints? Lenny, it doesn't make sense that a killer without a criminal record, not even a traffic infringement, would cover up so thoroughly.'

'Pitt might not have known that his prints weren't in the system. He might have decided that it was better to be safe than sorry,' suggested Lenny.

Anything was possible. I had to look at the case from the vantage point of the original investigators. Hindsight can be deceptive.

'Look,' said Lenny. 'Pitt died before he answered a long list of questions. There's no doubt there was plenty we never found out.

That's why I suggested you get the case files from Richmond. There are inconsistencies. And because the jewellery you showed me last time, from the Kellers Way victim, reminded me of the Pitt case.'

'As far as I'm concerned, the key question right now is whether Pitt killed the Kellers Way victim. Is that what you think happened, Lenny?'

'It's possible,' he shrugged. 'Maybe the Kellers Way victim was Pitt's girlfriend, or a working girl that he was infatuated with. Maybe he gave her jewellery as a gift, jewellery taken from the body of the victim that he burned.'

'He wouldn't do that.' I wasn't certain of much in the case, but I was absolutely sure of that point. 'According to the file, Pitt's financial situation was dire. Between jobs, he sometimes ate at soup kitchens. A man who is flat broke, who at times can't afford a proper meal, would not leave gold jewellery on a victim's body. Even if she was his ex-girlfriend.'

'You could be right,' said Lenny. 'I'm not saying you aren't.'

'And if I am right then there is a natural conclusion, isn't there, Lenny?' I needed him to confirm what I was thinking. That they'd botched the identification of Pitt's last victim. That she wasn't who they thought she was.

'If your hunch is right then one thing is for sure,' Lenny responded. 'We all screwed up. Me, Richmond police, and the coroner.'

I was interrupted by the insistent ring of my phone.

'Yeah,' I answered, mouthing an apology to Lenny.

'Mom.' Silence. 'It's me. Joe.' My son's voice was shaky. 'Mom, I, can you —' His incoherent words were cut off by sobs as he broke down.

'Joe,' I said. 'Joe.' I tried to keep my own voice steady. 'Where are you?'

'I'm at Nelson,' he sobbed. My mind ticked over, trying to figure out why my teenage son was in a town all the way on the other side of the county when he should have been in his classroom at school.

'Hello, ma'am.' A new voice. Gruff. Official.

'Your son was brought in this afternoon. We'll need you to be present when we question him.'

CHAPTER THIRTEEN

Julie

I press Matt's business shirt to my face and get the faintest whiff of a perfume scented with honeysuckle. Ever since our argument, he's been coming home late with alcohol on his breath and the milky scent of an unfamiliar soap on his skin. He always has a ready excuse: a racquetball game he'd forgotten to mention, a faculty meeting that ran over time, a post-grad student having a meltdown. There's always an explanation. It never rings true.

Been there, done that, I want to tell him. But I say nothing, because once I mention his infidelities there's no going back. No way to pretend they never happened. No way to pretend our marriage is anything other than flawed, and broken, and littered with lies.

I spray stain remover on his shirt collar to remove a lipstick smudge. Not mine. I wear coral, which suits my blond hair. This lipstick shade is a deep red, perfect for a girl with long, black hair. I feel a wave of nausea, and something else. Blind panic.

I furiously rub the fabric to remove the stubborn smudge.

I've turned a blind eye to Matt's affairs before. But this one, this one is different. That girl flirting with him at the lecture was the image of Laura at the same age, the age when they first met. He sees her as his second chance. Where does that leave me?

I throw Matt's shirt into the laundry sink to soak. I refuse to sit at home playing the helpless housewife when I should be staking my claim.

Thirty minutes later, I'm at the university, heading to the auditorium where Matt is lecturing. I buy two coffees from a vending machine in the lobby. I take a deep breath outside the wood-panelled door and walk in like it's the most natural thing in the world for me to turn up unannounced at my husband's psychology lecture. Nobody notices. They're watching Matt. He paces as he talks. Hands in pockets. The velvet timbre of his voice keeps everyone enthralled.

Usually when I sneak into his lectures I sit anonymously in a dark corner so I won't be seen. This time I want Matt to know that I'm here. I want him to know that I am watching. I want them to know too; all those sycophantic girls who follow my husband's every gesture with predatory eyes.

I inhale nervously and walk towards the lectern. My high-heeled boots click loudly as I cross the floor. It gets their attention. When I reach the podium, I smile and put the coffee cup on the table for Matt. I turn back and take an empty seat near the door.

I look my ice-blond best with my hair brushed into a slick knot and light makeup on my face. I wear taupe pants and a cream silk shirt with an azure scarf tied around my neck in the style made famous by Grace Kelly; all that's missing are the oversized sunglasses. I'm marking my territory. That's why I'm here. Pissing on a tree like a dog. I'm here to make sure they know Matt's mine.

We made up the day after the argument. Make-up sex. Me on top, riding him until he fell back onto his pillow exhausted. I collapsed on his chest. Twenty-four hours of the silent treatment was quite enough. I know how to get things back on track.

'Sorry,' I told him afterwards. 'It was completely out of character. I lost track of time. You know that I adore Alice. It will never happen again.' I curled up in his arms thinking that everything was fine.

Except there was wariness in his eyes the next morning. He tried to hide it but I could tell. He skipped breakfast and instead drank a mug of coffee, leaning against the kitchen counter. He mumbled something about being late and rushed out of the house. I happened to know his first class wasn't until after lunch. I wondered who else might have some free time that morning. He kissed me as he left, a pathetic effort at pretending we were back to normal.

So here I am at his lecture; a human 'trespassers will be prosecuted' sign. Every now and then his female groupies steal sideways glances at me. They're sizing me up. I smile serenely. It's why I am here looking my kick-ass best. Why would a man with a wife this hot want to stray? That's the question I want all of them to ask themselves the next time they try to catch his eye.

Matt lifts the coffee cup towards me in a gesture of gratitude before taking a sip. His eyes are hard. He's pissed as hell that I'm here. I smile innocently.

He's a performer. You have to give him that. When he turns it on, he lights up the room. His light-hearted jokes keep stupid smiles permanently stuck on his students' faces. They don't take their eyes off him, not even to check their cellphones. He has them all in the palm of his hand. And doesn't he just know it.

The lecture hall is almost full. I've heard that students fight to get a place in Matt's courses, especially girls. The seventy–thirty female-to-male ratio in the auditorium is confirmation.

Matt wears a bottle green blazer and dark pants. He uses his frameless glasses like an actor on a stage. He takes them off, waves them to emphasise a point, folds them and tucks them in his front shirt pocket, then puts them on again to read something in his notes. Each time, the faint click of the glasses frames opening and shutting fills the lecture hall with anticipation.

He doesn't even need reading glasses. They're like everything else in his life: an illusion. The loving father, devoted husband, empathetic therapist.

Today he's playing professor. He's charismatic, amusing, incredibly engaging. He revels in this role. That's why he refuses to dye his hair even though grey flecks are breaking out amid the brown strands. I bought him hair dye from a specialty store in town where the shop assistant matched the shade to a strand I pulled from his hairbrush. He flatly refuses to use it. You know what, I'll forgive him the hair dye if the grey strands discourage these college girls from acting on their crushes.

He asks two students onto the podium to illustrate a point about cognitive function. He gives them word games to play. Soon the room is filled with laughter as the students struggle to list the days of the week in alphabetical order.

With me watching, Matt is on his best behaviour. He tries hard not to look at the girl from last time; the girl with dark hair whose lipstick stained the shirt collar currently soaking in my laundry sink. Laura's clone. His eyes are drawn to her despite himself. She wears a pale blue cardigan with a tight black leotard underneath that exposes a sliver of cleavage. She puts up her hand with a studied elegance. She speaks loudly and confidently, though she blushes slightly under his attentive gaze.

'Good question, Emily,' Matt says, a little too enthusiastically. His students' eyes turn to me again to see my reaction. They know that something is going on between the two of them. Why else would they be watching my response so closely?

'I was hoping someone would ask me that question because it brings us to an interesting topic that I saved for last,' says Matt. 'Emily, since you asked the question you should come down and participate in this next exercise.' I watch their eyes connect for a millisecond. They give each other a look so intimate that it makes me shudder. I swallow hard and keep the serene smile fixed on my face like it's been pasted on with superglue. Everyone is watching. I won't let them see my humiliation.

Emily, I think to myself. Now I know my rival's name.

Emily flicks her hair behind her shoulders as she takes her place alongside Matt on the podium. Emily has two dimples in the left cheek that give the impression of a perpetual smile. Her posture is perfect. Her hair is dark and shiny.

Matt whispers instructions into Emily's ear. The students turn their heads towards me to watch my reaction to this show of intimacy. I respond with deliberate nonchalance.

'As you all know, memory is the process of encoding, storing and retrieving information.' Matt's voice reverberates across the room. 'If any one of these functions is disturbed then the quality of the memory may be affected. Or the ability to recall a stored memory. Sometimes it may even result in a false memory.

'What do I mean by this? Well, let me show you. I gave Emily a list of words to recall. They are on the screen behind her so that you can all follow along. After memorising the words, I asked Emily to watch a brief video on my computer with a neutral subject.

In this case, butterflies. Without looking, Emily will now recite as many words on the list behind her as she can remember. Go ahead, Emily.'

Emily stands with her back to the whiteboard, reeling off the words she has memorised. There are ten of them on the board behind her. She gets seven correct.

'Now,' Matt says. 'I am going to show Emily the same set of words, after which she will watch another video.'

We all wait as Emily memorises the same list of words. She nods her head when she is ready and Matt turns his computer screen towards her and plays another video.

'Go ahead, Emily,' says Matt when the video is finished. She names the words on the list. This time she gets just five correct.

'In this example, Emily should have been able to recall the words at least as well as she did the first time around. In actual fact, her performance was significantly worse. That's because this time she watched a traumatic video of a bus being struck by a train at a railway crossing. It affected her short-term memory recall. Now, these are hardly laboratory conditions, but I think you all get the point. Trauma affects memory.'

Emily walks back to her seat flicking her hair and looking like the cat that got every last drop of cream. How I wish I could wipe that smug smile off her pretty, dimpled face.

'Who here believes that memories can be tampered with? That memories can be deliberately introduced so that we can't tell if an event actually happened or if we just think it did? A show of hands.' About half of the room put up their hands.

'The lost in the mall experiment suggests that memories can be planted. A researcher gave his subjects booklets with a number of true anecdotes from their childhood. He also planted a false one, namely that as a child the subject was lost in a shopping mall. He found that a quarter of the participants not only remembered this supposed traumatic childhood event, but even added specific details to the memory. This is a hotly debated area of psychology, but there is plenty of research that shows memories can be caused by suggestion,' says Matt, looking at his watch.

'We'll pick this up next week when we discuss in more detail the factors that affect memory. Make sure to read page 142 to 165 of the textbook. And remember your term papers are due in exactly one week,' he says over the clatter of students stuffing their belongings into their bags.

Matt's groupies, including Emily, converge at his desk with questions. He answers them with good humour as he shuts down his laptop and packs his briefcase. I wait for him by the door. When he approaches, he leans in to kiss me with a lifeless brush of his lips on my cheek.

'What are you doing here, Julie?' His tone is cold.

'You forgot your papers.' I pull out a folder from my shoulder bag. 'I came to drop them off.'

'I thought I packed them in my briefcase,' he says. He did, but I removed them.

'I found them after you left,' I lie. 'They were on the floor near the coat stand. Alice probably pulled them out of your bag. She was playing with it this morning.'

'Was she?' His hand tightens on my arm as we walk through throngs of students. 'Let's go upstairs. It's too noisy here to talk.'

It's more of a threat than an invitation. I accompany him through the tide of students moving between classes, looking at their phone screens while they walk.

Matt guides me towards the elevator. It's almost full. We get inside and turn around to face the closed doors. My fingers brush against Matt's ever so softly. Ever so invitingly. I inhale his citrus scent and catch his eye. It's as if we are a single seething organism. He knows exactly what I'm thinking. We are incredibly attuned at the most basic, animal level, even though everything else between us is so complicated right now.

When we reach the third floor, we walk towards his office like impatient teenagers, except I'm wearing boots with high heels and I can barely keep up with his long strides. Matt's been stand-offish for days. Cold. Correct. The only time everything is normal is when we have sex.

That's what I want to do, right there in his office. Spice things up. Isn't that what the marriage therapists suggest in their magazine columns? We walk towards an office at the end of the corridor with 'Professor Matthew West' engraved on a plaque on the door. Matt holds the door ajar for me to enter. I am about to pull him towards me when I realise that we're not alone.

'Hello, Kate,' he says with a note of surprise. A woman sits on his couch with her legs neatly crossed. 'I hope I haven't kept you waiting.'

'Not at all. You're right on time,' she answers.

Her black-framed glasses are oversized and contrast with her linen pants and jacket. I suspect that she's a post-graduate student. Or maybe she works for the university.

'Kate, this is my wife, Julie. She dropped by to watch my lecture,' says Matt, putting his jacket over his chair and unpacking his leather briefcase.

For a psychologist Matt can be very insensitive to other people's feelings. I still have no idea who Kate is, all I know about her is her first name. What upsets me most is that he hasn't made the slightest effort to get rid of her. I shake her hand with a bland smile.

'I'm the new research assistant in Matt's department,' she says as she releases my hand. It annoys me that she feels the need to identify herself as someone non-threatening. She's just a research assistant. Nothing for me to worry about. Oh well, that's ok then, I want to tell her. Matt would never fuck a research assistant. Matt, of course, says nothing.

I stand waiting, with a stupid smile on my face, for Matt to reschedule the meeting with Kate. Or for him to ask me to meet up with him in an hour at the faculty club for lunch. Or something.

He does none of that. He leaves Kate and me to stand around awkwardly while he puts on his glasses and flicks through the file she dropped off.

'We can go over the initial study results together later, or tomorrow,' she offers.

'No, no,' says Matt, putting the document aside. 'We set this up days ago. Julie, you don't mind, do you?' It's hardly a request.

'Of course not.' I keep my voice upbeat. I don't want to show my embarrassment at being discarded so casually by my own husband. Let alone in front of a woman who treats him with such familiarity.

'Actually,' I say, making a show of looking at my watch, 'I have a lunch arrangement across town so I'd best get going. It was nice to meet you, Kate.' I smile. 'I'll see you later Matt.'

'Yes, enjoy your lunch, darling,' he says absently. He's forgotten about me already.

I close his office door behind me with a strange finality. Only then do I lean against the wall with my hand to my mouth to block the sobs. Tears blur my eyes. A door down the corridor opens. I don't want anyone to see me in this state. I run down the emergency stairs as if I'm escaping a fire.

Through a film of tears, I find my car and sit in the driver's seat, shaking uncontrollably, watching raindrops tap onto the windshield. When I've calmed down, I drive home robotically. I walk through the front door, without any memory of the drive. I don't even remember which route I took to get here. It's all a haze.

I go straight to our bedroom and swallow two sleeping tablets with a mouthful of water straight from the bathroom tap. I curl up on my bed still in my designer outfit. I don't have the energy to change. I'm overwhelmed by helplessness as I listen to the wind whipping up outside. I drift to sleep to the sound of tree branches scraping against my bedroom window. My last thought before unconsciousness envelops me is of a man with cloudy eyes and a bloodied face shaking his head in disappointment. 'You're not safe, Julie,' he says. The rest of his words are swallowed up by the roar of the storm.

CHAPTER FOURTEEN

Mel

Through the one-way mirror of the police interview room, I watched Joe nonchalantly leaning back in his chair, his legs stretched in front of him as if he was hanging out with his crew. His obnoxious smirk was all bravado and adolescent defiance. I could see the fear in his eyes. I'd seen it before; when he broke his arm when he was three, and when his dad died.

I left him to stew for a few minutes longer. I needed the time to switch gears from being a cop to being a parent. I wasn't sure I could pull it off when I opened the interview room door. It would be just the two of us in that grim room. Its narrow walls were painted a sickly green that wiped away all hope and left only despair. It was deliberate. That stifling room was a precursor to the prison system. A warning of what lay ahead.

Joe looked at the door uncertainly as I came inside. I wrapped my arms around him and hugged him. Deep racking sobs shook his body. I let him cry it out. When we finally broke the embrace his eyes were rimmed with red, though his cheeks were dry.

He wiped the tears in his eyes with his sleeve while I held him. When he finally sat down, he couldn't meet my eyes.

I suppose if you're the son of a cop and you want to get attention then you do exactly what Joe did. You get in trouble with the law. It was a cry for help.

'Joe,' I said. 'What's going on with you?'

'Nothing,' he said, showing inordinate fascination with his scuffed sneakers.

'They say you were spending time with an older kid who was dealing.'

'Last time I checked, hanging out with a friend was still legal in this country,' he said defensively, shifting his feet under the table. 'I didn't commit any crime.'

'You ran,' I said. 'When the police told you to stop. You ran. That's a crime.'

'A misdemeanour at best,' he retorted.

'Joe, your dad spent his entire career trying to catch these scumbags,' I said. 'He died for it. He was killed by a dealer. You know that. How do you think he would feel if he could see you now? Here? If he knew his eldest son was hanging out with drug dealers?'

'That's low, Mom.' Joe's voice cracked. I'd gotten through to him.

'It's the truth, Joe.'

I waited a moment before asking my next question.

'Were you dealing, Joe?' I searched his eyes. Whatever boyish fear I'd seen in them a moment before had disappeared. They were stubborn and defiant. 'Joe, were you dealing drugs?'

'Not exactly,' he said, crossing his arms.

'Explain,' I ordered.

'Derek, the dude I was with. He needed someone to run

deliveries for him. He promised to pay me ten dollars per delivery. You know, to deliver stock to his customers at school. I figured I'd make some pocket money.'

'You couldn't just get a job at McDonald's like other kids,' I said, furious. 'Look, Joe. Nobody here is stupid. Least of all me. You've been seen with this crowd before. I need you to tell me what's going on in order to help you. Do you understand?' He shifted his gaze away from me.

'Have you used?' I asked, making deliberate eye contact. No answer. 'Joe, have you used drugs?'

'No,' he said eventually. 'Well, maybe a bit of weed once, but nothing more. I swear.'

'Then what the hell were you doing with these guys?'

'I told you, they said they'd pay me to sell their stock at school. I was their delivery guy. That's all.'

'And did you?' I asked. 'Deliver?'

'A few joints,' he said. 'They wanted me to move on to bigger stuff. That's why I had that meeting with Derek. He said he'd give me ten per cent of his sales at school. You can earn a lot more money delivering pills and meth than weed.'

'Yeah, and you can go to prison for a whole lot longer as well. Do you really want to spend the next ten years of your life locked up in a cell about half this size, with maybe an hour of yard time a day?'

'Come on, Mom,' he said. 'Stop trying to scare me. They'd put me in a juvie centre is all. That's what Derek said.'

'Derek can say whatever he wants. He won't be serving the time,' I told him. 'I can tell you for sure, Joe, once you get in the system it's hard to get out. And don't kid yourself. Juvenile detention is no picnic. Now, I'm going to get myself a coffee. I'll come back in ten minutes. Make your decision. Either cooperate with the police or face whatever punishment they give you. You don't get a free pass just because your mom is a cop.'

'You can't use your, you know, influence to get me a warning or something?' asked Joe. Fear flared in his eyes. God help me, I wanted to tell him that it would all be alright. I had to stop myself cold.

'Joe, I don't know these cops. This isn't my station, or my town,' I said. 'You got yourself caught way outside my jurisdiction. They owe me nothing. In fact, I doubt I could talk them into bringing you a glass of water. They're super angry. They say you kicked the arresting officer when he tried to cuff you. They're talking about an assault charge.'

'Big deal,' he said as he dragged the side of his shoes against the floor.

'Joe. Look at me. This *is* a big deal. The only way you're going to get out of this mess is to tell them everything you know about this gang. Everything.'

'If I do that,' he said, 'Derek and his crew will come after me.'

'No, they won't,' I said flatly. 'We'll set it up so that you're the last person they come after. Believe me, I'll make sure you're not in danger for a second.'

I turned around before I opened the door. 'Think about what your dad would have said if he was here.'

'If Dad was alive,' said Joe, 'then I wouldn't be here in the first place.'

That was really the crux of it. I felt myself turn cold as I closed the interview room door behind me. It clicked as it locked itself. I leaned back against the closed door and stood there, drained. Joe was on the other side and I wasn't sure I'd ever be able to get him back. Really get him back.

'Did you get through to him?' asked the arresting officer when I arrived at his desk. He was a young cop in jeans and a casual shirt.

'God, I hope so,' I said. 'He's a good kid. Just a bit misguided, and angry.' I took a deep breath. 'Look, I'm going to get a coffee and then let's sit down and talk.'

The drug squad and I worked out a deal for Joe. They put him in a holding cell by himself for a few hours and gave him a warning to scare the hell out of him. They also made it perfectly clear it was the first and last time they would be extending such a courtesy.

When we arrived home, I confiscated Joe's phone and put him under a strict curfew with minimal computer access. That would be tough to enforce given the overtime I was pulling at work, but I was determined to do it, even if it meant hiring sitters to keep an eye on Joe. Whatever it took, I would do it.

The drug squad tracked down Derek a week later during a 'random' breath test of cars on the highway south of town. Purely by chance, they found packages of drugs taped under the front passenger seat. Exactly where Joe said they would be. I heard the sniffer dogs went crazy.

The night Joe returned from the police lockup, I called Bobby, Danny's younger brother. He's a detective in upstate New York. He suggested I send Joe and Sammy to him for the summer. 'To get Joe back on track,' he said. 'And to make sure that Sammy never needs an intervention.'

I hated the thought of being away from my kids for so long. But I saw the benefits. It's hard raising sons without their dad. They need a father figure. It's hardwired into their genes.

I didn't think much about the Kellers Way case during that week. I was busy with two other homicides.

What is it about spring that makes husbands and wives turn on each other? This time it was a wife who stabbed her husband with a steak knife after she found incriminating texts on his phone from a woman he was sleeping with. Her best friend, in fact. He died in the ambulance. She was stinking drunk when she killed him. When she sobered up, she tried to hang herself with bedsheets in her holding cell. She wrote a note to the effect that there was no point living without the love of her life. She should have thought about that before she stuck him in the belly with her dinner knife.

A couple of days later, a body was found wrapped in a plastic sheet in a field behind a remote gas station out near I-95. The victim had been shot. Execution style. Two bullets. Clean into the back of the head. The vic had gang tattoos on his knuckles. It was obviously drug-related. Based on a cash-register receipt for an unopened packet of gum that we'd found in his pocket, I figured it was most likely he'd been killed in Florida and the body dumped as the killers drove up north. I spent a fair bit of time down at the medical examiner's office for both of those cases.

When the autopsy report for the Kellers Way victim was ready, Mike offered to walk me through it. His office was on the second floor of the forensics building with a view of an elm tree and a sliver of sunlight running in a diagonal stripe across the carpet. I bought two coffees on the way over.

'You still take your coffee with two sugars?' I asked as I handed Mike his takeout coffee and a handful of sugar sachets.

'You'd think I'd know better, right?' he said as he tore open a sachet of brown sugar.

I sat down in a blue upholstered chair by Mike's desk. He had the build of a cyclist; thin and sinewy, with a slight tan from his daily ten-mile bike ride. He had thinning hair with a hint of silver. He handed me a thick bound booklet. It was 120 pages long, including an appendix of photographs and diagrams.

'I'll talk you through the highlights. You can read the full report later,' Mike said as he opened his copy and took a sip of coffee. 'The victim was female. She died approximately five years ago, give or take a few months either way. She was between thirty-five to forty years of age. Caucasian. Dark hair. Height would have been five foot nine. Weight, probably 130 to 150 pounds.'

'Cause of death?' I asked.

'Indeterminate,' he said. 'My suspicion is that she was suffocated. There aren't any obvious trauma injuries.'

'Was there any sign of a struggle?'

'There may have been, though probably nothing significant. It's impossible to tell for sure due to the decomposition.'

I listened to his summary, taking notes in the margins of my copy of the report. When he was done, I put it down and sat forward in my chair for the business end of our conversation.

'There's a theory, Mike, favoured by Richmond police that if correct will close this case right now.'

'And that theory is?'

'That Edward Pitt murdered the Kellers Way victim. Mike, from what you've seen, is there any physical evidence that supports the theory that Pitt was the killer?'

Mike sighed. 'Nobody is going to like the answer,' he said, choosing his words carefully. 'I know Pitt's work. Up close and personal. I was in the task force. I performed some of the autopsies. Let me tell you something about Pitt. His victims had two distinct features.'

'Which were?'

'Pitt broke his victims' fingers before he killed them. Sometimes he broke all their fingers, other times he broke a few of them.

The Kellers Way victim had no breaks in any of her fingers.'

'Maybe there was a reason. Maybe he didn't have enough time,' I suggested.

'It's not just that,' Mike said with a dismissive wave. 'The other defining feature is that Pitt stabbed all his victims as part of his killing ritual, usually in the stomach and chest. Due to the decomposed condition of the Kellers Way body, I can't determine whether there were stab wounds in the tissue, but I should see indications of a blade hitting bone. There is no sign of any blade being used. I've reviewed the X-rays thoroughly. I don't believe Edward Pitt had anything to do with the Kellers Way murder. If he did then he broke almost completely with his MO.'

'Ok, so let's say we both agree that Pitt had nothing to do with the Kellers Way vic. That brings us back to her identity,' I said. 'What are your thoughts on that, Mike?'

'Short of DNA tests, I can't say with certainty.' He sighed. 'In terms of a working theory, based on an initial analysis of the Kellers Way victim's measurements and facial structure, and a study of the jewellery she was found wearing, I'd say your gut is probably right on this, Mel. I'm betting the woman they thought was Pitt's final victim wasn't killed by Pitt at all. She was killed by someone else. And it's her body we found buried in Kellers Way.'

'You know, Mike,' I said, throwing my empty coffee cup straight into his waste paper bin, 'I was really hoping you wouldn't say that.'

I opened the case file of Pitt's final victim. He'd confessed to abducting a local woman in a forest near our town, killing her at his lair in West Virginia and then burning her body in an oil drum. It was increasingly apparent that Pitt falsely confessed to this murder, in a failed bid to claim the reward money offered by the victim's family. He wanted the money to fund his cancer treatment.

I contemplated the implications of turning a closed case into an active homicide investigation. Aside from the departmental politics, I'd have to contact this woman's loved ones and tell them that in fact her murder was still unsolved and that we were reopening the case.

I removed a photo of the woman from the file. She had a serene smile and lush black hair that contrasted with the golden fall leaves of the oak tree behind her. Her eyes were filled with intelligence and a hint of amusement. It was the last photo taken of Laura West before she died.

Who killed you, Laura?

CHAPTER FIFTEEN

Julie

Every two weeks, on a Tuesday evening, Matt comes home late after a faculty meeting. He usually arrives just past seven o'clock. Tonight he walks through the door after nine.

He throws his car keys in the drawer of the hall table and heads into the kitchen. His face is flushed. With guilt. And drink.

'Dinner will be ready in a couple of minutes.' My voice is wooden as I turn on the stove to heat up the food.

'I'm not hungry,' he says, leaning against the kitchen counter. 'They brought in food for the faculty meeting.' He avoids my eyes. Does he seriously think I can't tell when he's lying?

'I waited for you for dinner.' I keep up the charade as I dish up two serves. 'So you might as well keep me company while I eat.'

I bring the plates to the dining table, which I've set with wine and cutlery. I pour us each a glass of white wine. Matt gives me a warning look, but for once he doesn't try to argue. I drink my wine like it's water just to annoy him. Two glasses in the space of five minutes. Its warmth spreads through my body. My inhibitions disappear.

'Who was that girl at the lecture?' My tone is matter-of-fact.

'What girl?'

'The girl you called down to the podium at the lecture today.' I swirl my gnocchi around the blue-cheese sauce while I wait for his answer.

He takes a sip of wine and contemplates my loaded question.

'There were a few students on the podium. I'm not sure which one you're referring to.' His voice is patient, as if he is talking to a child. 'I often include students in demonstrations. It makes the lecture more engaging and it's an effective teaching tool.'

'There was a girl,' I say slowly (I too can patronise), 'who you brought down near the end. Black hair. Light blue cardigan. You asked her to memorise words you'd written on the whiteboard and then repeat them after watching a video of a train crash.'

'Oh.' His voice is over-dramatic as if hit by sudden recall. 'That's Emily.'

'She's very pretty,' I say. 'Seems smart, too.'

'Why this sudden interest in my students?' He puts down his fork. 'You're not jealous?'

'Why would I be jealous of your student, Matt?' I say sarcastically. 'She's stunning and smart. And she ogles you like a love-sick teenager.'

'Rubbish,' he says. 'You're far prettier. And I don't think of my students like that.'

'You thought of me like that,' I point out.

'A man's allowed one exception to a long-standing rule,' he says. 'And technically, you weren't my student at the time.'

'Touché,' I say as I lift a forkful of gnocchi into my mouth.

'Emily is a grad student,' he says in a reassuring tone that grates. 'Nothing more, nothing less. Now your turn. Why did you really sit in on the lecture?'

'I dropped by to bring you the papers you'd forgotten. You were teaching and I figured you wouldn't mind if I listened to your lecture. Are you annoyed with me?'

'I'm not annoyed,' he says patiently. 'I often get people sitting in on my lectures. There's no reason why my wife can't attend as well.'

'My point exactly.' I drain my third glass of wine. 'So why are you making an issue of it?'

'You're right, Julie,' he says. 'I was overreacting. It's just that when you walked into the lecture hall, you disrupted my train of thought. You're a distracting lady.' He leans forward to kiss me. 'You looked amazing today.'

'Doesn't she remind you of someone?' I ask later, when we're clearing up the dishes.

'Who reminds me of someone?'

'That girl from your lecture. Emily.'

'No. Who is she supposed to remind me of?' shrugs Matt.

'Nothing, nobody,' I mumble as I pile up the plates and take them to the kitchen.

When Matt goes upstairs to shower, I collect his clothes from the bathroom floor. I put my face into the fabric. The shirt smells of Matt's distinctive scent. If I close my eyes and concentrate very hard, I can also smell the scent of another woman's perfume. I put his clothes in the laundry basket and go through the connecting door into the garage where his car is parked.

I don't know what I'm expecting to find as I search Matt's car. Condom wrappers, maybe. There's nothing in the glove compartment or on the floor. I check the central console. Nothing except loose change. But when I slip my hand into the pocket on the driver's door, I find a brass key with an engraving that says it's the property of the university's off-campus housing department.

He has a key to her apartment. I want to be sick, physically sick, on Matt's Italian leather car seat. What has happened to us? We were never supposed to be this couple. We were supposed to have drawn the happily-ever-after card.

Damn Matt for making me take my meds. They leave me in a perpetual fog. They dull my senses. They give him the freedom to do whatever he likes; to cheat on me with impunity. I put the key back where I found it and return to the house. Matt's in the kitchen frothing up milk for hot chocolate.

'What were you doing in the garage?' he asks.

'I thought I left my car lights on.'

'I would have told you if you had,' he says, handing me a mug of hot chocolate. We sit on stools by the kitchen counter drinking from our steaming mugs.

'Matt,' I say. 'I don't want to take the pills anymore.' There, I said it. I watch his face tighten in disapproval as I wait for his response. We've had this conversation so many times. It rarely ends well.

'Julie,' he says after a long pause. 'We've discussed this before. The medication stabilises your mood. You can't just go on and off this kind of medication like a yo-yo.'

'I don't have mood swings anymore. I needed medication after the haemorrhage. And maybe after Roxy. But I'm fine now. I really am.'

'Why do you keep calling it a haemorrhage, Julie?' He sounds annoyed. 'It was a miscarriage.'

'I know what it was, Matt,' I snap. 'I was there. I went through it.' I take a deep breath to get hold of myself. 'Look, all I want is for things to go back to normal between us. And they won't if I'm taking those damn meds.'

'Everything is fine between us. You're getting yourself worked up about nothing.' He pulls me to him. The stubble on his jaw brushes again my skin. The reassuring beat of his heart melts away my distrust.

'Honey, you need to keep taking your medication,' he says, using his finger to wipe away an errant tear running down my cheek. 'To keep yourself healthy. For me. And for Alice.' He kisses me; a long, lingering kiss.

It's the first time in ages he has made the slightest effort to touch me with any tenderness. I wonder why? That makes me think of Emily. Later in our bedroom, as he makes love to me, I wonder who else's lips he has kissed today and who else's body he has thrust into.

When I hear his steady breathing in the middle of the night, I climb out of bed and sit on the edge of the mattress watching his hair rumpled and dark against the white of the pillow cover. His mouth is gently parted. I wish I knew what Matt dreams about. He knows everything about me; my deepest thoughts and my greatest fears. Yet he keeps so much of himself hidden.

I slide my hand under the mattress and remove the capsules that I've hidden there. Tonight he forgot to watch me taking them before we settled down to sleep. I flush the meds down the bathroom drain. Then I go downstairs to Matt's study as quietly as possible. I'm super careful on the landing, where a loose floorboard always creaks. I sit on the soft leather chair at his desk and boot up his computer in the dark.

I try his usual passwords. Each time, I receive a prompt that tells me it's not the right password. Finally, I think of another option. I type in a date; the date he married Laura. I press enter. The screen lights up. Rather than feeling elation at getting it right, it makes me miserable.

There's not a day when Laura is not in our lives. Her memory defines our family. We live in the two-storey house she and Matt bought when they were first married. The home Laura furnished like a doll's house. Except now I'm the doll. I cannot escape the fact that my house was once her home and my husband once belonged to her.

The very desk that I'm sitting at was once chosen by her, restored by her, put here for her husband to sit at and admire the tasteful selection of wall art that still hangs there today, mocking me from across the room. I would never have had the taste or imagination to decorate Matt's study the way she did. She knew him so much better than I do. His taste. His moods. His desires. No matter how hard I try, I will always fall short of Laura.

I search Matt's computer for his student files, which he's downloaded into a folder. I quickly find the file for Emily. Emily Morrison is her full name. She's a 23-year-old graduate student. Straight As. She's from Long Island. This semester she's doing four out of five courses with Matt. How nice for her. And how convenient that he's also her faculty advisor.

I check his calendar. They have a regular meeting on Fridays at 4.15 p.m. Matt sees all the students he is advising back to back. Each one gets a thirty-minute block on a Friday afternoon. Emily's slot is the last for the day. Now I know why he always comes home late on a Friday, face flushed, hair rumpled.

I scroll through his emails to see if there are any messages from Emily. I am looking for written confirmation of their affair. There's none in his inbox. I check his deleted items. There's nothing from Emily. There is, however, an email from the university office sent that afternoon saying: 'Please be advised that tonight's faculty meeting has been cancelled as several staff members are attending conferences out of town.' Matt was not at a faculty meeting this evening. Another lie. Another cover-up for his affair with Emily.

I find it strange that there's not a single message from Emily in any of his email folders. Not even in his archived or deleted items. She is, after all, his student. Rather than allay my fears, the absence of any correspondence between them whatsoever makes me more suspicious. Matt must have an email account that he keeps secret. How else would he communicate with her?

I've already checked his phone and it's clean. I sign into my own Facebook account to look her up, now that I have her full name. There are several people by the name Emily Morrison. Only one is a student at the university. I click on that profile. It's illustrated by a grainy photograph of a young woman in a soft pink ballet leotard with her leg extended on a dance bar. She's a dancer as well as an honor student. The perfect package.

Her profile says she's 'in a relationship'. She doesn't say with whom. I scroll through her recent photographs to find out. There is an assortment of photos with her college friends. There's a selfie outside the stage door at Lincoln Center holding an autographed program of *Swan Lake*. And a whole lot of photos of her family: at the Thanksgiving table, by the Christmas tree, on vacation in the Bahamas. Then there is a myriad of photos of artfully plated food at restaurants.

Emily has documented so much of her life; from the sublime to the mundane. Yet there is not a single photograph of her mysterious boyfriend. 'In a relationship.' I am incensed that she deems fucking my husband to be a relationship.

I return to Emily's student files. I copy her class schedule and save it in my own email's draft folder. I also copy her cellphone number and a street address back in Long Island. There's no information about her local campus address. When I've copied everything from Matt's laptop I can find on the subject of Emily Morrison, I sign out of Facebook and delete my browsing history.

I crawl back into bed. Matt instinctively pulls me to him. 'Where were you?' he mumbles in his sleep.

CHAPTER SIXTEEN

Mel

After dinner, I left my kids at home watching TV and drove to the most expensive neighbourhood in town. I pulled up outside a Georgian-style home with neatly clipped hedges and a black wrought-iron fence. The two-storey house was at the top of a cul-de-sac.

I arrived with a swab kit and an envelope filled with photographs. I'd be lying if I didn't admit I was apprehensive. For one thing, it's a bitch to reopen a closed case. Aside from the red tape, it makes enemies. Captain Howard in Richmond, for one. He was going to be a body short in the Pitt case. And he was going to blame me for it, especially if it meant a judicial review of the original case. Especially if there was blowback.

Captain Howard was the least of my problems that night. There are few things more excruciating than having to explain to the next of kin that there may have been a screw up in the investigation of their loved one's murder. Well, in truth there was one thing worse: telling a victim's family they might have buried the wrong body in the family plot. I'd be giving a double dose of bad news that night and I wasn't looking forward to it.

In an ideal world, I'd have had definitive answers on the victim's identity before I even arrived to talk with her family, because the lab would have crossmatched Laura West's DNA with the DNA of the Kellers Way victim.

In the real world of screw ups, I'd been unable to get that DNA crossmatch because we no longer had Laura West's DNA in the system. We also didn't have any personal effects that might have contained DNA traces, such as her hairbrush or toothbrush. As bad luck would have it, an entire box of Laura West's possessions had been thrown out of the evidence repository five months earlier. It was a closed case and everything had been purged from the system and the archives. Space costs money. Not surprisingly, I was mad as hell when I heard that piece of news.

I stood in the blustery evening air looking up at the house. This was where Laura West was last seen before she disappeared five years ago. I rang the intercom bell. A green light flashed on the console. I was being observed. Great. My hair was a mess from the wind and I was wearing jeans and a cable-knit sweater that I put on because of the chill. It was hardly standard detective gear. I probably looked like I was delivering religious pamphlets, or doing some shonky door-to-door sales pitch.

'Can I help you?' said a male voice through the speaker.

'Professor West,' I said loudly to be heard above the wind. 'I'm a police detective and I'd like to talk with you.'

A pause.

'Can I ask what it's regarding?'

'It's probably better if I discuss this matter with you in person.'

'Can't this wait until tomorrow?' He made little effort to

disguise his annoyance.

'I wish it could, sir,' I said, 'but I think it's best if we talk as soon as possible. I really am sorry to disturb your evening.'

A long beep and a click told me he was playing ball. 'It's open,' he said. 'Just push the gate and head up to the house.'

Motion-sensor lights turned on in slow succession as I walked up the sloping slate pathway.

'What's this about?' He was standing on the porch with his hair slightly ruffled by the evening breeze and his face taut with irritation. He kept his voice deliberately soft. It told me there were others in the house and he didn't want them to hear the conversation.

'It's with regard to the death of your wife.'

'My wife?' He turned his head instinctively to look upstairs.

'Laura West,' I clarified quickly. 'I'd rather talk with you inside if you don't mind. This won't be a five-minute conversation.'

'Come in.' He led me into a study off the entry hall. It was a severe room furnished with antiques and leather Brentwood armchairs. On the wall was a collection of old lithographs in brass frames.

'Have a seat,' he instructed me, closing the study door. He sat down on a leather armchair facing me. His jaw was tense as he waited for me to speak.

'I'm sorry if this brings up painful memories. Unfortunately, it can't be helped. I have a development that I'd like to discuss with you.'

'What development could you possibly have? Laura was brutally murdered. It was a nightmare. It still is,' he rasped. 'Death was too good for the bastard who killed her.'

'I'm sure it is incredibly difficult.'

'Detective, it took a long time, but I am trying to move ahead with my life and your presence here out of the blue is frankly, not to be rude, more than a little disconcerting.'

'You're right,' I agreed, trying to build rapport. 'I understand that, and I'll be quick.'

He stood abruptly and walked to a sideboard to pour himself a glass of whiskey. He drank it down neat in a single gulp. 'Would you like one?' he asked when he was done. I shook my head. He poured me a drink anyway.

There was no way to say it other than to spit it out. 'Professor West, I'm here because we have new evidence that suggests that Edward Pitt did not murder your wife.'

'What are you talking about?' His voice was raw. 'Are you suggesting Laura might still be alive?'

'No,' I said firmly. 'That's not at all what I'm suggesting. About ten days ago, we found a body at Kellers Way. It's a forest road just out of town,' I added.

'I know where it is,' he cut me off abruptly. 'I've lived here most of my life.'

'There was no identification found on the body,' I continued. 'But the victim was wearing certain clothing items and jewellery. I'd like you to look at photos of the items to see if any of them are familiar.'

I handed him photos taken in the lab of the personal effects found with the body. He went through them one at a time, under the soft glow of an antique lamp on his desk. When he was done, he said nothing. For a good two minutes there was no sound in the room except for an old clock ticking on the mantel of the fireplace. Matthew West stared into his whiskey glass as if it was a crystal ball.

'Do you recognise any of those items?' My voice broke through the silence.

'This looks like Laura's necklace.' He handed me a photograph of the pendant. 'I bought it when I visited South Africa for a conference. It was a gift to Laura to mark our first anniversary. The stone isn't precious but it's rare, a distinct colour only found in Africa.'

'Madagascar,' I said.

'Yes,' he looked up in surprise. 'That's right.'

'What about the jacket and the boots?'

'Laura had an extensive wardrobe,' he said. 'I was at a conference on the day she disappeared and I don't know what she wore that day. I told this to the police when I reported her missing.'

'Does any of the other jewellery look familiar?'

'I can't be sure,' he said. 'The earrings, maybe. My mother bought her a set like that for her birthday. It's hard to tell with the watch so damaged, but that could be Laura's.'

'What about Laura's wedding and engagement rings? Was she wearing them on the day she disappeared?'

'I'm sure she was.' He seemed very certain. 'Laura never took off her rings. She even insisted on wearing them when we were on holiday in Mexico, despite warnings that muggers were targeting tourists wearing expensive jewellery. Why do you ask? Did you find Laura's rings?'

'No,' I answered, without going into details.

He put his face into his hands for a moment. When he removed them, he was pale and drawn.

'You think the body in Kellers Way might be Laura? Don't you?' His eyes bored into me as he waited for my answer.

The brass door handle twisted and the heavy door slowly opened to reveal a child dressed in a fluffy dressing gown, with a teddy bear tucked under her arm. She ran into the room and wriggled onto Matt's lap.

'Mommy said I should kiss you goodnight.' She stood on tiptoe with her face turned up to her father.

'Well, of course you should, honey.' He lifted her into his arms and kissed her cheeks. 'Goodnight, Alice. I'll be up shortly to tuck you in, ok?'

'Ok, Daddy. I won't go to sleep until you come.' She ran out of the room and up the stairs.

'How do we find out for sure if there's a connection to Laura?' he asked once his daughter was out of earshot.

'I need Laura's DNA. You're the next of kin. I don't know how to reach her biological family. I understand that she was from New England originally? Or perhaps you've kept some of her personal effects that might still have her DNA. A hairbrush. Lipstick?'

'Laura's DNA.' His forehead creased as he considered the question. 'I'm sure I gave everything to the police when she went missing. I remember they took a whole box of items. Can't you use that?'

'When the case was closed, some of the forensics material was unfortunately destroyed. We need fresh DNA, either swabs or actual items I can give to the lab.'

'Whatever personal items weren't given to the police were thrown out. I gave Laura's shoes and clothes to charity. It was the only way I could move on with my life,' he said with a touch of defensiveness.

'What about Laura's parents? Siblings?' I asked. 'Can you put us in touch with them?'

'Her parents are dead. Laura was an only child.' He sighed. 'I know what you want. I'll be back in a moment.' He left the study and returned with his daughter in his arms.

'Alice,' he said. 'This nice lady is a doctor. She needs you to open your mouth while she makes sure you don't have a sore throat.

So when I tell you to, say "Ahhh" and open your mouth really big.'
She looked at him uncertainly.

'It won't hurt. I promise,' I reassured her as I opened the swab
kit. It took a second to swab the inside of her cheek and put the
sample into a sealed vial.

'You're the best patient I've had today,' I said gently. 'We're
checking lots of children in the neighbourhood because of whoop-
ing cough.'

He mouthed a thanks to me as he led her out of the room.

'Ask Mommy to put you to bed. It's very late,' he said. 'Oh, and
Alice, don't tell Mommy about the doctor doing the throat checks.
We don't want her to get worried.'

'Yes, Daddy.' She kissed him on the cheek before scuttling up
the stairs again.

'Thank you,' I said to him. 'I know this can't be easy.'

'No, it's not,' he agreed. 'Alice and I would do anything to help
you find Laura's killer. Anything,' he emphasised.

CHAPTER SEVENTEEN

Julie

Alice and I pretend not to notice that Matt's been in his study for the longest time with a woman I've never seen before. She arrived unannounced at the tail end of dinner, with curious eyes, and an aloof manner that gave the impression she was here on business.

The evening drags on as we wait in the kitchen for Matt to emerge. Alice is bent over her sketchbook drawing a picture with crayons that scrape noisily across the paper. I make her school lunch for tomorrow. When I'm done, I wipe the kitchen counter until the marble gleams.

I jump when I hear the echo of voices in the hall, followed by the click of the front door closing shut. Footsteps fade out as Matt returns to his study and shuts the door behind him. I desperately want to go to him, except Alice has been clingy all day and won't let me out of her sight. I don't want another tantrum. Not tonight.

Alice has been wetting her bed again, out of the blue, after two years without an accident. I'm at my wits' end with piles of sheets to wash each morning. Matt says I shouldn't say a word. He bought the sketchpad to encourage her to draw, so she can express her anxieties. Tonight she draws a house with jagged edges. There are three people in the house. 'Red people', she calls them. Each one is in a different room. I ask her why. She shrugs. Then, almost to punish me, she sketches a fourth person, this time drawn with a purple crayon that she rubs hard into the paper.

It's late and I'm about to tell Alice that it's time for bed when Matt enters the kitchen. He absent-mindedly tousles Alice's hair as he walks towards the living room couch. He holds a tumbler of whiskey in his hand. Judging by his flushed face, I'm sure it's not his first. His glazed eyes tell me he's in another place.

'It's about Laura, isn't it?' I whisper when I join him on the couch. He nods and looks into his drink.

'The police are reopening the investigation into her death. They say the bastard they thought killed her didn't do it. His confession was a lie.'

'If he didn't kill her, then who did?' I ask, blood draining from my face as shock sets in.

'They don't know.' His voice is strained. 'It means the real killer is free. I feel like I'm reliving the nightmare. Julie, I'm not sure I can go through this a second time.'

'You have me this time, Matt, darling.' I wrap my arms around him. 'We'll get through this together.'

All our married life, I've carried with me a feeling of dread that Laura would tear us apart from the grave. Her grip on our marriage has never felt tighter. Yet, as I lie here in Matt's arms on the couch, I realise that for once Matt needs me to help him through a crisis. Maybe this tragedy will, ironically, bring us closer.

Alice sits with her back to us at the kitchen counter, deep in concentration as she fills her book with drawings. I might not have given birth to her, but I'm her mother. I'm the one who holds her when she wakes in the middle of the night, who helps her with her homework, who reads to her, and gets down on the floor to play with her. I'm the one who listens to her tearfully recounting a playground argument at school. And who loves her. More than anything.

If my marriage falls apart then, as the mere stepmother, I'd lose Alice. That's not something I will allow to happen. If she takes Matt away from me Emily would destroy everything I've built. Unless I stop her.

I rise from the couch to shut the back blinds of the living room and lock up the house. Through the window I see the golden eyes of a deer reflecting in the dark. The rear gate has come loose and the deer has strayed into the back garden. It will eat up our flower-beds by morning if I let it stay. I let myself out of the French doors onto the patio.

'Scoot,' I tell the deer, clapping my hands as I walk towards it. It stands defiantly for a moment and then turns and runs through the open gate back into the forest. I walk across the garden in the dark to lock the gate.

The forest is filled with shadows. It's alive with a nocturnal music that reaches a crescendo and then ebbs away before rising once more. As I look into the mesmerising sway of trees I see the bloodied face of a man lying dead in the driver's seat of a car. A frisson of fear runs through me. I sprint back to the house as if I'm being chased.

Matt is slumped on the couch, fast asleep. I leave him there with the dimmers down. I whisper into Alice's ear that it's time for bed. She obeys without argument. I lie with her in bed and read her favourite book about a girl who wishes she was a goldfish.

When I look up, Matt is leaning against the doorframe watching us as he sips another whiskey.

'Thanks,' says Matt later as we get ready for bed in our room across the passage.

'For what?'

'For being here for me. And for Alice.'

'We're a family,' I tell him. 'We're here for each other.'

I rub my hand along the stubble on his jaw and lean forward to kiss him. I unbutton his shirt with clumsy fingers. He pushes me back onto the mattress. We kiss hard and rough. The way we used to before Laura disappeared.

CHAPTER EIGHTEEN

Mel

When I reviewed my notes from the first interview with Matthew West, what stood out were observations I had jotted in pencil in the margins of the transcript. They suggested I found him to be sympathetic. 'Sincere' was the word that I used. Sincerity. It's what you look for when you're interviewing potential suspects.

At the time that his wife Laura disappeared, Matthew West had been at a psychology conference on the other side of the state. The original investigator had written 'conveniently?' in his case notes. Matthew West, the notation implied, might have gone to an out-of-town conference to provide himself with an alibi. Perhaps the killing was a murder for hire; a husband wants to get rid of his wife without paying alimony, he hires a hit man to do his dirty work and makes sure he's out of town with an airtight alibi when the murder is committed.

It held together in theory. In reality there wasn't a single piece of direct or even indirect evidence that linked Matthew West to the death of his wife. At the time, the forensics team examined his car and searched his house, ostensibly to see if Laura had left behind clues to her disappearance. Perhaps she hadn't been abducted. Maybe she ran away. Every theory was checked. The forensics team found nothing when they examined the house for blood with ultra-violet light and fluorescence spray. There was no indication that anything violent had taken place on the premises, in his car, or in her car when they found it abandoned a few days later. There were no significant withdrawals of cash from their bank account, no life insurance policy on Laura West. And if that wasn't enough, her husband had no known motive for wanting her dead. There was not a single shred of evidence that Matthew West killed his wife.

His alibi was tight. At the time of her disappearance, he was a guest of honour at a conference in a city two hours' drive away. It was attended by over a hundred health professionals, all leaders in their field. If ever there was an ironclad alibi, that was it.

His reaction rang true. None of the video footage of Matthew West speaking to the media and police after Laura West disappeared suggested he was anything less than devastated, and I watched hours of footage.

He played the role of grieving husband in a way that struck people as both genuine and heartbreaking. The depth of emotion in his eyes, the pain in his voice, the dignified but palpable grief. That meant a lot to an investigating detective. You wouldn't believe how many husband or wife killers act without remorse after the crime, or ham it up for the police with crocodile tears. Sincerity. Matthew West was the real deal. Either that or he was one hell of an actor.

West called my cellphone first thing that morning. His voice was even, though he spoke too fast. He was nervous, or upset. I wasn't sure which. Maybe both. He hadn't slept, he said. The more he'd thought about the jewellery in the photos I'd shown him the night before, the more he was convinced it belonged to Laura. His voice cracked as he said her name.

He was apologetic when I suggested he come to the station straight away. He was scheduled to teach classes all morning and couldn't find a replacement lecturer at short notice. He asked if three o'clock would be convenient. I told him that was fine. I wanted time to go through the old case files and figure out a strategy for questioning him. He was a psychology professor. He knew interrogation techniques better than I did.

He arrived at the police station that afternoon straight from the university, wearing an open-collar shirt and a sports jacket, no tie. His eyes were bloodshot.

I took him upstairs to a meeting room on the third floor used for witnesses rather than suspects. It was an airy room that attracted afternoon light from a floor to ceiling window overlooking the street. It was furnished with upholstered chrome chairs and a white table. He sipped water as he spoke. I sensed it was more to break the tension than because he was thirsty.

'I didn't get much sleep last night,' he said. 'I couldn't stop thinking about Laura and what the bastard did to her. All these years and she was buried less than three miles from our house.'

'I intend to catch her killer,' I reassured him. 'But I'll need your help.'

When it comes to homicides, most are committed by someone known to the victim. More often than not, it's an immediate relative. A husband. Or a wife. They're also the easiest to catch because, when you dig deep enough, there's always evidence. I've had cases where we accessed old internet searches and found a husband who googled suffocation techniques, three months before his wife was suffocated by a supposed intruder who didn't so much as leave a footprint in the muddy garden outside.

There's often a money trail too; unusual transfers of money, or a prescient consolidation of assets that avoided probate issues after an extremely premature death that the spouse could not have anticipated – unless he or she orchestrated it.

I'm always on the lookout for an obvious motive. In this case, there was not a shred of evidence that Matthew West had anything to do with his wife's death. No motive. No opportunity. There wasn't even circumstantial evidence.

There was plenty of raw information from the time of Laura West's disappearance that I would have liked but was never collected. The original investigator seemed to have had a hard-on for Matthew West. I suspected it was because he was a betting man and he followed the odds: straight to the husband.

The trouble was that he didn't pursue any alternative suspects, and he did little in the way of investigating the secret corners of Laura West's life. What went on outside her marriage? What were her human frailties? What obsessed Laura West? What kept her up at night? He hadn't looked. It's those kinds of holes that make it that much harder to reinvestigate an old case years later.

'You were a speaker at a conference on the weekend Laura disappeared?' I looked up from the file as I asked Matthew West the question.

'Yes,' he said. 'I presented a paper.'

'Do you recall how you travelled to Charlotte for the conference?'

'I drove up on the Friday evening and returned on the Sunday afternoon. That's when I discovered that Laura had gone missing.'

'Why drive instead of fly? You could have gotten there in half the time by plane.'

'I like driving,' he said. 'It relaxes me. With a two-hour drive, it's a toss-up whether you get there quicker by plane or car, especially if the plane's delayed.'

'True,' I agreed. 'Flights can take longer than planned with airport security so vigilant these days. It's sometimes less hassle to drive.' He lifted an eyebrow as if to ask if that was the best I could do with the mirroring technique.

'Did you drive up with anyone?'

'No,' he said without hesitation. 'I drove there alone on the Friday evening and returned alone after lunch on the Sunday.'

'What time was your speech at the conference?'

'Saturday. Around lunchtime. I can't remember if it was before or after lunch. It was one of those awkward speaking slots where people are either hungry and don't want to listen, or they've just eaten and are inclined to nod off.'

'Are you sure of the timing?'

'As sure as I can be about an event this long ago. I speak at dozens of conferences a year. They tend to blend into one another after a while.'

'Do you recall what you did after your speech?' I asked.

'There were workshops. Other presentations. I probably networked. Grabbed a coffee with colleagues. That's what I usually do at these conferences.'

'Those are generalities. You may or may not have done any of those things. Can you give more detail about your movements that day? Perhaps you can recall the names of colleagues you talked with at the conference?'

'No,' he answered. 'I can't. It was years ago. I don't even remember what I did last month, let alone all those years ago. Surely all that information is in the file? The police questioned me extensively at the time.' He motioned to the dog-eared folder in front of me.

'I'm afraid the original detective is deceased,' I said. 'We have his old files, but there were some gaps in the information. We have confirmation you were at the conference. We also have confirmation that you delivered a speech early Saturday afternoon and that you attended a breakfast event on the Sunday morning. We have no specific confirmation that you were seen between Saturday afternoon and Sunday morning.'

That wasn't entirely true. In fact, according to the original case file, several people recalled seeing Matthew West during the Saturday afternoon and at the conference dinner that night. I conveniently forgot to mention that, because I wanted to see how he reacted to the possibility there might be cracks in his alibi.

'I was at the conference all weekend,' he insisted. 'I was at the main dinner and most of the seminars. I wouldn't leave my wife and baby daughter to attend a conference and then play hooky.'

'I understand that,' I said. 'Can you recall your specific movements in the afternoon after you gave your talk?'

'All these years later? I wish I could tell you but even my memory is not *that* good.' He rose to his feet and inspected the view of the street through the venetian blinds. A muscle flicked in his jaw. He was visibly trying to calm down.

'Do you seriously think I murdered Laura?' He turned to look at me directly. I said nothing. 'Things were great between us. We'd just had our first child after years of trying. We'd been together since we were students. We were – it sounds trite, but we were soul mates. Why are you wasting your time on me when you should be finding her killer?'

'Professor West, please don't mistake my questions for conclusions. I'm not making conclusions. I'm not suggesting that you had anything to do with your wife's murder. All I'm saying is that there's a certain period of time over that weekend that is not fully accounted for and it would be helpful if you were able to provide details so I could verify your movements.'

I said nothing more while my words sank in.

'If you don't suspect me for Laura's murder then why do you need to verify my movements?'

'Because,' I responded patiently, 'I need to officially rule you out as a suspect so I can focus my time and energy on finding the killer.'

'I'm sorry.' He put down his glass with a clatter and sat back down in the chair. 'I just don't want more time wasted when Laura's killer is still out there.'

'That's why I want to dispense with these preliminaries quickly. So please take a moment to think about whether there is anyone else who can verify your movements from Saturday afternoon to Sunday morning on the weekend that your wife was killed.'

'There's so much I've blocked out from that period, I think to shield myself from the trauma,' he said after a moment's thought. 'I'll need more time to remember.'

'There is some information from the original investigation that might jog your memory,' I announced as I opened another file.

'Such as?'

'Are you aware of a payment on one of your credit cards that indicates you bought gasoline twenty miles from your home at around 4 p.m. on the Saturday of the conference?'

'That's impossible,' he said. 'I was in Charlotte at the time. Perhaps I put fuel in the car on the drive to Charlotte and the gas station registered the payment with a delay?'

'Perhaps,' I conceded.

'Or perhaps Laura put gas into her car. She sometimes used my American Express for the points. In fact, she had three credit cards with her when she disappeared.'

'Yes,' I said, 'that was in the file too. Do you recall whether Laura's cards were used after her disappearance?'

He shook his head. 'They were never used again.'

'Did you cancel her credit cards once it became clear she'd disappeared?'

'It wasn't something that I thought about doing. It was stressful dealing with Laura's disappearance; the police, the media, the cloud of suspicion that seemed to inexplicably hang over me. And then I had to manage with a baby. Alice was a terrible sleeper. She'd scream for hours from colic and she missed Laura terribly. So for the first few days, it didn't sink in that something bad had happened to Laura.'

He took a sip of water.

'To tell you the truth, detective, I thought perhaps she needed a time-out,' he said. 'Laura was like that.'

'Like what?'

'Like a pressure cooker,' he answered. 'Everything would build up until she couldn't contain it anymore and then she'd go somewhere to pull herself together. That's what I thought had happened when she didn't come home. I never imagined that she'd been abducted and murdered. It didn't cross my mind to cancel her credit cards. What if she was lost and needed to pay for a ticket back to me? Or needed food? I left those credit cards open in case she needed to use them.'

'And they were never used? Not for a single purchase?'

'Laura's credit cards were never used again,' he said. 'I kept imagining that she'd walk through the door any minute. Then one day passed, and the next, and there was no sign of her. I still made excuses. She'd had a breakdown. She was in a fugue state. She'd lost track of time. When they found the car – that would have been four or five days after she went missing – that's when I realised she might not ever come back.'

'You mentioned that she sometimes went away,' I asked. 'Where would she go?'

'She had a friend with a beach house at Hilton Head. Or she'd stay at an old college friend's apartment in Manhattan. One time she flew to Amsterdam for the weekend. There was never any set place. She'd just go wherever, based on her mood.'

'After your daughter was born, did Laura frequently disappear on these trips?'

He paused as if to think through the question. 'Not really. Maybe a day here or there, but Laura wouldn't leave Alice's side for more than a couple of days. She was devoted to her. And she wouldn't go away without telling me and arranging suitable babysitters.'

My phone vibrated. It was a text from Sammy. 'Joe swore at me, Mom. And FYI, he was suspended from school.' I sighed. It was going to be a long night when I got home.

'Now, getting back to the conference,' I said, returning to my notepad. 'Do you recall specifically whether you attended the gala dinner on the Saturday night? It was at a French restaurant I believe.' I checked the file. 'Chez Marcel?'

'I don't have any particular recollection of the dinner. But I'm sure I was there. I almost always go to the dinners at these confer-ences. It's rude not to turn up, especially when you've presented a paper. They usually take group photographs at the dinners, perhaps the organisers still have photos?'

'I'll check,' I said. 'When did you first hear that Laura was missing?' I deliberately changed tack. I needed to hear it in his own words without him having time to think about his answer.

'The sitter,' he said. 'We had a lady taking care of the baby and she called me on Sunday morning to say that Laura wasn't there. That our bed didn't look slept in.'

'What did you do about it?'

'Nothing,' he said. 'I told her that Laura had probably come home late on Saturday and left the house early on Sunday. Laura was working on a research paper and she never worked from the house. She found it too disruptive. She worked at the university even on the weekend. She'd say a university campus on a Saturday afternoon or Sunday morning was the quietest place on earth.'

'You weren't worried about Laura's safety when you were told she hadn't come back?'

'Not at all. Mrs Dellamore wasn't either, from what I recall. She was annoyed because she'd expected the babysitting job to be finished by Sunday lunchtime and, with Laura not responding to her phone and me in Charlotte, it meant she'd have to be there at least until the afternoon. I offered to pay her extra for the inconvenience. That was all.'

'So your exchange with the babysitter was more transactional in nature?'

'Yes, you could say so,' he said. 'We – I – never suspected that anything bad had happened to Laura when Mrs Dellamore called me. It was really about calming Mrs Dellamore. She was upset her weekend plans had gone awry.'

'Do you remember when you started worrying?'

'It was while I was driving back from Charlotte on the Sunday afternoon. I don't recall the time but I'm pretty sure it was still light out. Mrs Dellamore called me again. Said she still hadn't heard a word from Laura but she needed to get going soon. I told her I would be there within an hour. I couldn't think of a single reason as to why Laura had been out of touch for, by then, twenty-four hours. Even if she'd been immersed in work, Laura would have called to find out how Alice was doing.'

'Why didn't you stay at the conference hotel?' I asked suddenly.

'Sorry?' he looked up at me in surprise at the switch in subjects.

'In Charlotte. You said you go to these conferences largely to network, yet you didn't stay at the hotel where the event was being held. Why not?'

'I can't remember. It was so long ago. Perhaps they didn't have vacancies that weekend and I had to stay at an overflow hotel.'

'Perhaps,' I said. I'd already checked with the hotel where the conference was held and according to their records they had not been at full occupancy that weekend. 'If you didn't stay at the conference hotel, then it would be most logical that you'd stay nearby. A hotel a short walk away.'

'Yes, I suppose that would make sense,' he admitted.

'Yet you stayed at the Clairmont.' It was a boutique hotel on the other side of town from the conference centre. It was one of those places with separate villas set around a garden. The website marketed it as a romantic getaway for couples. Privacy guaranteed.

'Why did you book at the Clairmont?'

'No idea,' he said quickly. 'My travel agent usually made my bookings. Or sometimes Laura would book if she was coming with me. Actually,' he said, as if struck by a sudden recollection, 'that's probably the reason. Laura must have made the hotel booking. She had initially been scheduled to give speak at the conference as well. Laura was very particular about the places she stayed. If memory serves, the Clairmont was roomy and private. It would have been an ideal place to stay with the baby.'

'Do you recall why your wife cancelled her speaking engagement at the conference?' This piece of information was new to me.

'God, I wish she had gone.' He rubbed his temple. 'If she had then none of this would have happened.'

'Why didn't she go?' I repeated.

'I really don't remember. Do you remember what happened five years ago?'

I remembered where I was four years ago. I remembered every last detail from the day Danny was killed. What I was doing in the minutes before he was shot. Where I was at that exact moment in time when he lay bleeding on the side of the road. Where I was when the paramedics shocked him back to life with a defibrillator. I remembered the entire day as if it happened in slow motion.

Yes, it was years ago. Yes, who can possibly remember what they were doing last month let alone years ago? But when your 'soul mate' disappears, and has possibly been murdered, then every second of every moment around the time that it happened is ingrained in your mind for ever. Do you know why? Guilt. The survivor always wonders what he or she could have done differently to have changed the course of events..

That's why I didn't quite believe Matthew West when he said he couldn't remember what he'd done on the day his wife disappeared. It was the only part of his story that didn't ring true.

'I'm sorry,' he said. 'I don't recall why Laura didn't attend the conference. It was a tough year for her, adjusting to having a baby. She tried to cut her workload. These conference presentations take hours of work. Laura probably pulled out because she didn't have the bandwidth.'

'Did Laura spend time in the country?' I changed the subject again. 'Hiking or horseback riding?'

'No,' he said emphatically. 'Laura was never an outdoors person. She was fair-skinned. She burned easily and as a result she tended to avoid the sun. Also, she was allergic to animal fur. We had to give away my pet dog when we first married. Why do you ask?'

'The body we found in Kellers Way was wearing riding gear when she was killed,' I said.

'What do you mean, riding gear?'

'Her body was found wearing knee-high black boots with a thick heel used for riding. She wore a tailor-made riding jacket as well.'

'Laura was afraid of horses,' he said. 'Are you sure?'

'Yes, we're quite certain,' I said. 'We found traces of horse manure and hay in the tread of the boots. There's a good chance that Laura would have been around horses shortly before her death.'

CHAPTER NINETEEN

Julie

It's easy enough finding Emily on campus once I have her class schedule. Thank you, Matt, for keeping meticulous records of your students.

Emily has back-to-back classes most mornings from nine to eleven. I arrive a few minutes before eleven and wait for her on a polished timber bench outside the psychology department lecture halls.

Not even Matt would recognise me if he walked past me in the corridor. I'm wearing a college sweatshirt, paid for in cash at the campus store, and a baseball cap that covers a shoulder-length light brown wig made from real human hair, which I rented at a costume store. My face is framed by navy-rimmed glasses with clear lenses, bought at a discount pharmacy at a strip mall across town.

I stifle a yawn as I wait for Emily's lecture to finish. I slept badly last night, troubled by the latest fault line to run through our marriage. I can't compete with a dead woman.

Matt is mourning Laura all over again. Who better to console him than Emily? Her resemblance to Laura is uncanny. It makes me more determined than ever to fight for Matt. I won't lose Alice just because that bitch Emily wants to steal my husband.

Right on the hour, the auditorium door swings open with a thud and students stream out. Emily is at the rear, deep in conversation with two other girls.

I fall into place behind them as they leave the building. They cross the quadrangle to a campus cafe where she and her friends take an outdoor table. I sit at an adjacent table with my back to them. I open my laptop and pretend that I'm working while I listen to their every word.

One of them goes inside the cafe and returns carrying a cardboard carrier with three coffees. They talk mostly about a group assignment. Their discussion is tedious and useless for my purposes. I'm rewarded for my patience because, as they are wrapping up their little get-together, I get a scrap of information that makes it all worthwhile.

'We're going to need another meeting,' sighs a girl with a Midwest twang. She pulls out her phone to check her calendar. 'How about Thursday at six?'

'I can't,' says Emily. 'I'm teaching ballet.'

'Damn, Em. I thought you only taught on Mondays and Saturdays?'

'They asked me to fill in on Thursdays for the rest of the semester. One of the teachers tore a tendon and can't teach for six weeks.'

I mentally file away that information as I follow Emily to her next class. I telephone every dance school in town while I wait outside the lecture hall.

'Hello, can you tell me which ballet session Emily teaches?' I ask repeatedly. On the fourth call, I hit the jackpot.

'Emily,' says the receptionist. 'Emily teaches on Saturday mornings and Monday evenings. Actually, just a moment,' the receptionist says, pausing while she checks on her computer. 'Emily's also doing Thursdays now, until 7.30 p.m.'

'Emily Morrison?' I ask, to make sure we're talking about the same person.

'Yes that's right,' the woman confirms. 'Emily's a wonderful teacher, especially with the younger kids.'

'That's what I've heard,' I respond enthusiastically as I jot down the details.

When Emily emerges from her class, she goes straight to the cafeteria with another group of friends; two girls and a guy, all around her age. Emily shows no interest in the guy, who anyway is paying way too much attention to her petite blond friend. They sit at an empty corner table and take turns going to the self-service counter to collect their meals. I can't get a seat at a table close enough to hear them talk so I am forced to watch from a distance.

After lunch, Emily goes straight to the fitness centre. I look at fitness class timetables pinned to the wall by the reception as she disappears into a change room at the end of the corridor. She emerges a few minutes later in pastel yoga gear and heads to a hot yoga class in the first studio. It's an hour-long class. I am torn. I desperately want to stay but it's getting close to school pick-up time.

Day two is not much different. Emily eats lunch at the campus cafeteria, a few tables away from where Matt sits with two colleagues; a psychology professor from his department, who I know from Christmas functions over the years, and Kate, the research assistant I met at his office. She's wearing the same oversized glasses and her straw blond hair is knotted with a brown clip on top of her head.

Matt eats fried chicken and mash. That makes me mad. He had his cholesterol checked only last week and the doctor warned him that his triglyceride levels were too high. And now he's eating the unhealthiest meal on the cafeteria menu. I am so furious that I have to restrain myself from going over there and snatching the plate away from him.

I get even more annoyed when Emily beams at Matt from her seat in the cafeteria. He ignores her as he bites into his chicken. I'm kind of relieved by his lack of interest. Then I remember that it's just a facade. He could get fired if the university found out he was having an affair with a student.

I shadow Emily for the next few days, moving with her between classes and following her to the fitness centre, where she goes every day she has a break between lectures. Gradually, I piece together Emily's life. At least during school hours. What happens after 2.30 p.m. is still a mystery to me because I have to leave to collect Alice from school.

I learn the names of Emily's friends, and collect snippets of information about their lives. It's remarkable what you can pick up from eavesdropping on other people's conversations. I buy a second college sweatshirt in reverse colours so that I remain invisible as I burrow deep into Emily's life. Sometimes I wear a baseball cap. Sometimes I take it off. I buy a pair of squarish glasses that make me look quite different from the other pair. I change my look while I wait for Emily's lectures to end so that, when she comes out of the auditorium, I look completely different from the way I looked when she went in.

'When're we going to meet the new man in your life, Em?' asks Charmaine, her study partner, as they sit in the campus cafeteria. Charmaine, I've learned, is a Californian who talks constantly about transferring to USC so she can be close to her boyfriend, Greg, who is in the first year of medical school.

'Not sure. I'm still testing him out,' Emily teases.

On the fourth day of tailing Emily, I'm in the change room when she comes out of her Pilates class. I go through the motions of buttoning up my shirt at the other side of the change room while Emily strips off her sweaty leotard and walks to the shower stalls with a towel wrapped around her. When she returns I'm standing by the basin fixing my hair. She drops her towel and, without any self-consciousness, stands naked in the middle of the change room to dress herself in white lace panties and a low-cut bra.

Emily has a particular aesthetic. She wears yoga pants with tight undershirts, cardigans and sometimes slip dresses. I'm yet to see her in a pair of jeans. Her preferred palette is frosty pastels. It makes her look feminine and super pretty with her dimples and fresh-faced complexion.

Her hair is always worn down except when she works out in the gym. I know this because, after a few days of watching her, I finally have the nerve to join her hot yoga class. This time I come in as myself with my hair scraped back and no makeup. I arrive late and leave before the class ends. I pick a spot behind Emily from where I watch her contort her body in a series of poses well beyond my abilities.

I'm sitting so close to Emily that I can see drops of sweat roll down her neck into the gap between her breasts. Her sweet, cloying scent is achingly familiar. Matt brings it home to our bed most nights.

Emily's home address is still a mystery. One day I arrange for Alice to go home with a friend after school so I won't have to rush to the school pick-up. I'm hoping that a few more hours of tailing Emily in the late afternoon might lead me to her apartment. Instead, she goes to the library for a marathon group study session.

In desperation, I access Matt's computer again while he's asleep. I find nothing on his hard drive. He has a link to a student database bookmarked in his browser but it's password protected and none of my guesses work.

I decide to move to plan B. I pick up Alice from school and drive across town to the ballet studio. It's in a yuppified warehouse district in the centre of town, surrounded by hipster cafes. In fact, it's quite near the park where I sometimes take Alice to play on the weekends.

Alice looks pretty as a picture when she walks into the ballet studio in white tights and a pink leotard. Her hair is in plaits dressed in matching ribbons.

Emily arrives in her dance gear. Her hair is tied in a bun. Her deportment is perfect as the first notes of music signal the class has begun.

As the lesson goes on, I have to grudgingly admit that Emily is a good teacher. She patiently corrects each child's foot position and gently moves their bodies into the right posture at the barre. She gives clear instructions and plenty of praise. 'Good girl, Alice.' Alice beams. 'Lana,' Emily says. 'Your arms are wonderful. Pretend you're a butterfly. That's right, girls. Let's try it again.'

'Mommy, did you see how I danced?' Alice shrieks as she runs to me at the end of the lesson. She stumbles over the words in her excitement. 'Emily says my toes were pointed perfectly.'

'You were great, honey.' I put her sweatshirt on her by the reception desk and zip it all the way up before we go out in the evening cold. I've timed our departure so that Emily is behind me.

'Can I come again? Please, Mommy. Please.'

'We'll see,' I tell her. Alice's face suddenly lights up. I don't need to turn my head to know that Emily is behind me. She wears a denim jacket over her ballet gear.

'Alice really enjoyed the class. You're a great teacher,' I compliment her as we walk onto the street. It's bustling with the evening cafe crowd. 'This is a lovely neighbourhood. Do you live around here as well?'

'I wish,' she answers, with a dimpled smile so charming that it's almost infectious. 'I'm a grad student. I live in off-campus apartments up in the student district.'

'That's all the way across town. I suppose you have a car.'

'I take the bus. Actually it's two interconnecting buses. It takes about half an hour all up, which isn't too bad.'

'We live close to the campus. Would you like a ride? I can drop you home in under fifteen minutes.'

'That would be great,' she says after a brief hesitation. It's worked out just as I'd hoped.

We walk to my car parked a block away. There are five minutes left on the parking meter. Emily unknots her hair and lets it fall to her shoulders. Whatever doubts I had about her relationship with Matt disappear as the smell of honeysuckle fills my car. It's the scent of Matt's betrayal.

We talk inanities during the drive. How long has she worked at the ballet school? Where does she come from originally? That sort of thing. She tries to ask me questions too, but I deflect.

'It's off Peterson Avenue,' she says as we approach the university housing district.

'This is me, here,' she says, pointing to an apartment block on the corner. 'Maybe I'll see you next week.' She thanks me and gives us a little wave as she gets out. Alice smiles and waves back.

I wait with the engine running as Emily disappears through the apartment building entrance. A moment later, light floods the windows of a ground floor apartment. The ballet class has served its purpose. I finally know where Emily lives.

CHAPTER TWENTY

Mel

When the only lead you have involves a wild-goose chase, you go chasing geese. That's what ran through my mind as I pulled into a parking lot at a horseback riding school about forty minutes' drive out of town.

'Stay here,' I told Joe. He was slumped in the back of the car, overdoing the bored teenager act. My words were like a red rag to a bull. He climbed straight out of the car and followed behind me. It was the first time that day he actually did what I wanted. But hell, reverse psychology works a treat.

The reception area was in a cabin overlooking a white-fenced paddock where a rider was taking a horse through its paces.

'Anyone here?' I called out as we entered a wood-panelled office. A whiteboard above the counter listed prices for riding lessons and trail rides. On the walls were tattered posters of horses and a montage of faded photos with curled edges.

'Come on, Mom, this is the fifth horseback riding place we've been to today,' complained Joe. 'Can't we just go back home now?'

'Sit down, Joe.' I pointed to a threadbare couch. 'Read a magazine or something.'

The owner came out, a short man in his sixties with ruddy cheeks and a clump of grey hair. He was wearing a plaid shirt, a brown leather vest, jeans and boots up to his knees. He smelled of horses and perspiration.

'Sorry,' he said. 'I was cleaning out the stable. Didn't hear you. Are you looking to ride? Charlie over there would be perfect for your boy.' He pointed through the window to a chestnut lazily chewing hay in a pen next to the paddock.

'Not today I'm afraid,' I said, flashing my police badge. 'I have a few questions for you.' I showed him a photograph of Laura.

'Can you recall this woman ever coming here to ride? It would have been around six years ago,' I said.

He pulled out his reading glasses from his top right pocket.

'Well, I can't say that I recall this lady,' he said, 'but that would have been around the time I had my triple-bypass surgery. The person who'd know best is my daughter, Lacey. I'll go find her for you.'

Joe sat on the reception room couch staring blankly at the wall. Last night, while I was at the station interviewing Matthew West, Joe and Sammy had an all-out fight. By the time they were done, the sofa cushions had been tossed all over the house, including in the kitchen where a cushion had knocked over the sugar bowl. They tried to clean it up so I wouldn't notice, but they did it with water: I came home to find the floor covered with syrup. It took me two hours to scrub it clean. I told my kids it was a textbook case of the cover-up being worse than the crime.

The cherry on top was when Joe gave me his suspension note. It didn't say why he was suspended, but it asked me to contact the school immediately. Joe's monosyllabic response when I asked him what had happened didn't exactly improve my mood. It was too late to call the school. I had an anxious night until the morning when I finally managed to get hold of the principal. He told me Joe had brawled with another boy and they'd both been suspended for a week.

Joe acted as if the suspension was some kind of badge of honour. He joked the principal was doing him a favour letting him off classes for a whole week. He teased Sammy he'd be sleeping until lunch and gaming all afternoon while Sammy was at school.

That was the final straw. Joe was coming with me to work. At the very least, I would keep an eye on him. Who knows, maybe he'd learn something.

That's how Joe ended up being with me at the Sommerville Horse Ranch. It was southwest of town, about ten miles from where Laura's car had been found, and well within the search area that I'd delineated on a map when I'd put together a list of horse ranches to investigate.

The older man with the ruddy face returned through the rear door. He was breathless and his face was even more flushed from his exertions. Behind him was a woman with a solid build and a plain face framed by black curls. She wore jeans and a denim shirt.

'This is Lacey,' he wheezed. 'It took a while to find her. She was working in the top paddock.'

'I understand you have a photograph to show me, detective?' she asked as she shook my hand.

'That's right,' I said. 'Do you recall whether this woman might have come here about six years ago?'

She studied the photo of Laura under the overhead fluorescent light. 'The face is vaguely familiar. But we get a lot of visitors here. It's hard to remember them all,' she said finally.

'Is there someone else who might remember?' I asked.

'You could try Dylan, our riding instructor. He's not here today, though. Dylan only works on weekends unless we have special bookings.'

'Do all your riders fill out registration forms before they ride?' I asked.

'New riders register. Return riders sign a booking sheet before they're allowed on a horse,' she answered. 'It's for our insurance.'

'How long do you keep your paperwork? I'm thinking credit card payments, booking forms, guest books, waivers. Business records. Whatever you have.'

'Until we run out of room,' she said. 'If Dad had it his way then we'd keep every last scrap of paper. Just like his photo collection.' She indicated the faded photo montage on the reception wall.

'Do you think you still have the records from around this date?' I asked, writing down the date Laura West went missing.

'Maybe in the basement up at the house,' she said. 'There's a stack of boxes in storage there. I can take a look, but I won't have time today. I'll have to get back to you.'

As we walked out, we passed another wall covered with photos of people riding horses. Most were unframed and simply pinned to a giant cork board. Some of the photos looked as if they dated back years, with washed out colours and out-of-date clothing and hairstyles. I scanned them, looking for Laura.

'She's not there,' said Joe.

I spun around. 'Who's not there?'

'Your victim,' Joe said. 'I already looked. She's not in any of the photos.'

CHAPTER TWENTY-ONE

Julie

Dinner at Anne's house is a once-a-month chore to be endured. Death by a thousand cuts. None physical. All emotional. That's how Matt's mother works. She chips away at me slowly; my self-confidence, my peace of mind, my happiness. She's so delicate with her surgical strikes that her darling son, an eminent psychologist who prides himself on being perceptive, never notices. He actually thinks she likes me. He said that to me once. With a straight face.

Anne wears her hair short and dresses in neutrals. Colours are gauche; so middle-class. She wears whites and creams and taupes. Her jewellery is tasteful and plentiful. Always gold.

Anne's from a family of politicians going back five generations. Her father was a state senator. She married Matt's father at the age of twenty-one. He was years older than her, a childless widower who'd made a fortune buying up swampland in Boca Raton and Fort Lauderdale when they were scrappy beach towns where working-class Miami families took their vacations in the fifties.

Ever since Matt's dad passed away from a heart attack two decades ago, she holds the purse strings. Tightly, I might add.

Matt sees a sweet lady in her early seventies, filled with energy and generous to a fault with her money and time. She's overdoing it, he tells me after each visit, shaking his head in admiration as we drive back from Greensboro after one of her excruciating dinners. He doesn't realise that his mother is a prize bitch. What is it about mothers that blinds their sons to their faults?

Anne's always busy organising one charity event or another. Matt sees it as generosity. He doesn't get that it is ego. Pure and simple. Anne likes everyone to kowtow to her. That's why she has a finger in so many charities. It's ironic, because that woman doesn't have a charitable bone in her body.

Mercifully, in the summer, Anne travels to Europe or stays at a friend's house in Martha's Vineyard. She says the weather there is more pleasant than the incessant humidity of home in the high summer.

Matt drives into her circular driveway and parks under a magnolia tree. We are on time for once so at least she can't criticise me for not being punctual.

I'm wearing a wraparound designer dress. My nails are painted. Anne thinks that women who don't polish their nails are uncivilised so I make sure to go to the manicurist before our monthly dinners, lest I give her extra ammunition to use against me. Anne lives in Greensboro, which is the only saving grace of this arrangement because it's far enough away that we see very little of her.

Her house is a linen-white antebellum, impeccably restored and filled with period furniture. It's beyond me why someone would live alone in such an enormous house. Anne insists that she has no need to downsize. It's another reason why Matt shakes his head after every visit.

I ring the doorbell. Matt is on his cellphone and has lagged behind.

'Hello Julie,' Anne says as she kisses me coldly on my cheek. 'What an extraordinary dress.'

To Matt's ear, anyone's ear, that is a compliment. In reality, it is loaded with venom. Anne knows how to cut me down to size. I am garish and so excruciatingly lower middle class. I overdress. I underdress. I try too hard. I don't try enough. Usually all at the same time.

'Thank you, Anne,' I respond, ignoring her sarcasm. 'You look lovely too.'

'Alice, honey,' I gently push my daughter forward. 'Give your grandmother a hug.'

'Oh, aren't you just as pretty as a picture today,' Anne says as she kisses Alice on the forehead. She takes Alice's hand and escorts her to the couch in the formal living room. Pretty soon Matt joins us and it's the three of them on one couch and me alone on a two-seater. Alice looks at me longingly. She wants to sit with me but Anne is holding on to her arm as if she will never let go. I give Alice an encouraging smile and gesture discreetly that she should stay with her grandma.

'Matthew,' Anne says, surveying her son's appearance. 'You look gaunt. You're working too hard again.'

He's too blockheaded to read between the lines and recognise that her comment is aimed at me. It's my fault that he looks exhausted. And underfed. I don't take care of him properly.

At least he won't be able to take me to task over her grand-daughter's attire. Alice is dressed in a crisp dress, perfectly ironed.

I've plaited her hair in a single braid. Matt, on the other hand, could come in his underwear and Anne wouldn't mind.

Matt can do no wrong. Except marry me. His one transgression. Anne was overseas when we got engaged. She arrived back two days before the wedding. I had the distinct impression she attended only because it would have caused talk if she'd missed her son's wedding. Anne is very concerned about appearances so it would not have been a trivial matter.

The wedding was immediate family only. I had no family to invite. Or none that I wanted to attend. So it was a small wedding. Matt's mother, his brother Stuart and his wife, and a couple of Matt's cousins who I'd never met before, or since.

Anne made it clear she found the idea of our marriage to be distasteful. It was too soon after Laura died. I was too young for Matt. He's twelve years older than me. She gave Matt a list of reasons as to why he shouldn't marry me. Thank goodness Matt didn't pay attention.

She and I have since fallen into a pattern of tolerance, but that doesn't stop her from taking a stab at me whenever the opportunity arises.

'Alice looks the image of Laura, don't you think, Matthew?' Anne says, smoothing Alice's hair. Incidentally, Alice doesn't have a hair out of place because I spent twenty minutes brushing it and tying it before we left the house. Me. Not Laura.

'Mother,' says Matt in warning. He knows I get upset when they speak about Laura as if I don't exist. Laura gave birth to Alice, but I'm her mother now. I'm the one raising her. I deserve some acknowledgement. I deserve some semblance of respect from her grandmother. That's what I told Matt after the last visit. He just nodded his head and said nothing to his mother. She's the only person in the world that he's afraid of. He will do anything to avoid upsetting her.

Anne swiftly changes the subject by asking Alice if she'd like to accompany her to a musical in New York over summer vacation. Alice says she's not sure and then looks back at me for approval. It puts me in an awkward position, exactly as Anne intended. If I say no, I come out looking mean. And if I say yes, I'm sending Alice to New York with a grandmother who can barely stand me and would undoubtedly do her best to turn Alice against me.

Matthew is so blind to Anne's faults that there's not a word I can say to him about her behaviour without him somehow blaming me. I have no choice but to sit there and smile, enduring being picked at by Anne.

Did I mention that Anne keeps a photograph of Laura in a silver frame on a vanity cabinet in her bedroom? The photo used to be in the living room but I think Matt had a word with Anne and she moved it. He knows I get upset having Laura shoved in my face at every turn. Anne even has a framed photo of Stuart's stripper wife wearing a demure lace wedding dress. That's rich, given her tawdry past. I know all this, by the way, because I went into Anne's bedroom once when they were all eating dinner and I needed the bathroom. There was an array of family photographs in various silver frames on her cabinet. I didn't appear in any of them. There wasn't even a photograph of our wedding. It's as if Anne has decided that our marriage will be fleeting and there is no point keeping a permanent record of my existence.

Anne adored Laura. She was the daughter she'd never had. She invited her to join the boards of her arts charities. I've never so much as been invited to a meeting. It's Anne who set up the scholarship trust in Laura's honour. Even though Matt hasn't said a word, I know it was Anne who decided that I shouldn't attend Laura's memorial scholarship dinner.

I've heard that Anne and Laura would meet for lunch every couple of weeks. They were by all accounts a mutual admiration society, which in my book says as much about Laura as it does about Anne. Though one doesn't want to speak ill of the dead.

Tonight Anne snipes at me more than usual. Matt is preoccupied. He telephoned the medical examiner before we left home. It left him shaken.

I listened to the conversation on the other house phone, which I turned onto mute so that Matt wouldn't know I was on the line. The medical examiner told Matt the DNA tests had confirmed that it was Laura's remains they'd found in Kellers Way. The confirmation was expected but it was still upsetting. I heard Matt asking questions about Laura's injuries. Would she have suffered? Where exactly had her body been buried? When would her body be released for burial?

As the medical examiner answered Matt's questions about Laura's body, how it had been found in an unmarked grave in the forest, I saw a blurry image of someone digging a hole with a shovel. When the person looked up, it was me. The image shook me so badly that I was silent for the duration of the drive over here.

I often tell Matt about my dreams. Matt says it's therapeutic. I don't tell him about this one, just as I've never again mentioned the recurring dreams of the dead man in the car, even though not a night passes when his image doesn't infiltrate my sleep. Matt would undoubtedly tell me that my anxiety is creating false memories. He'd tell me it's time to increase the dosage of my meds. He doesn't know that I'm not taking them regularly. And there's no way that I want him to find out.

The dining room table is set formally with Anne's best china service and crystal glasses. Anne's view is that there's no point having beautiful dinnerware if it's never used. Her maid moves invisibly among us, serving us and taking away our dishes. I've never become used to being served by a maid. The only help we have at home is a woman who comes twice a week to clean and iron. Even that feels alien to me.

There's a sadness about Anne tonight. Matt telephoned her right after the medical examiner's call to tell her that Laura's body had been identified.

After dinner, Matt takes Anne aside to talk on the rear porch. I move to an armchair near an open window so I can listen to their conversation.

'Poor darling Laura. It breaks my heart all over again. Matthew, you look terrible; drawn and stressed. I've never seen you looking like this before. I'll ask Emmerson to liaise with the police so you don't have to carry this burden alone. That's why we have a family lawyer, after all. You already have your hands full with your wife.'

'No,' Matt tells her. 'I want to help the police as much as I can so they find the son of a bitch who did this to Laura.'

'If you think that's best,' Anne sighs. 'Maybe you should go to the lake house. Take a few days off.'

'You know I can't stand the place, mother.'

'Of course, darling. I forgot,' she says. 'I just want the best for you. When I think how different your life would be if Laura was still alive.' Her tone is wistful. I rush into the bathroom and run the water from the faucet to cover my sobs.

CHAPTER TWENTY-TWO

Mel

Angela Dellamore lived in a one-storey prefabricated house with rosebushes along the front lawn in lieu of a fence. It was the only well-tended house in an otherwise unkempt street marred by front yards with rusting furniture strewn among overgrown grass.

I called ahead to see if she was home. 'I don't go anywhere much these days,' she said in response. I didn't tell her that I wanted to discuss her time working as a babysitter for Laura West. I figured I'd get into the details in person. By the time Joe and I arrived at her front door, five horse ranches later, her house smelled like a bakery.

As far as Mrs Dellamore was concerned, cop or no cop, we were company. She set up her dining room table as if for bridge day, with a wipeable plastic cloth and her best napkins artistically folded in a porcelain holder. On the table was a jug of fresh lemonade, a pot of coffee, a platter of banana muffins and chocolate chip cookies still warm from the oven.

'My mama told me long before you were born that it's not polite to have company without anything to serve,' she said when I told her she really didn't need to go to all that bother.

I figured her for mid-seventies. Maybe older. Her hair was dyed a bright brown that seemed to emphasise rather than disguise her age. She was dressed for guests in a cardigan two-set and a pearl necklace.

Her house was spotless. It was furnished with sixties pieces that were in perfect condition and a lemon-yellow kitchen that dated from the same period. Metal bars on the windows were the only sign that she was living in a neighbourhood with the worst crime rate in town.

Joe and I sat at the dinner table while Mrs Dellamore hovered around us pouring our drinks. Joe beelined for the cookies. He might act like a tough teenager but put a plate of cookies in front of him and he's all kid. So much so that I had to give him a warning look when he took his third cookie, just the same as I used to give him when he was a toddler.

The moment we were done eating, Mrs Dellamore disappeared into the kitchen and returned with a container of cookies for Joe to take home.

'He's a growing boy,' she said, waving off my insistence it was unnecessary.

'Now, you didn't come just for cookies. What can I do to help?' She showed me into the living room, where she lowered herself into a deep armchair covered with an embroidered throw cloth.

'I'm investigating the Laura West murder.'

'Laura West,' she gasped. 'Why, I haven't heard that name for the longest time. It was such a terrible tragedy. There's not a day that I don't think about poor Mrs West and her beautiful baby being left without a mother. But I thought the police caught the murderer?'

'I'm conducting a review of the investigation,' I said quickly, trying to keep the details to a minimum. 'I was hoping you might be able to tell me what happened the weekend she disappeared.'

'Gosh,' she said, rubbing her temples. 'That was a long time ago. I'll try to remember as best I can. What is it that you want to know exactly?'

'Let's start with some basic information. Can you tell me how long you were working for the Wests?'

'I'd help out when they entertained, which they did quite frequently. Once the baby came, Mrs West sometimes asked ask me to babysit when their nanny was on leave.'

'And that is what you were doing on the weekend that Laura West disappeared?' I asked.

'That's right,' she said. 'Mr West was away if I remember correctly. Mrs West asked me to take care of the child. I believe she said that she had to work all weekend.'

'Was it a longstanding arrangement? Or did she ask you at the last minute?'

'Well, I don't recall exactly,' she said, closing her eyes as if trying to remember. 'Mrs West usually booked me in advance.'

'Tell me about when you last saw Mrs West.'

'I arrived on Saturday morning. Early, just after breakfast. The baby was in her highchair and Mrs West was sitting opposite her, feeding her from a bowl of mashed fruit. When I came in, she asked me to finish feeding the baby while she dressed. She came down some time afterwards and left,' said Mrs Dellamore, unwittingly recounting almost word for word the testimony she'd given to the police after the incident.

'Did she telephone at any time during the day?'

'I believe the police asked me that question at the time,' she said.

'Unless my memory is failing me, Mrs West called after lunch to check that the baby was sleeping. That was the last I heard from her. She was supposed to be back by 4 p.m. so I could go home and feed my cats. We'd agreed I'd return at 6 p.m. for the night shift so she could go out again. That didn't happen because Mrs West didn't come back.'

'What did you do when she didn't return?'

'I waited. I assumed she was running late. After a while, I called her cellphone. It was turned off. I think I left a message. Eventually, I called Mr West.'

'And what did he say?'

'He said she probably got caught up in her work and lost track of time. He asked me to stay until she came home.'

'So that's what you did?'

'I telephoned my neighbour and asked her to put out a tin of tuna for the cats. I slept that night on a couch in the baby's bedroom. That sweet child didn't even know her mamma wasn't there.'

'And the next morning? Was there any sign of Mrs West?'

'No,' she shook her head vehemently. 'Her bed didn't appear to have been slept in. I had the impression that she hadn't come home at all. I stayed all day on Sunday. I called Mr West when she didn't turn up or telephone by early Sunday afternoon. By then I was very worried.'

'Was it unusual for her to disappear like that? Not to call, or check on the child?'

'She did have a tendency to get immersed in her work, and she would sometimes forget to call. Or she'd come back hours late and would be very apologetic. That's why I wasn't too concerned at first. A little put out, but not worried,' she said.

'Do you recall what she was wearing on the day she disappeared?' I asked.

'Pants, perhaps?' She looked at me inquiringly to see whether I was happy with her answer. I kept my face expressionless. 'I'm not actually sure,' she said finally. 'I don't recall seeing her when she left the house. Mrs West wasn't one of those ladies who walked around in jeans or sports clothes. She was always well dressed. Even on the weekends.'

'Do any of these items look familiar?' I passed her photographs of the clothes we'd found on the Kellers Way body, which by then the lab had confirmed were Laura's remains.

'I'll need to take a closer look.' She turned on a lamp and put on her reading glasses to pore over the details of each photo. 'I'm sorry. I couldn't really say for sure.'

'Did Laura say anything about where she was going when she left on that Saturday morning?'

'She said she was going shopping and then she had to work. I assumed that she was working at the university but the police said afterwards that she hadn't been there at all.'

'Did you have much to do with her husband? Matthew West?'

'A little,' Mrs Dellamore said. 'He drove me home once when my car was at the mechanic. He asked if he could take a few roses for Laura from my rosebush. It was in full bloom, covered with white roses. He said white roses were his wife's favourite flower. I thought that was rather charming.'

'How well did you know him?'

'Not that well,' she said. 'I suppose it's often like that. Taking care of kids and all, I usually see more of the mother than the father.'

'What about their marriage? When you were around, did they argue? Was there tension between them?'

'Their marriage seemed strong,' she said. 'Of course, one never knows what happens behind closed doors.'

'Did Laura have any men in her life? Aside from her husband, of course.'

'I used to help out at the parties they'd throw at the house in the summer and over Christmas. They were fine affairs with catered buffets, and a bartender in a tuxedo. Why, Mr and Mrs West were inseparable at those parties,' said Mrs Dellamore, with more than a hint of nostalgia in her voice. 'I never saw Mrs West show interest in any man other than her husband. Not at their parties, and not any other time.'

'You've been very helpful, Mrs Dellamore,' I said. 'Just one last question for you. Do you recall seeing any changes in Mr and Mrs West's relationship after Laura became pregnant? Or once she gave birth?'

'Well, call me old-fashioned, detective, but I found that very curious, now that you mention it. You see, Mrs West wasn't ever pregnant.'

CHAPTER TWENTY-THREE

Julie

Matt's late. Again. I don't know why. He hasn't bothered to tell me. He treats me like a housekeeper. Like I have no right to know about his comings and goings. Like he owes me nothing.

I call. His cellphone rings and rings. He doesn't pick up. The next time I call, it goes straight to voicemail. I try his office. There's no answer. He's left me no messages on my cellphone or the home phone. He hasn't bothered to call or text.

Come to think of it, he doesn't need to tell me anything. I already know where he is. He's at Emily's apartment, no doubt decorated with black-and-white photographs of ballet dancers and colourful cushions thrown on her student sofa. And Matt in her bed, under her organic cotton sheets.

I feel incredibly sad. And angry. I thought this business with Laura might bring us closer. Instead, Matt is more remote than ever. It's as if Laura's died all over again and he's back in mourning. Except this time he has a chance to bring her back to life through her clone, Emily.

He said nothing to me on the drive back from his mother's house last night. He was in one of his strange, intense moods. Not a single word passed his lips. From the moment Matt switched on the car engine, we sat in an uncomfortable silence until he turned up the radio loud enough to cover the awkwardness. The only sound other than music was the gentle hum of Alice's breathing, asleep in the back of the car.

Since then, nothing much has changed. We step around each other like strangers sharing the same house.

I open the fridge. There's half a bottle of milk in the door, and three-quarters of a loaf of bread. I pour the milk down the drain. I push the remaining bread into the garbage disposal in the sink until there's nothing left except the plastic bag.

'We're going for a drive, Alice,' I announce as I snatch my car keys from the kitchen counter. She's sitting on the floor in her pyjamas, bent over her sketchbook. 'Put on your slippers and a dressing gown so you don't get cold.'

'Where are we driving to, Mommy?' She looks up at me expectantly, holding a marker in her hand.

'We've run out of milk and bread,' I tell her. 'I need to swing by the supermarket. Otherwise there won't be anything to eat tomorrow for breakfast.'

I know the way to Emily's apartment without having to use the GPS. It's on a street corner, two blocks from campus, in a four-storey building with distinctive red-flecked bricks. There's a willow tree on the front lawn and an entryway flanked by neatly trimmed hedges.

I park outside the building. The windows of Emily's apartment are dark. Nobody's home. Or maybe they're in the bedroom. My stomach churns. After a minute of staring at Emily's dark windows,

I drive along the street looking for Matt's parked car. I don't see his Lincoln. That doesn't mean much. He probably parked it around the block. Or left it on campus, which is only a ten-minute walk away. Matt is nothing if not discreet.

I turn the car around and stop on the opposite side of the road. Now there's a light in Emily's living room. Through the closed blinds, I see two silhouettes. I watch Matt and Emily's shadows flicker through the blinds until Alice's high-pitched voice cuts through like a sharp knife.

'Mommy! When do we get to the shops?'

'In a couple of minutes,' I tell her as I turn on the car engine. I drive to a shopping strip with fast-food joints and cafes set around a paved square. It bustles with students hanging out. A busker holding an acoustic guitar on his knee plays sixties music at one end of the plaza. A silver-painted mime artist collects money in a black fedora hat. On the other side of the square, hip-hop music blasts from a street performance that I can't see because of the crowd.

We head into an all-night store where I buy milk and bread to replace what I threw out. On the way home, I slowly drive past Emily's apartment again. This time the lights are off.

When I arrive home, Matt's in the hallway checking the mail. His car keys are still in his hand.

'I was wondering where you two were,' he says, scooping up Alice in his arms.

'We ran out of milk,' I say, carrying the grocery bag into the kitchen.

'You should have asked me to pick up milk on the way home.'

'I tried. Twice. I couldn't get hold of you, Matt,' I respond defensively. I'm still furious he abandoned us for the evening without the slightest explanation.

'I was in a meeting.' He unpacks the shopping bag and puts the milk in the fridge.

'You didn't answer any of my calls. Or my text messages.'

'I forgot to turn on my phone.' He gives me an apologetic shrug that riles me even more.

'What was the meeting about?'

'We're working on the course syllabus for summer school and we ran over,' he says. 'I told you this morning that I'd be late.'

'No, you didn't,' I tell him, but he's already deep in conversation with Alice as he carries her up the stairs to bed. I stand in the upstairs landing listening to him reading her a bedtime story. He makes her laugh by using difference voices for each character.

I return to the kitchen and reheat his meatball dinner in the convection oven. I take a handful of washed vegetables from the crisper and cut them into a salad with my chef's knife. The crunch of carrots being sliced on the chopping board is so loud that I don't hear Matt approach.

'I missed you,' he says, wrapping his arms around my waist. I put down the knife with a clatter and turn to face him. I remind myself his affection is an act. Deceit is etched into his face.

'You look exhausted, Julie.' He gently pushes the hair off my forehead.

'I guess I'm sleeping badly these days,' I say looking up at him. 'With everything that's going on and all.' I want to tell him his constant shifts in mood from hot to cold throw me off balance, but I'm afraid he'll say it's my imagination. Or that I'm being insensitive to his emotional needs after Laura's body was found.

'You need to sleep properly,' he says firmly. 'You haven't stopped taking your meds, have you?'

'Of course not,' I say, looking at a tiny crack on the wall behind him so he won't notice that I'm lying.

'If you're not sleeping properly, you probably need something to help you sleep. Or maybe we need to increase the dosage.'

'No, Matt.' I try not to sound as if I'm begging. 'I want to go running in the morning.' He knows that when I take my meds I struggle to get out of bed the next day.

'Not after what happened last time you went running,' he says firmly. 'You still have the bruises from the fall. Use the treadmill if you want exercise. Or go to the gym. Julie, we've discussed this before, I don't want you running alone anymore. It's dangerous. There are bad people out there. Plus it's not good for you to be so isolated. You need to mix more with other people.'

'I will. I promise,' I say. I'll tell him whatever he wants to hear if it means he won't bother me with talk of medication. Tomorrow, when Matt's at work, I'll go running.

We eat dinner at the kitchen table. I prattle on about Alice and whatever else comes to mind as I desperately try to recreate normality between us. Matt makes the requisite responses. I can tell his mind is somewhere else too.

After dinner, I go upstairs and dress for bed. On a whim, I put on a cute satin-lace set that I bought at Victoria's Secret ages ago and never had the nerve to wear. It's ivory and ridiculously sexy. When Matt comes upstairs, he shows precisely zero interest in my skimpy lingerie. I might be wearing a paper bag for all the attention he gives me.

He hands me a glass of chilled water and two capsules he tears from an aluminium strip. 'The doctor says it does more harm than good when you skip doses,' he tells me when I make a face. He doesn't leave me with any choice but to swallow the capsules, which I do in one reluctant gulp.

'I'll drop Alice at school tomorrow morning so you can sleep late,' he says as he leans forward to kiss my temple. 'It'll be good for you, Julie. Sleep in. Pamper yourself. You deserve it.'

'You know, Matt,' I tell him later as I lie my head on my pillow, punch-drunk from the meds. I'm making a mistake by saying anything but I can't control my tongue. 'I keep dreaming of the car accident. And the driver. He told me something very strange. It frightened me.'

'What was it?' Matt asks.

'I don't remember.' I slur my words as I'm overcome by a wave of exhaustion so great that I feel incapable of moving.

'Go to sleep, sweetheart,' Matt sighs. His face turns into an unrecognisable blur as I drift off.

CHAPTER TWENTY-FOUR

Mel

Joe and I arrived at Matthew West's office at the university at the tail end of an open-office session. There was a printed sign stuck on his door instructing students to take a seat and wait patiently. Every student would get ten minutes only.

By my count, the student in his office had more than used up the ten-minute slot. Joe shifted about in his seat restlessly as the meeting ran way over. Eventually, his office door opened and a pretty girl with long hair and a short skirt walked out. She gave a nervous smile before striding down the corridor swinging a leather satchel in her right hand.

I knocked on the office door and immediately walked inside.

'Office hours are over,' Matthew West said, lifting his eyes briefly from his laptop screen as he spoke from behind his desk. 'Come earlier next time.'

'I hope you have a few minutes for me at least, Professor West,' I said with a touch of amusement that he'd taken me for a student. Yes, I am petite, and I admit I keep my makeup to a minimum, mostly because I don't have time, but it had been quite a while since I was taken for a twenty-year-old.

'Of course, detective,' he said, as recognition dawned. 'Take a seat.'

'This is my son, Joe.' My eldest son followed behind into the office with fake nonchalance and a desperately bored expression. 'Joe's doing a work experience day with me,' I said dryly. I handed Joe my phone and indicated with a tilt of my head that he should wait outside. 'Take a message if anyone calls, ok?'

'Sure, Mom.' He took the phone and slumped back to his seat in the corridor.

Professor West looked at his watch with an expression that told me he was behind schedule and wasn't sure how much time he could spare. The stubble on his unshaven face and crisp shirt pushed up to his elbows gave the impression of an investment banker closing a high-stakes deal rather than a tenured university professor cocooned in an academic bubble.

'What do you need to know, detective?' His tone was cooperative but there was an underlying warning in his voice that told me to tread carefully. He obviously didn't like me turning up unannounced. I ignored his irritation. It's my job to make people feel uncomfortable.

'Laura didn't give birth to your daughter? Though she is listed on the birth certificate as Alice's biological mother?'

'The two things are not mutually exclusive,' he snapped. His face took on an angry flush.

'No,' I conceded. 'They are certainly not. But I would like you to provide more information. Anything could be relevant to our investigation. Also, as you know, we used Alice's DNA to identify Laura's body, so this issue is important to clarify.'

'We used a surrogate,' he said flatly. 'Laura was not able to carry a baby to term. She'd had several miscarriages. The doctors said there was a weakness in her uterus. A surrogate was the only way we could have a child.'

'How did you find the surrogate?'

'The usual way. We went to a clinic,' he said, writing on a sticky note. 'This is the doctor's name. They harvested eggs and semen from us and found the surrogate. Nine months later, we had a baby. It was straightforward. Expensive but uncomplicated. And one hundred per cent legal.'

'I don't doubt it,' I said. 'Is there anything else that might be relevant to my investigation that you'd like to mention?'

'What do you mean?' His blue eyes met mine without flinching.

'As far as I know, the original detective had no idea you used a surrogate to have your child. Is there anything else from your past, Laura's past, no matter how minor, that might help me find the killer?'

He contemplated my question. 'I can't think of anything,' he said. 'And frankly I don't think the surrogacy had anything to do with Laura's murder.'

'Perhaps,' I said. 'But if I'm to do my job then I need you to be open with me. For example, I was able to obtain the hotel bill from your visit to Charlotte on the weekend your wife disappeared. At 10 p.m. on the Saturday night, you ordered from room service a grilled Atlantic salmon, an entrecote steak, two side dishes and a rather expensive bottle of white wine. That sounds awfully like a romantic dinner for two.'

Irritation flicked in his eyes though the rest of his expression didn't change. I passed him a stapled photocopy of the three-page hotel bill. 'As you'll see on page two of the bill, the following morning an order of two continental breakfasts was brought to your room.'

'I don't recall why I would have ordered dinner at all,' West said as he paged through the bill. 'I'd eaten at the conference dinner. Maybe the hotel mixed up another room's order with my room? And as for the breakfast, the hotel might have assumed there were two people staying that night given that it says here on the bill that the room rate was for a twin-share.'

'Was Laura with you at the hotel?'

'No,' he sighed. 'I wish she had been.'

'Then who was in the room with you, Professor West?'

'Nobody.' He spoke a little too quickly for my liking. 'You have a vivid imagination, detective. All based on a hotel bill. Do you have any idea how many mistakes hotels make in their billing?'

'Tell me about Laura's rings.' I changed the subject abruptly.

'What rings?'

'Her wedding ring and her engagement ring,' I said. 'Do you have photographs of those rings?'

'I have our wedding photos. I doubt there are any close-ups of the rings, though.'

'What about for insurance purposes? Presumably the rings were insured. Insurance companies often require photographs for valuation reports.'

'I don't recall,' he said after a moment's thought. 'I'd have to look through my old papers.'

'Did you make an insurance claim for the jewellery?' I asked. 'After Laura disappeared.'

'You know, detective,' he said quietly, his tone offended, 'the thought never entered my mind.'

'Laura disappeared wearing $40 000 worth of jewellery and you never filed an insurance claim?' I exclaimed in exaggerated shock. 'Why?'

'Maybe it was my way of hoping that she'd return,' he said sadly. 'An insurance claim has a finality to it. Once Laura disappeared, all I had left was hope.'

I felt a pang of guilt for dredging up a subject that was palpably painful for him. I kept going, though. You have to have skin like an elephant in my line of work.

'You met your current wife not long after Laura disappeared?' I waited to see if he'd rise to the bait.

'It was a year,' he corrected me. 'One long, extremely lonely, and very dark year. I mourned Laura every day, detective. I still do. But the world keeps turning. I needed to rebuild a life for myself and for Alice and I won't apologise for it.'

'I wouldn't expect you to,' I said. 'I understand, Professor West, that your professional area of interest is human memory?'

'Yes,' he said. 'I've written a number of papers on the subject.'

'What's your expert opinion on how much a detective should rely on the memories of people such as yourself when investigating a case that's six years old?'

'Not a lot,' he said. 'Memories are far more fluid than people realise. So much of what we remember is coloured by our perception. If you're relying purely on recollection, mine or anyone else's, then you may never find Laura's killer.'

Professor West rose from his desk. 'I'm sorry to have to cut this conversation short, but I have a faculty meeting in ten minutes on the other side of the campus. You're welcome to walk with me if you have more questions. Or otherwise we can schedule another meeting.'

'There's no need,' I said as I rose from my seat. 'I'll be in touch if I have more questions.'

I left the office and walked with Joe down the corridor to the elevator. 'You had a call, Mom,' he said. 'Someone by the name of Samantha. From an events company.'

I called Samantha back as we walked to the car. She was the office manager of the events company that had organised the psychology conference Matthew West attended the weekend Laura West disappeared. I'd contacted them to see if they had video from the conference or anything else that might help me create a timeline for Matthew West's movements on the day his wife disappeared.

Samantha told me that they routinely videotape conferences. 'It's part of the package. We keep the footage on hard drives in our office.' She couldn't guarantee they still had footage from a conference six years ago, but she'd have a look and get back to me.

'Mom,' said Joe when I finished the call. 'Did you notice that photo on his desk?'

'What photo?' I asked as I climbed into the car.

'The dude you just spoke with, Professor whatever,' said Joe. 'There was a photo on his desk. I saw it from the doorway. You didn't notice it?'

'Yes, I saw it, Joe.' It was in a prominent position on his desk. You'd have to be blind to miss the photo. 'The blond woman in the photo is his second wife, Julie, and the little girl is his daughter. Why the interest, Joe?'

'I just noticed it,' he said sullenly as he clipped in his seatbelt. 'You know what's weird, Mom?'

'What, Joe?'

'I could swear the blond woman in that photo was in one of the photos at the Sommerville riding school.'

CHAPTER TWENTY-FIVE

Julie

I wake with a bitter taste in my mouth and a pounding headache. It's late morning. The sun streams into my bedroom. The house is quiet save for the reassuring hum of the dishwasher in the kitchen. I lie in bed and listen to it for a while. The familiar mechanical rhythm lulls me back to sleep.

When I wake again, the dishwasher is no longer running. I'm unsure whether the cycle is over or if it's a different day. I crawl deeper under the covers and drift off.

Each day blurs into the next. Some days I wake so late that I don't bother getting out of bed. Other days I blindly make my way to the shower and go through the motions of getting dressed and fixing my hair. Usually my pathetic efforts at restoring normality exhaust me so much that I'm back in bed by early afternoon. The lethargy that fills me is overwhelming.

Matt's been amazing. When he's home from work, he spoils me with freshly squeezed orange juice and fruit shakes that I don't really feel like drinking. He brings me newspapers and magazines and leaves bouquets of flowers from the garden in a vase next to my bed. He has arranged for a neighbour to pick up Alice from school until I feel better. Even the groceries are delivered to the house. I don't need to do any shopping. He cooks dinner some nights and on others he buys prepared food from a delicatessen in our local strip mall. There's really nothing to do except sleep.

'Relax, Julie,' he tells me. 'Get some rest. It will make you feel better.'

The thing is that it doesn't make me feel better. It makes me feel as if I'm in quicksand. The more I struggle to get out, the deeper I am dragged in.

I don't know how many days have passed since Matt became vigilant about my medication. 'It's for your own good,' he says every time I make a face during the nightly ritual of him handing me capsules and watching intently as I swallow them with a glass of water.

I wake again. Another morning. Rays of sunlight pour in. Time is passing without me noticing. The cloudless sky shimmering an incandescent azure gives me a new purpose to get up, to break out of the monotony of this new daily routine.

I stumble to the bathroom feeling light-headed. I sit on the toilet seat long after I've finished peeing, trying to think of what I need to do next. I decide to shower and wash every part of me so that I feel new and reinvigorated.

In the shower, I lean forwards with my hands against the wall tiles as hot water runs down my back. Steam condenses on the glass shower doors. It reminds me of the windshield of a car, shattered into a spiderweb of cracks.

'You're not safe, Julie.' A rasping voice suddenly comes into my head. 'You need to get away.'

The words run in a loop. My legs buckle. I slide down the tiled wall until I'm sitting on the marble shower floor with water hitting me in a steady barrage.

I lose track of time. Eventually I muster whatever strength I have left and scramble out. In the bathroom mirror I'm confronted by a naked woman, slippery and wet, with translucent skin and frightened eyes.

'Julie, you need to get away,' says a raspy voice. 'You're not safe.'

My wet hands slip clumsily on the door as I try to escape. When it opens, I'm suddenly afraid to leave the safety of the bathroom. I'm terrified of what awaits me on the other side. I feel as if I am drowning a little bit more each day. The more I fight, the more I descend into an abyss.

CHAPTER TWENTY-SIX

Mel

No matter how hard Joe tried to project boredom, it was obvious that he'd gotten a kick out of the day. His shoulders were straight for a change, not slumped. He was more animated than I'd seen him in ages. Best of all was the smile on his face. It had been too long since I'd seen anything but a petulant scowl.

'You have a real knack for this type of work, Joe,' I told him. We were in the kitchen and I was cutting vegetables for a garden salad.

'It was kind of fun,' he said. 'I wouldn't mind going out with you again, Mom.'

'Well, you're not done working yet. There's something else I need you to help with.'

'What?'

'Start up the computer and I'll show you,' I said as I put spaghetti in a pot of salted boiling water. On the way home we'd picked up a hard drive from the events company that had organised the psychology conference. Their head office was in the downtown precinct. I'd intended to watch the conference footage later when the boys were asleep, but if the investigation kept up Joe's enthusiasm then I'd milk it for all it was worth.

'Ready,' Joe called out once the hard drive was connected to the computer. I pulled up a chair alongside him at the work desk in the niche in the kitchen. I scrolled through the files until I found the video from the conference. I fast-forwarded through it until I reached the footage of Matthew West's address on the Saturday that Laura West was last seen alive.

'Hypnotism,' Professor West said, 'is highly controversial. Some say it's quackery and others say it's a placebo effect; the power of suggestion. In a study that I conducted, I found that among certain subjects, hypnotism actually affects brain function on an organic level.' He clicked to a slide with a graphic of the human brain.

'We chose thirty subjects who we found responded to hypnotism more than the average person. We conducted a range of experiments on them. For example, we gave the men a brick and timed how long they could hold it out front with one hand. They lasted, on average, two minutes and thirty-three seconds.'

He put up a slide with a photograph of the test subjects holding out bricks.

'Then we hypnotised the subjects and asked them to do the same thing, except this time we told them they were holding a feather, not a brick. Under hypnosis, they held the brick in front of them for twenty minutes and eleven seconds, on average.

'We took those same subjects to a medical facility and put them in an MRI machine to monitor their brain activity under hypnosis,' he explained. 'While they were in the machine we showed them various objects and asked them to identify the colour of each. When we hypnotised them with the suggestion that every object was blue, twenty-nine out of thirty of our test subjects

identified every colour shown to them as blue. It didn't matter
what colour we put before them – red, pink, orange, yellow, green,
black – you name it, they said they were all blue. Now, let's look at
the brain scans of subjects under hypnosis.'

I fast-forwarded through his address until the audience
applauded and he walked off the podium to return to his place at
the speakers' table.

'Here's what I need, Joe.' I paused the video. 'I need you to go
through the other video files after this one and let me know if at
any point you don't see Matthew West sitting at that table. Ok?
If he gets up for any reason, write down the time code he leaves the
room and the time code when you see him coming back.'

'Sure thing, Mom.'

'Good. But let's eat dinner first.'

We sat down with Sammy to spaghetti bolognese and a bowl of
fresh salad that nobody touched except me. After dinner, Sammy
did his English homework at the table, while Joe went through the
rest of the conference video on the computer.

'Mom,' he called out to me twenty minutes later as I was
unloading the dishwasher. 'Mom. He's gone.' I watched the video
over his shoulder.

'That professor dude,' he said. 'Check this out.' Joe rewound
the video and played it. 'He gets up from the table here,' he pointed
to the screen. 'Then he goes out of the room. And he doesn't return
back to his table.'

'Are you sure he doesn't move to a different table, Joe?' I asked.
I scrolled through the video backwards and forwards. Joe was right.
There was no sign of Matthew West in the audience during the
subsequent speakers' presentations. Matthew West's disappearance
in this video was a possible chink in his alibi. But did it give him

enough of a window to drive across the state, murder his wife, and return for the conference dinner that night?

'Great work, Joe,' I said. 'Watch the rest of the footage in case he comes back.'

'You know, Mom,' he said, looking up from the monitor, 'I'm thinking that maybe I should be a cop after all.'

I worked on my laptop at the dinner table next to Sammy, researching Matthew West's professional profile. He'd written several papers in the years before Laura's death. From what I could tell they were all published in minor psychology journals. His career had only really taken off four years ago, after he'd published a landmark study in a prominent journal. It had been extremely well received. I found write-ups and profiles, referring to him as an up-and-coming figure in the field of cognitive psychology.

Still, when I looked closely at his resume, I noticed that for a number of years early on in his career Matthew West was teaching at minor universities as an adjunct professor until, seemingly out of the blue, he received a full professorship at the leading university in our town, an institution with a national reputation. Why the sudden change in fortune?

I looked up Laura West. She was also Ivy League. Unlike her husband, she won a slew of awards for her work even when she was still in graduate school. She had so many fellowships and honours, including one at Oxford for a year, that I had to make a list in my notebook to keep track of them. Matthew West's progression seemed lacklustre by comparison.

Laura West moved to this university with Matthew, her husband of two years at the time. She was a full professor while he was an adjunct professor. I suspected that it might have been a two-for-one deal. The university got her as long as they took him as well.

My phone vibrated on the table. The number of the forensics lab flashed on the screen.

'Hey Dennis. You're up late.'

'I'm on vacation next week. Trying to clear the backlog before I go.' He sounded tired. 'Remember I told you we found fibres on the red jacket from the Kellers Way vic?'

'Sure, did you manage to source them?'

'We did,' he said. 'We found two types of trace material on her clothes. The first seems to indicate the victim, or at least her clothes, had been around lake water some time before she died. Possibly on a boat.'

'When you say some time, are you talking about hours or days before she died?'

'It's hard to tell,' he said.

'What about the second trace material on her clothes?'

'They match a carpet fibre used in Korean cars back around six, seven years ago. Both Hyundai and Kia used that particular carpet at that time. They no longer use it because it doesn't meet the new rules for flame-retardant textiles. It's been out of circulation for at least five years. That's why it took us so long to match it,' he said. 'The fibres were largely concentrated on the left side of the jacket and pants, so it looks as if the vic was lying on her left side in a car, or more likely, a car trunk.'

'So you think the victim's body might have been brought to the burial site in a Hyundai or Kia. Probably transported in the trunk?'

'Yes,' he said. 'That's exactly what I think.'

The moment I got off the phone I logged into the police database on my laptop and searched Matthew West's car history. He was not a Korean car sort of guy. This man liked his cars American and high-end.

But I discovered the same could not be said for his second wife, Julie, when her name came up against the Lincoln they currently owned. At the time that Laura West disappeared, Julie was registered as the owner of a Hyundai sedan.

CHAPTER TWENTY-SEVEN

Julie

I've thought about it long and hard, and I've decided I won't take my meds anymore. They make me passive. They fill me with inertia. They destroy any clarity of thought.

Every night Matt brings me the medication along with a glass of water. Such solicitude. He's the model of a perfect husband. When I look at his expression as he watches me swallow my meds, I have to wonder why he's so diligent about keeping me drugged out of my mind.

'You're not safe, Julie.' That raspy voice intrudes on my sleep every night. I see the bloody face of a man, dying. I smell smoke that chokes my lungs, and the unmistakable scent of blood. If the car accident didn't happen then why does it feel so real?

Tonight I make a show of taking my meds. I shove the capsules into my mouth and drink half the glass of water he hands me, washing them down without complaint. What Matt doesn't notice is that I'm holding the capsules underneath my tongue when I drink the water. It's taken me two weeks to perfect that trick. When Matt leaves to brush his teeth in the bathroom, I spit the capsules into my hand and hide them underneath the mattress. The next day, thanks to that little trick I pulled on Matt, I wake up med-free and energised. It's a minor victory. I collect the capsules from under my mattress and wash them down the bathroom sink. It's mid-morning and the only sound in our neighbourhood is the drone of a mower on someone's lawn.

I strip off my pyjamas and step into the shower. The cold water is invigorating. It wakes me. Not just my body, but my mind. I haven't gone running for ages and I'm probably out of shape, but I put on my running clothes and shoes and quickly head out the front door before I change my mind.

Minutes later I'm running down the gentle slope of our street. I should do an easy loop around the neighbourhood and build up to a more ambitious run. I don't. I turn right, in the direction of the toughest route in the area. I run towards Kellers Way.

I tell myself it's because I want to be challenged. To see if I can still do it. That's a lie. Deep down, I know it. I run towards Kellers Way because I don't want to be afraid anymore. Because I want to remember.

There's nobody on our street except for a handyman hammering on a front porch. A dog goes berserk as I run past the house on the corner. I cross the road and run through the local park, which is blooming with pink and white flowers on otherwise unremarkable trees that will return to being plain once the petals fall.

It doesn't take long until I'm descending down Kellers Way under a canopy thick enough to shroud the forest in an eerie darkness, broken only by irregular sunlight stealing through gaps between branches. It's only when I'm surrounded by the rustling of trees that I'm hit with the uncomfortable thought that this is where Laura's body was found. It's too late to turn back. And why the hell should I? Kellers Way is my sanctuary. I won't let Laura take that from me as well.

My feet thump heavily against the asphalt as I get into my stride, the beat of crickets rises and falls as I move deeper along Kellers Way. I inhale and exhale the crisp air in short bursts.

Down an incline off the road, a piece of torn plastic tape with the words 'Crime Scene' hangs from a branch. I slip underneath and reach a clearing. A section of ground has been freshly filled with soil. This must be the place where they found Laura's body.

It makes me inexplicably sad. I pick a wildflower and toss it gently towards the dark patch of topsoil near the gravesite. It seems like the right thing to do.

I turn back to the road and resume my run. Five, ten minutes later, I reach a sharp bend by a poplar tree. I stop to drink water and tighten my laces. This tree is my unofficial halfway point when I make this run. I look down an embankment covered with shrubs and I'm assailed by a memory of me frantically crawling up the slope, getting mud under my fingernails as I pull myself up to the top.

'You're not safe, Julie. You need to get away.'

A glint of red in the dirt catches my eye. I scrape away a thin layer of soil with the edge of my sneaker until lying in front of me is a piece of translucent red plastic. I poke around in the foliage with a stick to see if I can find more. The stick hits something hard. I slide the object out from under the bush and pick it up. It's a much larger piece of broken plastic. The two pieces of red plastic fit together to form the cover of a car headlight.

It confirms what I've always known deep in my heart; there really was a car accident here that morning. Matt's wrong. My memory hasn't been playing tricks on me. I remember what happened in Kellers Way.

CHAPTER TWENTY-EIGHT

Mel

I arrived at my office to find my partner Will back at his desk with a bronze tan and a clipped hairstyle that made him look more marine than cop.

'Good thing you came back today, Will. I was about to file a missing persons report,' I said. Truth be told, it was a relief to have Will back. It had been an intense few weeks managing single-handedly, especially with all my troubles at home with Joe.

'First proper vacation I've had in a decade. I should get married every year just for the honeymoon,' he joked, before strolling to the lunchroom to make morning coffee. Will is a master coffee maker and a coffee snob to boot, which means the only coffee he drinks is his own. His dream is to open a coffee shop in the gentrified warehouse district downtown and sell coffee and chocolate chip cookies. Nothing else. I've warned him that he'd last two minutes out of this job. He was born to be a cop, just like me.

Will and I are currently the only dedicated homicide detectives in this town. When things get really bad, a detective from the drug squad is assigned to help out. That rarely happens these days. They're badly stretched too. The town has recently become a stop-off on the east coast drug trafficking route from Miami to New York. Added to that, there's a thriving industry of dealers who sell drugs to students at the three colleges around town. Those kids buy everything from study drugs used to boost concentration come exam time to recreational drugs to help them unwind.

'You'll have to give me more than one of your famous lattes to soften me up,' I told Will when he returned with two steaming coffees. 'You can't imagine how crazy it's been running cases solo while you were tanning in Cancun.'

'It was Marcia's idea to get married in the spring,' he laughed. 'You'll have to take it up with her.'

'I will,' I answered with a smile. 'How is Marcia?'

'She's doing great. Back at work today as well.'

'She still works at the university admin office, doesn't she?'

'Sure does,' he says. 'Why're you asking?'

'I'm wondering if she might know someone I could talk to about a case I'm working on. We're working on,' I corrected myself. 'I need to talk with someone who knows all the university gossip going back years.'

'Which case?'

'A decomp,' I said. 'We found the body earlier this month. The victim was a professor at the university, although that part is still under wraps.'

'I'll call Marcia. See if she knows anyone,' Will offered. 'Meanwhile, let's get me up to speed on what's been going on here while I've been away.'

For the next hour, I took Will through the open cases, starting with the discovery of Laura West's body.

'Don't you think it's strange that the killer left jewellery on the body but took her wedding and engagement rings?' Will asked.

'Maybe the killer kept the rings as mementos,' I suggested. 'But you're right. It bothers me too. Usually the killer takes everything. Or takes nothing.'

'How valuable was the jewellery left on the victim's body?'

'It was all gold. The real deal,' I said. 'Even fenced, it would have fetched a couple of grand.'

'What about the missing rings?'

'They would have been worth forty, fifty grand in those days. The engagement ring had a two-carat diamond. The wedding ring was diamond-encrusted.'

Will turned the pages in the file until he came to Matthew West's profile. 'You interviewed the husband. Do you think he's good for it?'

Thanks to Joe's meticulous observation of the conference video on the day Laura West disappeared, I knew that Matthew West left the conference room and didn't return for the other sessions that Saturday afternoon. I also knew for certain he made it back by evening because the conference organisers emailed me a group photo from the gala dinner in which Matthew West appears prominently in the middle row. I figured there might have been as much as a six-hour gap during which Matthew West's movements were unaccounted for. Or as little as a three-hour gap, depending on the accuracy of statements made at the time by a couple of witnesses who vaguely recalled seeing Matthew West in the hotel lobby that afternoon.

'The husband is a suspect,' I told Will. 'There's a six-hour gap in his alibi that has never properly been accounted for but in my view it's not enough time for him to do the crime.'

I'd thought about the timelines on my way into work. It would be a serious stretch for West to make the two-hour drive home, find his wife, murder her and bury her body in a forest – all on a weekend in the full light of day – and still have enough time to drive back to Charlotte, get dressed and attend the gala dinner. He'd have broken speed limits to make the journey there and back in that narrow a window of time. His car plates didn't come up on any speed-camera violations that weekend and there was no indication that he'd hired a rental car. His name wasn't on any plane manifests either, so it was unlikely that he'd flown back home, killed his wife and disposed of her body, and then flown back to Charlotte to rejoin the conference.

'We don't know the time of death,' Will said, looking through the file I'd put together. 'That alone plays havoc with his alibi.'

'There was no signal coming from Laura West's cellphone from just after 4 p.m. on the Saturday. That's the time I'm assuming she was taken.'

After going through the case files, we decided Will would focus on wrapping up the other homicides I'd been working on and handling any new cases while I gave most of my attention to the Laura West case.

I had a pile of boxes to go through to reconstruct the original investigation. It would take the best part of a week even if no other cases fell on my desk.

'I almost forgot,' said Will. 'The medical examiner's office left a message for you to call them back.'

When I called the ME's phone, it rang through to voice mail. Thirty minutes later I finally got through.

'Hey Mike, it's Mel. I'm returning your call,' I said when he answered.

'Mel,' he said, putting something metal down with a clatter.

I'd caught him in the autopsy room. 'I have an interesting development with regard to the Henderson case.'

'The what case?'

'The car accident vic found in Kellers Way in the first week of spring.'

'That's being handled by highway patrol. It's not a homicide case,' I said, perplexed.

'Well, I'm sorry to be the bearer of bad news, Mel. Looks like the case might be coming back your way.' I hated it when Mike went cryptic on me.

'Why?'

'We have the toxicology tests back.'

'And?'

'That guy was pumped with scopolamine,' he said, as though I was supposed to know what that meant.

'What's scopolamine?'

'It's a drug that comes from a tree in Colombia called *borrachero*. It's a pretty white and yellow flower. The type of flower you'd put in a vase on your dinner table,' he said. 'Though I would highly recommend that you don't do that.'

'Mike, are you saying that this drug is what killed him? That he wasn't killed in the crash?'

'I have never before seen that concentration of scopolamine in a person's blood. Scopolamine is used in low doses in prescription patches for motion sickness. Sometimes to treat Parkinson's disease symptoms. Always in minuscule amounts.'

'What happens when the levels are not that small?'

'In large doses it can cause delusional behaviour and psychosis.'

'And the driver had taken a large dose of scopolamine before he died?' I asked.

'A potentially lethal dose,' said Mike.

'Which means what? That he overdosed on motion sickness tablets.'

'Not at these levels. He'd have had to consume hundreds of motion sickness tablets to get anywhere close to this concentration. It's not just abnormal, it's bizarre that he had that much scopolamine in his blood.'

'Maybe that was his drug of choice, Mike.'

'Not scopolamine,' he said adamantly. 'There's no buzz from scopolamine. It's like going down the darkest, scariest rabbit hole. It makes you manic in the worst possible way. I can't imagine anyone taking it by choice in those quantities. It's no surprise he crashed the car, with that amount in his blood.'

'You think he might have been deliberately poisoned?'

'I can't think of any other explanation.'

'Thanks for letting me know, Mike,' I sighed. 'I'll let highway patrol know that we're taking the case back. The good news is that Will's returned from vacation. I'll fill him in on my involvement, but he'll take the lead from here.'

I don't usually handle fatal car accidents, but I had gotten stuck with the Henderson case when it first came in.

Two days after Will left for Cancun, I got a call from Henry Dawson, a veteran cop in highway patrol. They'd found a body in a car in Kellers Way. This was a couple of weeks before we found what turned out to be Laura West's body, so that didn't mean much to me at the time. Henry told me it looked like a car accident but that there was something strange about the scene. He figured I might want to take a look. Henry was about two years from retirement; I trusted his instincts.

When I arrived at the scene, Henry was deep in conversation

with a cyclist who was still wearing his helmet. Over Henry's shoulder I saw a silver Toyota smashed into a tree. A body was in the driver's seat, slumped against the window.

The cyclist's name was Kevin. Early twenties. Tall, lanky. He would have been handsome if his cheeks hadn't been pitted with acne scars. He was a student at the university. I could tell from the sweatshirt he wore with the university logo, and the suburban Boston accent.

'I was riding past and saw the car wreck.' Kevin started talking before my first question. He seemed to want to get it off his chest. I jotted down the raw flow of his testimony. It's always more reliable getting an account from the gut, before witnesses have time to refine, or over-think by filling in gaps about what they assume happened, rather than what they actually saw.'

'You approached the vehicle?'

'I saw the driver's head against the window. I couldn't get to him because the driver's door was pressed up against the tree. Like it is now. So I leaned through the front passenger door and took his pulse,' he told me. 'I didn't need to, actually, but I did it anyway.'

'Why didn't you need to take his pulse, Kevin?'

'Just by touching him, I knew the guy was gone.' He was hesitant. Nervous. 'I'm pre-med. I've done enough anatomy classes to know when someone's dead.'

'So what did you do once you realised he was dead?'

'I closed the door and cycled uphill to get a signal on my phone so I could call 911. I didn't have cellphone reception here.' Kevin inspected the screen of his phone. 'I still don't.'

'Riding up the hill took what, five minutes?'

'More like ten. It's a steep ride. After I called 911, they asked me to wait for the police car.' He motioned towards Henry's black-

and-white patrol car. 'They met me at the top and I rode down to show them the location.'

Henry nodded his head to verify his part of the story. He slapped Kevin's shoulder reassuringly. Kevin was trembling.

'Are you ok?' I asked.

He nodded and swallowed hard. Despite the initial bravado, he was clearly traumatised. 'I thought anatomy classes prepared me for everything,' he joked weakly.

I offered him a ride back into town but he declined. He scribbled his contact details in my notebook in an unsteady hand and then climbed on his bike and pushed off up the hill.

When he was gone, I put on gloves and examined the car. The driver was wearing a checked shirt and was unshaven. He looked to be in his thirties. There was an ugly cut on his upper arm that looked like a stab wound, which is what had prompted Henry to get me involved in the first place. Lying alongside the brake pedal was a bottle of Jack Daniel's. The neck of the whiskey bottle was jagged and covered in blood. It had broken off in the crash. It explained why the car stunk of whiskey. And death. But mostly whiskey.

It also explained the cause of the nasty wound on the driver's arm. I figured the whiskey bottle broke at the moment of impact, went flying and cut his arm. People don't realise how dangerous loose objects in a car can be in a high-speed accident.

I'd seen enough bodies to figure the driver had probably only been dead for a couple of hours. I took photos and put the broken bottle in an evidence bag.

I checked the glove compartment and the driver's pockets. There was no ID on the victim. No wallet. I found a thick wad of well-thumbed twenty-dollar bills shoved into the middle console. Deep in the glove compartment, I retrieved a ziplock bag with two joints rolled tightly in cheap cigarette paper.

I walked around the car wreck. There was no sign of any other vehicle being involved. Or an animal, for that matter. Deer sometimes run into roads and cause collisions. There was nothing here except a car wrapped around a tree.

I took photographs of the tyre marks on the road, in case the rain threatening in the sky washed away all traces before the accident investigator arrived. I figured the driver was swigging whiskey straight from the bottle while taking a notoriously dangerous road at speed. He lost control and hit a tree. Probably died on impact.

'What do you think, Mel?' asked Henry, leaning back against his patrol car as I wrote my notes.

'We'll have to run this past forensics, but from what I can see this is a fatal car accident, Henry. There's no sign of a homicide here, unless you count a redneck idiot committing homicide on himself by driving under the influence,' I said dryly.

That's what I thought, right until the moment that Mike told me about the scopolamine. That changed everything.

I walked back into the squad room. Will was leaning back in his desk chair while chatting with one of his buddies in narcotics.

'Don't get too comfortable, Will,' I told him. 'I have a case for you.'

CHAPTER TWENTY-NINE

Julie

It takes me three days to get to the downtown library. Three days of tricking Matt into thinking I am still medicated. Three days of indecision over whether to go looking for answers. Or to forget. Forgetting would be easier, but questions gnaw at me. In the end, I decide the answers couldn't possibly be worse than the questions.

I arrive at the library not long after it opens, wearing jeans and a navy cable-knit sweater that makes me look thick and middle-aged.

I grab a stack of local papers from the last month and page through them next to an elderly man with Coke bottle glasses. His lips move soundlessly as he reads from a broadsheet newspaper that he holds in front of him, savouring every word.

I, on the other hand, race through each newspaper, efficiently scanning the headlines on each page before moving to the next. When I'm done with one paper, I fold it and put it on the floor by my feet, then flip through the pages of the next newspaper on my pile. And the next, until the pile of newspapers on my lap gradually dwindles, replaced by an unruly heap on the floor.

Time slips by until I find an article that makes me sit up. It's in the top right hand corner of an inside page, in a paper from two weeks ago. The headline says 'Motorist Dies In Fatal Accident'. Below it is a hazy photograph of a middle-aged man with a scraggly beard and uncertain features. 'The victim,' the caption says. 'Alexander Henderson. Age thirty-eight. Unemployed.'

'Mr Henderson,' the article says, 'drove his car into a tree on Kellers Way. Police say he was killed in the crash. There does not appear to have been any other vehicle involved in the accident. Police say his car may have skidded on ice, or swerved to avoid a deer. Police remind motorists to drive slowly, especially in the mornings and evenings on country roads, when frost increases the risk of skids.'

Alexander Henderson. I type the name into the search engine of my phone. I get hundreds of random results. I narrow the results by adding our location. That gives me the profile of an Alexander Henderson living in our town. The last time this Alexander Henderson was active on social media was seven months ago, when he posted a cartoon with a drug recovery message. His Facebook profile says he's a graduate of the Carolinas Community College. He once managed Mick's Burger Bar, an institution at the local community college. Within minutes I'm in my car driving towards the campus.

The Carolinas Community College campus hasn't changed much since my time there. It's on the opposite side of town from the academic universities with the big names and even bigger tuition fees. That makes plenty of sense because this working-class side of town is the community college's catchment area. The vast majority of its students are juggling jobs and families, trying to finish a diploma or get credits towards a degree. They're hoping for something better than dead-end jobs and a lifetime of debt.

Seven years ago, I was one of those students juggling work and studies. I had to pay my own way. There was no family to foot my tuition bills. I only realised the importance of education when I was twenty and facing the prospect of being a department store attendant – or, as they liked to call us, a customer service executive – for the rest of my life. Or until my legs couldn't take the punishment anymore. You can't know how hard it is standing on your feet for nine, ten hours a day until you've actually done it. It's what made me realise there are choices in life. My choice was to try for something better.

I pass the administration buildings at the main entrance of the campus. The path is fringed by magnolia trees. Outside the library is a cafe with a canvas sun shade hanging over an outdoor deck. Students relax on sun chairs while they work on their laptops.

I keep walking until I reach a strip of campus restaurants. Mick's Burger Bar has changed in the intervening years. The tinted windows are gone, along with the trademark red awnings of my time. Instead there's a hipster vibe with chalkboard menus hanging on whitewashed walls and vintage tables that spill out onto a timber deck.

When I walk inside they're preparing for the lunchtime rush. I head straight over to the college kid on the cash register. His head snaps up as I ask for the manager.

The manager comes out a minute later with a combative expression on his face. He thinks I'm here to complain. He lumbers towards me, a heavy-set man with a prominent nose and bunched up features. Mid-fifties, I guess. His name badge says 'Paul'. I tell him that I'm a reporter and that I am writing an article on a man killed in a car accident a couple of weeks ago.

'He used to work here,' I say. 'I'm hoping you might be able to tell me about him for my article.'

'It depends,' he shrugs. 'What's his name?'

I show him the copy of the newspaper article about the car accident that I'd photographed on my phone. He reads the article and hands back the phone with an audible sigh.

'Used to be my shift manager. Years ago. Best I ever had. I thought he was going places. Then . . .' he breaks off with a shrug.

'What happened?' I push.

'Drugs is what happened,' he says. 'Cocaine. And meth. And who knows what else. He'd been depressed for a while before he started using. Girl troubles.'

'What kind?'

'Got dumped. She was fooling around with someone else,' he says. 'Not long after that, he started drinking and then using. Eventually I had to fire him because I caught him pocketing money from the register,' said Paul. 'I can't have a thief for a shift manager.'

'Absolutely not,' I say sympathetically.

'Sad thing was that he came from a tough background. He was determined to get out of it. The drugs ruined him in the end. Yup,' he says. 'I'm pretty cut up to hear that he was killed.'

'I'd be interested in talking with the family. Do you have any names or contact addresses?'

'I may still have the employment file.' He takes me through a door with the sign 'Staff Only'. We walk down a narrow passage to a staff room at the back.

He unlocks a door and pushes it open to reveal a cluttered room with filing cabinets pushed against one wall. On the desk are a thick pile of invoices on a spike, alongside an abandoned breakfast special still in its wrapping and a mug of coffee with congealed milk floating on the surface. On the back wall is a whiteboard with notes written in blue marker, mostly reminders about staff schedules.

He unlocks the top cabinet drawer with a key on the ring hanging from his belt.

'Here it is,' says Paul, pulling out a file. It's a thin file. Not much inside except tax and payroll records and an employee information sheet. He hands me the sheet with the personal details for a closer look. It lists a residential address a few blocks away from the campus.

'It's double-sided,' says Paul helpfully. I turn it over to read the second page. It lists health questions about pre-existing medical conditions.

At the bottom of the form is a section for an emergency contact. There's a name and a cellphone number scrawled in almost illegible handwriting. I lift the form closer so I can read it properly.

The name says 'Julie' and the contact number is my old cellphone number, the one that I had before I married Matt.

CHAPTER THIRTY

Mel

There's one of them at every workplace: a fly on the wall, an inveterate gossip who knows everyone and everything there is to know, the good and the bad. It was the bad that I wanted in my search for a motive for Laura West's murder.

Diane Lester had worked in the previous dean's office for eight years before her recent transfer to the alumni association, which I gathered was the university equivalent of being put out to pasture. She was a slim woman on the wrong side of fifty, all bone and hard edges.

I met with her at an off-campus cafe for an early lunch. I ordered a Greek salad. She had a chicken caesar salad; hold the egg and the croutons, and a half serve of fat-free dressing on the side.

'A woman my age has to watch her weight,' she confided with a light laugh. She was full of nervous energy and an underlying resentment that I figured might work in my favour.

I'd chosen an outdoor corner table where we could talk freely without being overheard. So far, I'd managed to keep a lid on the identity of the Kellers Way victim. Media attention has a nasty way of biting you on the ass. You get a flood of pseudo witnesses coming out of the woodwork, lying for the publicity or making up stories for a shot at reward money. Either way it creates more work and solves nothing.

'How well did you know Laura West?' I dived straight in when the waiter left with our orders. Diane had only thirty minutes for her lunch break and I wasn't going to waste it on social niceties.

'I was the dean's personal assistant when Laura was hired, so I was privy to everything there was to know about her hiring; salary, negotiations, all of that. Most of that information is confidential of course,' she added hastily.

'Of course,' I agreed smoothly. That was not why I was here. I could get that information from Laura West's personnel files and bank accounts. I was here for nuance, for the type of information that didn't appear in employment records or official documents. I wanted the dirt.

'How would you describe Laura, as a person?'

'Well, that's a difficult question.' The hesitation on her face told me she needed coaxing. Not because she was loath to gossip, but because she didn't want to appear overly eager to bitch about a dead woman.

'This discussion is between us. It's important I hear an unfiltered account,' I reassured her, 'so I can get an understanding of Laura.'

'Well,' she said, fidgeting with her napkin. 'Laura was not the easiest person to work with. She was highly respected. Brilliant in her field. Don't get me wrong. It was well deserved. But as with most exceptional people, Laura was arrogant, self-obsessed and very much an individualist. There was always conflict or drama around her. Often both.'

'Who did she argue with?'

'I wouldn't say argue exactly,' Diane corrected herself, taking a sip of water. 'She simply wasn't the type of person to meekly accept decisions or policies that she didn't agree with.'

'What sorts of decisions?'

'I can't remember all the details, but I do remember there was a lot of back and forth on funding cuts to research.'

'The university cut her funding?' I paused as the waiter brought our salads in large glass bowls, along with a basket of freshly baked bread rolls and a dish of herbed butter.

'No, not her funding. Funding for her husband. The university was not comfortable with some of his research. When they had to cut spending in the overall budget, they reduced Matthew West's funding. It didn't go down well with either of them.'

'That was loyal of Laura, to battle the university on her husband's behalf to get his research funding reinstated,' I observed.

'She didn't see it that way. Matthew was probably her greatest weakness.'

'How do you mean?'

'Laura would do anything for him. She'd already sacrificed her career for him.'

'Sacrificed in what way?'

'Laura was headhunted by the country's top universities to head their neuropsychology programs. She chose to come here on the condition that we'd offer a position to her husband as well. The university agreed to hire him and give him the necessary research funding. Afterwards, I think the university regretted the arrangement.'

'Why was that?'

'There were issues over his research.' Her tone was vague as she picked at her salad with her fork. I knew that I'd stepped into sensitive territory.

'What issues?'

'I'm not sure exactly, but I believe there were concerns that his research didn't adhere to the standards set by the university. I think there were ethical concerns.'

'Do you know what his research was on?'

'I can't recall exactly,' she said with a shrug, though I had the impression she knew more than she was letting on. 'But about six months before Laura died, her husband's funding was cut as part of overall budget cuts. Laura barged into the dean's office the day it was announced. I heard raised voices.'

'So she gave the Dean a dressing down because her husband's funding was cut?'

'From what I could tell, yes,' Diane said. 'If you ask me, I'm not sure if her husband appreciated the lengths she went to for him. I don't think he showed the same loyalty.'

I took a sip of water as I contemplated her words. Diane was filled with resentment. And information. It was a dangerous combination in a disillusioned employee. Will's wife had come through big time. All I had to do was ask the right questions and Diane would unload whatever she knew.

'In what way was Matthew West disloyal to his wife?' I asked matter-of-factly.

'There were plenty of rumours that he was sleeping around. With his students mostly, sometimes other faculty. That was why he'd left two other universities before he moved here. He had that sort of a reputation. You know, a playboy professor.'

'Did you ever see anything that substantiated the gossip?'

'Not that I can remember,' she answered. 'Matthew West's a

good-looking man. He oozes charisma. You almost expect a man like that to be unfaithful. It may well have been malicious gossip. Laura was assertive, outspoken. She was hardly the doormat type. I wondered whether they might have had an open marriage. I mean, how could she not have known? The biggest blow-up that I recall was when the two of them were up for tenure.'

'What happened?'

'Laura and Matthew were supposed to get tenure immediately after their mandatory probationary period. Laura received hers as soon as the waiting period elapsed. But the university made up one excuse after the other as to why Matthew West wasn't eligible for tenure yet.'

'Do you know the reason for the delay?'

'I think it was because of the controversy over his research. There were concerns. I remember that Laura met with the dean and insisted that her husband's tenure be approved as well or else, she threatened, she'd quit.'

'That was audacious. She must have been confident of her position to give an ultimatum,' I remarked.

'It was very Laura,' answered Diane. 'Laura could be as sweet as pie or hard as nails, depending on whether she needed something from you. At the same time, she inspired loyalty in her students. They would walk through fire for her. She was like her husband in that regard. Their students were their biggest fans. She knew the university would never get rid of her. She was an academic superstar; a drawcard for endowments and students. Laura knew she could play the prima donna and get away with it. And she did. Until she was killed.'

'Do you recall how Matthew West reacted when Laura disappeared?'

'He was devastated. Completely torn up. The student body held candlelight vigils and memorials. He was at them all. When the university finally approved his tenure, the student newspaper wrote an article about it. He was enormously popular with his students and they were thrilled.'

'But not the staff?'

'There were eyebrows raised among some members of the faculty. As for management, well the dean was not one of his fans. Though he rarely showed it. He passed away last year, otherwise I'd have suggested you talk with him. Hiring Laura West was a big coup for the university and the dean tried his best to keep her happy. In the end, he wasn't able to turn a blind eye to the ethical implications of her husband's research. He asked Matthew to move his research program to the community college.'

'That's unusual,' I said. 'Do you know the reason?'

'Well, the standards are laxer there,' she said. 'The agreement was that he would teach seminars at the community college and transfer his research there under a cooperation agreement between the two colleges. The arrangement allowed him to get his funding on the condition the research was done off-campus.'

'Is that arrangement still going on?'

'No, not at all,' she said. 'After Laura's death, he dropped the study and eventually submitted a new proposal on impulse control that was accepted by the ethics board. By all accounts it was a very interesting area of research. He's since published in several important journals.'

I made a mental note to text Joe after the meeting so that he could photocopy Professor West's most recent journal articles. I'd left Joe at the campus library to do some research for me while I met with Diane.

'It sounds like Professor West had quite a dramatic change of fortune with his new research,' I observed.

'Without a doubt,' said Diane. 'He's turned into one of our most acclaimed academics, with a national profile. It's hard to believe he was on the verge of being fired six, seven years ago.'

Diane put down her fork.

'May I ask you a question, detective? Why all these questions about Laura? I thought this was all dead and buried, as it were.' She flushed under her makeup at her poor choice of words. 'I mean, I thought that her murder was solved.'

'I'm working on a related investigation,' I said, trying to keep things vague without lying outright. 'One last question Diane. From what you know, did Laura West have enemies? People who were substantially better off once she was out of the picture?'

I registered more hesitation on Diane's face. She knew something but she wasn't sure whether she should tell me. I watched the expression on her face change as she debated with herself how much to divulge. In the end she put down her fork and sighed.

'Despite her popularity with students and benefactors, not everyone liked Laura,' she said carefully. 'The admin staff found her arrogant. Some of the faculty were jealous of her research grants. Others were put out by the support she received from the university in terms of resources. She had two research assistants when most researchers had only one, and that was if they were lucky. That sort of thing. But I don't think that anyone outright hated her. And frankly, even though Laura sometimes rubbed people the wrong way, she was very charming and quite good at smoothing over any unpleasantness. She was the type of person to buy everyone a generous Christmas gift, which would usually ingratiate her with them for another year.'

'Did anyone work closely with Laura?' I asked.

Diane pursed her lips as she thought.

'She had a researcher, Helen, who was her assistant for quite a long time. They were close,' she said, looking up at me. 'Helen is now an adjunct professor. You could ask her. Except —' She stopped talking abruptly and looked down at her salad bowl as if she had just realised she'd spoken out of turn and hoped that I hadn't noticed.

'Except what?' I asked.

'Well, I gather they had a falling out before Laura's death.'

'What makes you think that?'

'Laura came to see the dean about a week before she disappeared. She wanted Helen transferred out of her department. I don't know the reason, but Laura was adamant.'

CHAPTER THIRTY-ONE

Julie

I find Alexander Henderson's old apartment at a run-down building near the community college. It's a seedy complex that overlooks the back of a strip club with pink neon lights that flash desperately in the daylight. The stairs are raw concrete. White paint peels from the metal handrail and cigarette butts are scattered on the ground.

When I reach the fourth floor I walk along an open-air corridor that overlooks the parking lot. A television blares so loudly that I hear it long before I reach the apartment in question. I knock on the door several times. There's no answer. I resort to tapping on the window with my car keys.

The television volume goes down and eventually the front door swings open. The man who opens the door is wearing a stained T-shirt stretched over a morbidly obese belly. The irritated look on his face immediately tells me that he's not happy about the disruption.

'I'm watching *Dr. Phil*,' he snaps.

'Sorry.' I try to sound contrite. 'Is this Alexander Henderson's old apartment?'

'Who?' he bellows.

'Henderson.' He lived here until earlier in the year. The guy scratches his scraggly beard as he contemplates the question. His expression remains blank.

'Never heard of him before,' he says and makes to shut the door.

'He used to live here.' I move my foot to block the doorway. 'He was killed in a car accident a few weeks ago. I'm trying to find his next of kin.'

'Well, it's not me, lady.' He twists to look back at the television screen as we talk.

'Ok, I get that. How long have you been living here?'

'Five, six weeks.' He's still twisting his head around to watch the show. 'The previous guy was kicked out for not paying his rent. Then I moved in.'

'What was the name of the guy they evicted?'

'I didn't ask,' he shrugs, without looking at me. 'Are you a cop?'

'I'm with the probate court,' I answer, thinking on my feet. 'Did the previous tenant leave anything behind? Any belongings?'

'Well, all the furniture was his. The landlord confiscated it to cover his unpaid rent, so you can't have it if that's what you're thinking.'

'I don't want it,' I respond. 'I'm wondering whether he might have left any papers behind. It might help us find his next of kin.'

'I put away all the personal stuff at the top of the back cupboard,' he says. 'Take a look. If you can reach the shelf.'

He opens the apartment door and stands back to let me through. This guy seems more concerned with watching *Dr. Phil* than letting a stranger into his home. And he clearly does not believe in fresh air. There's a rancid smell from the kitchen, where a garbage bin is overflowing and dishes are piled up in the sink. A half-eaten meal is on a tray on the floor. He returns to his armchair by the television set and turns the volume so high that I want to pull out the electrical cord.

'The cupboard is in the laundry,' he shouts out. His eyes are fixed on the television set as he waves in the general direction.

I walk through the galley kitchen to the laundry room in the back. A sour smell hangs over a basket overflowing with dirty clothes and towels. I stand on a kitchen stool that wobbles on the uneven floor as I open the cupboard door.

I find a heap of sporting equipment; a tennis racquet, baseball gear, that sort of stuff. I doubt they belong to the current tenant. I even find a lime green dog's bowl. It looks weirdly familiar. When I remove it I find a small box shoved behind it, stuffed with all sorts of random papers. There are letters and other documents addressed to Alexander or Alex Henderson.

'This may be what I'm looking for,' I tell the tenant as I walk out of the apartment carrying the box. He says nothing. He doesn't budge. He's engrossed in some sort of mother–daughter dispute going down on the *Dr. Phil* set. I slam the door behind me.

I head down to my car in the lot below and go through the box while sitting in the front seat. There are old utility bills. Most of them are stamped 'overdue'. I find a pile of letters from debt collectors with varying levels of threat. Most have never been opened. Some are torn in half.

The only personal letter is a Christmas card sent by 'Aunt Nancy'. There's an address on the back of the envelope with her full name, Nancy Poole. I look up her contact details on my phone and dial the listed home number. It rings through immediately.

'Nancy?' I say when a woman answers the phone.

'Yes,' she answers. 'Who is this?'

'I'm a friend of Alexander Henderson,' I say.

'A friend of Alex? Which friend?' she asks, suspicious.

'From his college days. I'd like to stop by and talk to you about him.'

'Well, I don't see the point,' she says. 'Alex is dead and ain't nothing gonna bring him back.'

'I just found out about what happened. I'm in shock.' I let my voice break. 'I want to be with people who cared about him.'

'I don't know why it should be a shock,' she says flatly. 'The only wonder is that it didn't happen sooner. Alex had been troubled for a very long time.'

'I remember him as an outstanding student at college,' I say. 'What changed?'

'Where do I start,' she says after a long pause. 'Well, I'm home tomorrow, so you might as well come over and I'll tell you all about it.'

That night Matt is so preoccupied with funeral arrangements for Laura that he only does a cursory check that I took my meds. To fool him, I leave the empty foil capsule strip on the table next to my bed along with a half-drunk glass of water.

My mind is drug-free and crystal clear as I drive to Nancy Poole's house the next morning. She lives off a main road two counties away, with a chicken farm and a dairy a half-mile down the road in either direction. My chest is tight. I feel anxiety building like storm clouds as I approach the house. But I don't care because my mind is clear again.

Matt thinks I've adjusted to the new dosage. He believes my mood has stabilised. He has no idea of the lengths that I go to, to avoid swallowing those capsules. There is so much that I'm keeping from him these days. I haven't said a single word to him about finding the broken headlight down at Kellers Way, or the article that I found about the car accident there. He'll tell me that I'm making it up, and I'll get confused again about what really happened there.

Nancy Poole's flat-roof house is at the end of a long concrete driveway with weeds breaking out between the cracks.

'Are you Alex's friend?' says a shrill voice as I get out of my car. I turn to see a woman in her sixties with a straw sunhat on her head, squatting in front of a raggedy garden bed that she's trimming with pruning scissors.

'Yes. My name is Stacy.' I have no idea why I lie to her about my name, but in the moment it seems a smart precaution.

'Come in and have something cool to drink,' she offers as she takes off her gardening gloves, leading me inside the house. I follow her into the kitchen and perch on a linoleum-covered bar stool. She pours two glasses from a pitcher of homemade lemonade and drops ice cubes into them.

'How did you know Alex?' She hands me one of the glasses.

'We knew each other at college,' I tell her. 'We were in the same study group. I kind of lost track of him after college. You said things had been tough lately. I didn't know,' I say. 'I've only recently come back to town.'

'He was using. Drugs,' she says. 'Not just marijuana. Hard drugs. It's a damn shame. He always swore he wouldn't grow up to be like his daddy, and there he was injecting heroin and smoking crack just the same. It broke my heart to bits.'

'I'm sorry. I never realised that things were so bad for him.'

'It was all on account of that no-good girlfriend of his,' she says bitterly. 'Dumped him for another boy just like that.' She clicks her fingers loudly to emphasise the point. 'He never recovered from the disappointment. I think that's why he turned to drugs.'

'In college, he was a top student.'

'It all fell apart after college,' she sighed. 'He went to rehab. Several times, in fact. It took years of going in and out of rehab until Alex was finally off the drugs. Finally clean. Even then, it wasn't easy for him to get a job. He had no references. A few days before he died, he told me that he had a job offer. He said the pay was good and he'd have enough money to get his life back together. He even talked about starting his own store, eventually.'

As she speaks, she walks over to a closet down the hall and opens it to display neatly packed shelves.

'I keep all Alex's things here,' she says. 'Even his college notes and files.'

'Do you mind if I have a look?'

'Knock yourself out,' she says.

I spend a good ten minutes going through the papers. I find a file containing notes from a psychology experiment that Alex participated in while at college. It includes a list of all the participants in the experiment. My name is on that list too. That's how I first met Matt. It was his study and he ran the experiment.

I'm afraid of what else I might find among the papers. I hastily push the box back onto the shelf. Lying on a higher shelf is a framed photograph of a man in his twenties, young and clean-shaven. He's wearing sunglasses and a baseball cap. He has his arm around a girl with shoulder-length hair. They're both smiling into the camera. It's obvious they're a couple.

'That was the last time he was happy,' says Nancy, her voice cracking over the last word. She stands behind me looking on.

The girl in the photo has her hand out over her forehead to block the sun from her eyes. It throws a shadow over her face. That's probably why Nancy doesn't realise the woman in the photograph is me.

CHAPTER THIRTY-TWO

Mel

When she was a student, Helen Williams was plucked from the anonymity of graduate school to work as Laura West's assistant. Laura mentored Helen and arranged a fellowship that allowed her to complete her PhD at a time when she had been considering dropping out for financial reasons.

From the photographs that I'd pulled up in an online search, Helen fashioned herself after her boss in more than just her professional aspirations. She wore her hair in a similar style to Laura and dressed in classic clothes and suits that seemed odd when she was a student in her early twenties, but were less out of place for the position of adjunct professor she now held.

On the walk across campus, I toyed with the idea of calling ahead. That would have been the polite way to do it, but I wanted to see Helen's raw reaction to my questions. Facial expressions can be the most revealing part of an interview, if you read the person right. I gave a cursory knock on her office door and walked straight in.

'Why are you asking about Laura?' she asked, after I flashed my badge and introduced myself. 'That case was closed years ago.'

I sensed more than curiosity in her manner. There was a wariness.

'I'm investigating a related case.'

She looked like she wished I'd disappear into thin air as she reluctantly pushed her laptop out of the way and motioned for me to take a seat on the other side of her desk.

'What was Laura like?' I deliberately asked an open question. I wasn't sure which side of the fence Helen stood when it came to Laura West. I had realised by then that people had strong opinions about Laura, one way or the other.

'Laura?' she asked as if trying to figure out my angle. 'Laura was amazing. She was one of the most brilliant people I've ever encountered. It was an honour to have worked with her and a tragedy that she died so violently.' Her answer seemed rehearsed yet there was sincerity in her delivery.

'Did Laura have enemies here?' I asked. 'Anyone who might have wanted to harm her? Perhaps even kill her?'

'There's always politics at a university campus, but I can't imagine anyone wanting to hurt Laura.'

'Including her husband?'

'Especially her husband,' answered Helen. 'They were very close.'

'I understand you were Laura's assistant?'

'Yes, that's right. My desk was in a cubicle adjacent to Laura's office and I was very involved in her work and research.'

'So you probably knew more about Laura's habits than most people at the university?'

'We worked together closely for a long time,' she responded.

'Did Laura take medication? Did she drink? Did she have any addictions?'

'I never saw her taking any regular medication, except headache tablets. She was prone to migraines. When they came, she'd immediately leave the office. She once told me that she needed total quiet when one of those headaches hit. The slightest noise was excruciating for her. She rarely drank. Wine, especially red wine, was one of the triggers for her migraines.'

'What about recreational drugs?'

'Are you seriously asking whether Laura was a drug addict?' she said.

'I am.'

'No,' she snapped, offended. 'Laura did not take recreational drugs of any sort.'

'Was Laura going through a difficult time at home? In her marriage? Or in some other aspect of her private life? Was she troubled about anything in the months or weeks before she died?'

'Not that I know of,' said Helen. I could tell she was uncomfortable with the direction of the questions. We were in sensitive territory. 'Laura was a very private person. I don't think she confided in anyone. She kept a notebook in her purse and wrote in it every now and again. I think she only really confided to her journal.'

It was the first time that I'd heard that Laura kept a journal. I made a mental note to check the case files in case we had a copy.

'Were there any students who had a grudge against her?'

'None that I can think of. Laura was very popular with the student body. Her students were hand-picked. They'd gone through a rigorous intake process to be accepted into the program. Laura was a big name in the field and she attracted big donations. When she died, some of those funds dried up and we had to downsize the department considerably. So no, I can't think of a single student who had a grudge against Laura. Except perhaps a student who wasn't offered a place in her program. There were thirty places offered each year and we had thousands of applicants from around the country, and abroad.'

'Did Laura have rivals among the faculty?' I asked.

'The entire faculty are rivals in some way,' Helen said. 'We're all competing for funding and grants. And of course recognition. But it never spills over into the realm of violence.'

'Did you ever sense tension between Laura West and her husband? Did you overhear arguments in the weeks before she died?'

'I overheard the usual couples conversation. Weekend plans. Cancelled dinners due to work commitments. That sort of thing. He came around sometimes to talk about a research project they were both working on. Their discussions sounded heated at times. My desk was in the other room, so I never actually heard what they discussed.'

'I didn't know they worked together,' I said with genuine surprise. 'What were they researching?'

'They were in the early stages of a collaboration. I don't know the details. She kept it under wraps. Even from me. Laura was excited about it at first, and then she lost interest. I'm not sure if it's because the preliminary findings were disappointing or because she didn't have the bandwidth once her baby was born. I had the impression it sort of tapered off.' I didn't miss the fact that Helen hadn't once met my eyes throughout this rather vague and lengthy response to a direct question. This was a woman who was not telling the truth. I chose to back off. For now.

'Did Laura have anyone in her life besides her husband? A lover?'

'That's ridiculous,' she said hotly. 'Laura reduced her hours at the university to spend more time with the baby. She said that after so many years of waiting for a baby, she wasn't going to miss out on watching her grow up.'

'What about her husband. Was he faithful to her?'

'What have you heard?' Her tone became wary. I said nothing. I wanted her to do the talking.

'There are always rumours about handsome male professors and their female students,' she answered carefully. 'It's a cliché really. The joke on campus is that they were Matt's harem. I took it for what it was: malicious gossip.'

'Matt?' I said. I could tell from her guilty expression that she'd hoped I hadn't noticed the slip. 'It sounds like you know him quite well?'

'That's what Laura always called him,' she responded quickly. 'I guess it rubbed off on me.' She looked at her watch abruptly. 'Look, I hope I've been of help, detective. If you don't mind, I have a lecture to deliver after lunch and I need to finish preparing my slides.'

'Absolutely. Just one last question. Is it true that Laura was trying to kick you out of her department before she died?'

'Where did you hear that?' Helen looked rattled, even though she tried to hide it. Her cheeks flushed and she tightened her fist until her knuckles turned white.

'Why didn't Laura want you to work for her anymore, Helen?'

'I don't have the faintest idea, detective,' she said. 'Now if you don't mind, I really do need to get on with my work.'

CHAPTER THIRTY-THREE

Julie

After my meeting with Nancy Poole I head towards a place I haven't visited in years. The back roads of the lake district are narrow asphalt, but my mind is not on the road. I'm lulled by the hum of the car engine as I keep going over what I found out at Nancy Poole's house.

Back in college I knew Nancy's nephew as Alex Trent. I'd never known that Trent wasn't his real family name. I knew that he'd had had a falling out with his father, I guess that extended to him not wanting to go by his father's name.

We dated briefly, brought together by our difficult backgrounds. I'd come through foster homes. Whenever social services couldn't place me with a foster family my extended family would move me around among themselves like an unwanted pet. Alex also came from a broken home, the son of drug addicts, which made him all the more determined to avoid drugs. His aunt was right. Alex had first-hand knowledge of where that could lead.

Alex was smart and driven. He'd been hell-bent on going to

law school even though his real passion was teaching. He often complained that a teacher's salary wouldn't dent the mountain of student debt he'd accumulated.

As for our relationship, he took it more seriously than I did. All I really wanted was to get away from this town. Ironic that after all these years I'm still here.

I'm so immersed in the past that I lose track of my surroundings. I come out of my reverie to realise that I've stopped the car on the banks of a lake, next to a house that I haven't seen in years.

The lake house looks the same as it did the last time I was here, with Matt, except for the air of neglect that surrounds it. I slam the car door shut. Gravel crunches under my shoes as I walk down the path towards the house. It has its own private cove and a jetty.

I vaguely register the decay wrought by time. The exterior of the house has faded and turned cream. It was once a brilliant white. The garden has gone to seed. It's not the same as in those heady days when Matt and I would sneak out here to be together while Laura was immersed in her work and out of the way.

The lake house has been in Matt's family for decades. Every once in a while, Matt and his mother argue over what to do with it. Usually they agree to do nothing. Matt says it's derelict and should be torn down. Anne won't hear of getting rid of it, even though she never visits. She's not really into bucolic vacation homes, even if she did bring her sons here when they were children.

The lake house is a piece of family history, she tells Matt whenever he pressures her to sell it. Anne is sentimental in that way. It's probably why she rattles around in that old Southern mansion of hers with its leaky roof and poor insulation in the winter.

Matt's hated the house ever since he almost drowned in the lake as a kid. He probably would have died if his father hadn't jumped in and pulled him to the jetty, where Matt vomited up the water he had swallowed. Anne remembers it differently. She says Matt's leg was caught in the reeds and he panicked until someone threw him a lifebuoy and he was pulled to shore. Other than splashing his arms about wildly, she insists Matt never went underwater. It's strange how two people remember the same incident completely differently.

What the lake house lacked in fond childhood memories, it made up for as a bolthole for Matt's extramarital affairs. I don't kid myself that I was the first woman he brought here. It's the perfect place for assignations, less than an hour's drive from town and offering complete privacy. There aren't any neighbours, as the house is on the edge of a national park.

The first time Matt took me here was on a late afternoon in early summer, about a fortnight after we'd first slept together. Ostensibly we came to the house for a swim. Laura had gone up to New York for the wedding of an old college friend. She had the keys with her, but there was a spare set hidden in case of emergencies. Matt counted the white painted rocks along the garden path leading from the house to the lake until he reached the eleventh rock in the row. He lifted it to reveal a keyring in a plastic bag caked with mud.

I do the same now, counting off the rocks. The key is still there in its hiding place.

Inside the lake house, slivers of sun creep through the gaps in the drawn curtains, leaving rays of dust hanging in the air. I open the front windows to let in light and to air out the musty smell. The furnishings have a Southern grace that gives the place a laid-back charm. I see Laura's hand in the interior design.

There are drop cloths over some of the furniture and cobwebs in the light fittings. It's been a long time since anyone was here.

I am relieved. It means that Matt hasn't brought Emily here. Yet.

In the kitchen pantry are old tins of soup and a jar of coffee that's long out of date. The fridge is unplugged and partially open.

There are two bedrooms down the hall. The mattresses are stripped bare. The cupboards are empty. The third bedroom is in an attic loft, up a set of timber stairs. The stairs rattle as I climb up. When I reach the top, it's just as I remembered, the bed looking directly out at the lake through a long window. I lie on my side on the bare mattress and watch a bird skim its wings along the water before soaring up again. How many times did Matt and I take in the view from this very bed?

Our relationship was never planned. Emily may say the same one day. Matt told me the usual things that cheating husbands tell their lovers. That his wife wasn't there for him anymore. Their marriage was falling apart. That he couldn't keep his hands off me. These days it's the exact opposite. Alice is the only reason that Matt comes home at all.

Matt's returned late every single night this week. Never able to meet my eyes. He lowers his head as he walks past me, muttering one story or another to explain why he has arrived home at a ridiculously late hour. Exam preparations. An unscheduled faculty meeting. When he ran out of work-related excuses, he even tried the old flat tyre excuse the other night. He is running out of lies. I might not have a graduate degree, but stupid I am not.

I never intended to become involved with Matt. It just sort of happened. He taught a seminar at my community college. That's how I found out about the psychology study he was running. I volunteered to be a subject. More out of curiosity than for the meagre pay. Even then, for the longest time we had nothing to do with each other.

Then one evening, after a night class, I stayed back to ask him a question. He was aloof and dispassionate as he answered my question while the other students streamed out.

By the time he finished his detailed explanation there was nobody left in the lecture hall.

It was already dark out. He insisted on walking me to my car. There had been an attempted rape a few weeks earlier and he said it wasn't safe for me to walk alone after late lectures.

'How about we get a drink?' he said casually as he opened my car door for me. I could feel his eyes run down my body with obvious interest. The truth is that I wanted him too.

We met up fifteen minutes later at a nondescript bar downtown. He ordered me a margarita and a whiskey sour for himself. The drink loosened me up. I flirted like crazy and drank too many tequila shots, which have always been my Achilles heel. He drove me to my one-bedroom apartment. An hour later, he left me in my bed, sated, as he drove back to his wife. It was my first affair with a married man.

I have slivers of memories of the weeks that followed. Matt and me on the living room floor, in my bed, in the lake house loft where I lie now. We never used the master bedroom downstairs. That belonged to Laura. Matt was always very adept at compartmentalising his life.

Now that I'm off my meds, memories return piecemeal like a strobe light flashing in my head. I try to catch them and keep them, though they are terribly elusive.

I remember exactly what happened on the day that Roxy was killed. Matt and I had a fight, a really bad one. He'd been invited to talk at a conference in Montreal. I wanted to go with him, just the two of us. I suggested we ask Anne to take care of Alice. I told him it wouldn't kill his mother to help out for once.

He refused. He said I wasn't making enough of an effort to bond with Anne. I stormed out of the house, taking Roxy with me on her leash. We walked up and down the neighbourhood until I'd cooled down. Then, just as I was about to cross the road to head home, a car sped around the corner. I stepped back onto the curb but it was too late for Roxy who, with her usual labrador enthusiasm, had pulled ahead of me on the leash. She bled something awful. I held her in my arms until her whimpers faded away. The driver didn't stop.

I think about that awful day as I lie on the bare mattress and look at the clear blue sky above the lake until it blurs into nothing. When I wake, it's early afternoon. My head is pounding and my mouth is dry. Mostly, I'm hungry. I open a can of soup from the cupboard and heat it on the gas stove. I drink it out of a mug as I stand on the front porch and watch the lake waters lap gently against the jetty.

This place relaxes me. I'll come here again, when Alice is at school. It's only a thirty-minute drive. I could bring groceries and fix up the garden. Maybe repaint the porch. I could restore it to its glory days, the way Laura did. When it's all fixed up, I'll bring Matt and Alice here as a surprise. We could swim in the lake and have a picnic on the shore.

The door of the boatshed rattles in the breeze, as if to remind me that Alice would love rowing. I walk over and open the latch of the door. The metal fastener is rusted through. It comes loose in my hands. The timber door opens with a creak. The smell of mildew is so strong that I cover my nose with my palm. Along the wall is a shelf with deflated swimming toys stained with patches of dark mould. They haven't been touched in years. Hanging off the wall is a row of tangled fishing rods. I lift up the canvas covering the rowboat to see if there are oars, to take Alice rowing. It's empty except for an old, broken torch and a rusted pocket knife with its blade open.

CHAPTER THIRTY-FOUR

Mel

The boys and I leaned against the whitewashed timber fence as we watched riders take their horses through their paces in the dirt paddock. The Sommerville Horse Ranch was busy with weekend horseback riding lessons and trail riders heading into the forest for mountain treks.

I'd been meaning to stop back at the ranch to inspect the photo montage on the wall after Joe said he was certain he'd seen a photograph of Julie West. I'd initially dismissed it as a case of Joe being overenthusiastic. I'd since learned that Joe had good instincts. Like his dad.

I figured I might as well get my kids outdoors while I followed up on Joe's lead. I'd booked them in for a riding lesson, to make an outing out of a trip I had to make anyway. Let's just say it didn't go down too well at home when it actually came time for them to get into the car. Apparently playing virtual sports on electronic devices is preferable these days to doing sport yourself, or riding horses, or for that matter, just getting out of the house on a sunny Saturday afternoon.

The bells tied to the handle of the reception door chimed when I pushed it open. Joe silently pointed out the photo at the top left of the montage as we walked into the reception area.

'Sure is nice to see you here again so soon, detective,' said Lacey, who was standing at the counter.

'I thought it was about time for my sons to learn to ride.' I gave both boys a warning look as they stood with pained expressions on their faces.

'Do they have any riding experience?' Lacey asked, taking off her reading glasses.

'Not unless you count riding ponies at fairs when they were five.'

'Mom,' Joe groaned in embarrassment.

'By the time we're done with them, they'll be naturals,' Lacey said. She pushed over a clipboard with registration and waiver forms to sign.

I helped the boys adjust their helmets while she led two horses to the paddock. When the boys were mounted, she opened the gate to let them inside the oval paddock, where an instructor with a weathered face and stetson hat was waiting for them.

'Would you like to ride as well?' Lacey asked me as she closed the gate.

'I'd love to,' I said, and meant it. 'But not today. I have a few questions I'd like to ask you back in your office.'

We walked together up the grassy slope to the reception building. 'By the way,' she said, with a note of embarrassment in her voice, 'with the good weather we've been so busy that I haven't had a chance to get into our basement to look for the files that you asked for last time. I'll do it first thing on Monday.'

'That would be great,' I said as we walked into the reception area. 'Can I take a closer look at that photo on your wall?'

'Sure, which one?'

'Over there.' I pointed at a dusty black frame in the top left of the photo montage. Lacey stood on the couch and took it down. It was a photograph of a young woman helping a child mount a horse. I was impressed. Joe had a good memory for faces.

'Who is she?' I asked, even though I knew the answer.

'That's Julie,' Lacey said. 'She used to work here. Loveliest girl you'll ever meet. A heart of pure gold.'

'She doesn't work here now?'

'She got married. Moved away. It was a real shame. The kids just adored her, especially the autistic kids who came for therapy lessons. Julie had a magic touch with kids. And horses.'

'You mentioned last time that I should speak with your weekend instructor.'

'Yes, that's right. Dylan has been working here for over a decade. In fact, he's the instructor teaching your sons,' she said.

I went back down the hill to watch the rest of the lesson. By the last few minutes, the boys looked pretty comfortable on their horses as they trotted around the paddock.

'That was awesome, Mom.' Sammy's eyes were glowing when he and Joe climbed off their horses.

'Why don't you boys go help brush down the horses. Then you can buy yourselves each an ice-cream,' I said, handing them money. 'I want to have a word with Dylan.' I flashed Joe a look that told him not to hurry back.

Dylan was sitting on the paddock fence with his sandy hair blowing in the wind. 'They did well for their first ride,' he said.

'They enjoyed it,' I said. 'Listen, I work as a detective back in town. Besides bringing the boys here for a lesson, I also stopped by for help on a case. Do you have a minute?'

'Sure,' he said, jumping down from the fence.

'Is this woman familiar?' I showed him a photo of Laura West taken in the months before she disappeared.

'She looks like a former student. From years ago. I don't recall her name but I remember her quite clearly because she was the most horse-scared person I'd ever met.'

'Is it usual for someone with a horse phobia to take lessons?'

'Some people don't want to be afraid anymore. In most cases, they fell from a horse when they were young and have never ridden since. I don't recall her reason, though,' he said. 'I didn't work with her.'

'Do you remember who trained her?'

'An instructor called Julie,' he said. 'She hasn't worked here for a long time. She mostly taught young riders. It was unusual for Julie to have an adult student. But this lady and Julie built a rapport. By the time she stopped coming here,' he said, tapping Laura's photo, 'Julie had taught her how to ride a horse around the paddock. It might not sound like much, but for a lady that afraid of horses, it was one hell of a breakthrough.'

'Where is Julie now? Do you know?'

'She left to study full time at a college in town,' he said. 'I kind of lost touch with her after that.' The slight flush on his tanned face suggested that Dylan had been sweet on young Julie. 'I'd best get going. The next riders are ready for their class.'

'Just one last question.' I walked alongside him to the paddock gate. 'Do you by any chance recall what time of the year it was when she came here for lessons?'

'In the fall. It was just before I moved to Argentina for a year to work at a horse ranch there.'

'I've left my card at the reception office,' I said. 'Call me if you remember anything else.'

'There's one other thing that I've never forgotten, now that you mention it,' he turned to tell me as he opened the white timber gate to the paddock. 'The last time I saw the woman in the photo, she came all dressed up in fancy riding boots and a red jacket. That get-up must have cost a small fortune. She rode by herself for the first time. Without any help. One loop around the paddock. When she was done, she dismounted from the horse, thanked us, and said she wouldn't need any more lessons.'

CHAPTER THIRTY-FIVE

Julie

I have a new routine. I drop Alice at school and drive straight to the lake house. I jog along the banks of the lake and then strip off my running clothes, down to my swimsuit, and dive into the water. I swim laps parallel to the jetty, backwards and forwards until I'm exhausted.

After my swim, I lie on the rough timber of the jetty to dry off. Sometimes I fall asleep and wake languidly in the early afternoon. Other times I take a fishing rod from the boatshed and sit with my feet hanging over the jetty trying to catch a fish. I haven't had a single bite but I still do it.

This morning I dig weeds out of the garden bed and plant a dozen shrubs that I picked up from the nursery on the way over here. My work is paying off. The lake house is looking vibrant again. Reluctantly, I leave to collect Alice from school. How she would love it in this peaceful forest clearing. Instead, I take her back to our lonely house where most evenings it's just her and me.

Matt hasn't been home for dinner in ages. He's late tonight

as well. After Alice and I have eaten dinner, I go out again with her, ostensibly to buy milk. Emily's apartment lights are on. I can see inside through the partly open blinds. Matt is sitting at her kitchen counter with his back to the window. I can't see his face but I recognised his posture. And his shirt, the blue chequered shirt I bought him for Father's Day.

I want to ring her doorbell and confront them. Enough with the deception. Then I remind myself those lies are the only reason we're still together. Our marriage is based on deception. Matt lies to me and I lie to him. As long as neither of us acknowledges our lies then everything goes on as usual. It's the lies that hold our marriage together like fast-drying glue.

Matt still believes I am taking my meds, albeit a lower dosage because my mood has improved. In reality, I haven't taken them for over a week. I feel amazing. The clarity of thought, the energy. I'm a different person.

In the end, I sit in the car with Alice half asleep in the back seat watching Emily's living room light flicker. I wonder what I've done to push him away from us.

Three hours later, Matt is back at home. It's close to 10 p.m. He has liquor on his breath. A cloud of Emily's sickly sweet perfume hangs over him. It's on his clothes, his skin, his hair. He makes no effort to disguise the increasingly obvious signs of his affair, sheepishly hoping I haven't realised he is home three hours late. The cheating, lying bastard still won't meet my eyes. He bends down to give me a dutiful chaste kiss. Our daily ritual.

'Sorry I'm late,' he sighs, as if he's exhausted from a long day at work. I know why he's tired and it has nothing to do with work.

'I got caught up correcting term papers,' he says as he thumbs through the mail on the hall table. That way he doesn't have to look at me while he spits out his string of lies.

'You should have brought the papers home,' I say. 'You could have marked them in the study.'

'I seem to focus better in my office,' he says, rubbing his neck to reinforce the lie he's spent the evening slumped over his desk at the university when he was actually in bed with Emily. He walks past me to the kitchen and opens the fridge. 'Anything to eat?'

'Sure,' I say lightly, thinking to myself that bitch Emily does everything except feed him. 'We have lasagne. I'll heat up a piece.'

I swill down a glass of white wine while the lasagne warms up in the microwave. When it's ready, I take his plate to the table along with the wine bottle and two clean glasses. I sip my second glass of wine while I watch him eat.

'I've never known you to stay this late marking papers,' I blurt out. My voice is accusing. I regret saying anything. I don't want a confrontation.

'What's your point, Julie?' he snaps.

'No point.' I back off. 'I don't remember you working as hard as you're working this semester. That's all. It worries me that you might be, you know, overdoing it.'

His eyes are still on my face.

'I have a lot of students this year,' he says. He speaks slowly. Like I'm an imbecile. 'The university increased the intake to raise more money. It means more work and headaches for me. You know that. I've complained about it often enough.'

'Yes, of course,' I say. I sip more wine. 'Isn't your teaching assistant supposed to help with marking papers?'

'At the end of the day, I have to give the grades, so I have to read the papers,' he says sharply. 'I'd be doing my students a disservice if I did any less.'

Matt does not like being second-guessed. I'm on thin ice. I need to get off before it cracks. As long as everything has the veneer of normality then we might get through this crisis. Until the next one.

'I'm sorry, Matt.' I act contrite. 'It's just that Alice was disappointed she didn't get to spend time with you today.'

'I'll make it up to her.' His voice softens. 'The bulk of my marking will be done by next week and then there'll be less pressure.'

Give the man an Oscar. He is so convincing he almost makes me believe he spent the evening hungry and tired in his office, bent over his desk, diligently marking his students' work.

Except his phone vibrates. A message pops up that he quickly blocks with his cupped hand.

'Who's texting you so late?' I ask. Nausea wells in my throat as I wait for his answer.

'Just an alert from the bank about a payment that went through.' I can tell from how smoothly he says it that he is lying.

As I get up to clear the dishes, I kiss him on the back of the neck, hoping to get a look at the screen of his phone. He quickly shuts it off and turns around to unbutton my shirt. He kisses my mouth. I remember where those lips have been and feel sick.

'You've had a long day. I bet you're tired.' I move away. He tries to pull me back but I'm already out of reach.

'I know that I'm exhausted,' I say with an exaggerated yawn. I go upstairs and change for bed. To my relief, he doesn't follow. I hear him watching television downstairs. The light flickers faintly up the stairs into the landing by our bedroom.

Later, as we lie in our king-size bed with a giant gap between, us he says to me, 'You're not taking your medication, are you? You told me you were cutting it back to one capsule a day but we never agreed you could stop entirely.'

I ignore him and maintain my fiction of sleep, my head pressed into the pillow and my chest rising and falling in deep, even breaths. He turns around so that he is leaning on his elbow, looking over me. I can see his shadow through my closed eyelids.

'Julie, you're not asleep. We need to talk. I can tell you aren't taking your meds.'

'How can you tell?' I respond sleepily.

'You're tense and you're constantly flying off the handle for no reason at all.'

'Don't you dare suggest that I'm not holding it together.' I sit up abruptly. 'I barely get to see you these days. I feel like a single mom.'

'Julie.' He leans over me, talking quietly, patiently. 'Stop changing the subject. You still haven't answered my question. Have you been taking your medication?'

'Yes,' I say, meeting his eyes steadily. 'Of course. I took it this morning and spent most of the day sleeping.'

'Good girl.' He kisses me on my forehead like I'm a child. We lie there for a few more minutes, both of us pretending to be sleeping. My heart beats rapidly while I wait for his next move. He gets out of bed and returns carrying a glass of water.

'You're so tense, honey,' he says, sitting down next to me on the mattress. He passes me two dark green capsules and the water. His eyes don't waver until I've swallowed the capsules. Then he takes the tumbler from me and puts it on the table next to my bed. He turns me on my stomach and lifts up my nightgown. He massages my back, pressing deeply into the muscles with his thumbs so that it's both excruciating and pleasurable at the same time.

'I've never felt muscles so tight before,' he whispers in my ear as he kneads his hands into my back. 'I'm pleased you took those tablets. You'll wake up refreshed. Back to your old self.'

The medicine is kicking in. I'm floating under the sure touch of his hands.

'Matt,' I say drowsily.

'Yes, honey?' His voice seems so far away.

'Why don't we ever go to the lake house?'

He stops massaging for a split second. Long enough for me to know, even through the medicated haze, that the question bothers him.

'I don't like the place. It's run-down,' he answers curtly. 'And it has unpleasant memories.'

'You told me once that you almost drowned there.'

'I did. When I was a child. Why are you asking me about that place now?'

'No reason,' I say, oblivious to everything. 'Your mother says that Laura loved it there.'

'My mother over-exaggerates,' he says. 'Laura and I barely went there.'

'It's very pretty around there,' I say as a wave of sleep washes over me. 'But the house badly needs a new coat of paint. We really should paint it, Matt.'

I drift off. When I wake in the morning, I am naked and wrapped in his arms.

CHAPTER THIRTY-SIX

Julie

Alice is sitting on our homemade swing in the sunlit rear garden, catching bubbles that I blow towards her. She giggles so loudly that at first I don't hear the doorbell ring. It's only after the third or fourth ring that Alice with her acute hearing points out that we have a visitor.

'I was in the neighbourhood and I had a few questions,' the woman says when I open the door. She tells me her name and shows me a detective shield. A flash of panic runs through me. We've never spoken directly. We've never even met. I know who she is only because I watched from the landing as Matt took her straight from the front door to his study when she last stopped by.

I tell her that Matt isn't home and won't be here until much later. Then I realise from the expression on her face that she isn't here to talk to him. It's me she wants.

I take her into the rear garden where Alice is still on the swing. I give Alice a couple of big pushes to get her going and then retreat to the patio. We sit opposite each other on hessian chairs. I pour us each a long glass of iced peach tea from a pitcher on the outdoor table.

My hand trembles and I spill some of the liquid. She notices. I want to tell her it's not from nerves but from my medication. That may lead to a whole host of questions that are frankly none of her business. So I flush at my clumsiness and say nothing.

'How can I help you, detective?' I ask. I feel sleepy as I talk, as if I'm slurring my words. I'm back in the haze.

Matt's back to being diligent about making sure I'm taking my meds. The more I take them, the less I'm able to resist him, and his nightly routine of capsules washed down with a glass of water. I haven't gone for a run in days. I feel bloated and unhealthy. I worry about the lake house plants dying without regular watering, and weeds taking over the freshly planted garden beds overlooking the lake. Every morning I wake wanting to visit the lake house, and yet most days I can't even get out of bed. The truth is that I can't drive to the store without getting sleepy.

'I'm sorry if my timing isn't good,' the detective says. I notice she doesn't offer to come back another time. 'I have a few questions for you about Laura West's death.'

'Of course.' I try to inject energy into my voice. 'Anything I can do to help.'

'Did you once work at the Sommerville Horse Ranch? It's about thirty miles out of town.'

My mind is blank as I contemplate the question. Sommerville Horse Ranch? It's there somewhere in my memory. I am distracted by the groaning of the ropes as they rub against the oak tree branch each time Alice goes up and down on the swing. The detective stares at me, waiting for an answer. I force myself to focus.

'Sorry. What was the name of the place?'

'The Sommerville Horse Ranch,' she says slowly. She looks at me oddly.

'I worked there,' I say. 'Years ago. When I was a student.'

'Do you recall whether your husband's first wife, Laura, came there for lessons?'

'That was a long time ago.' I scramble to get my thoughts together, to stop my mind from drifting. 'I haven't thought about that place for ages.'

'To make it easier for you to recollect,' she says, taking a blue folder from her bag, 'I've spoken with the staff at the ranch and they mentioned that you were Laura West's riding teacher. In fact, they say the two of you built a rapport during the weeks she came for horse riding lessons with you.'

'That's strange,' I say. My voice is thin. 'I worked with kids mostly, not adults. I don't recall meeting Laura but I suppose if the horse ranch says I taught her then they must be right . . .' My voice trails off. Surely I would remember teaching Matt's wife to ride a horse?

'This might help jog your memory.' The detective removes photocopies of documents from a folder and places them before me on the table. 'They're the horse ranch's records. They show that Laura West came to the school for riding lessons on six occasions between September and November in the year she disappeared,' she says. 'In all but her first lesson, she was assigned to you.'

I recognise the familiar horse ranch letterhead. The writing is cramped. My vision blurs suddenly as I lose focus. After two failed attempts, I force myself to concentrate and read the words.

'You were the only Julie working there.' The detective's voice cuts through my confusion. 'So it must refer to you.'

'I suppose I must have taught Laura,' I say helplessly. I'm not sure what to say. 'The paperwork must be correct.'

'Is this your signature?' she asks, showing me another document. It's a photocopy of a logbook entry for a one-hour class with Laura West. In the column under 'Trainer' it says 'Julie'. Alongside it is the signature that I used in those days.

'That's my signature,' I say.

'Would it surprise you to know that this is the exact day that Laura West went missing?' The detective looks at me again. To see my reaction. It makes me uncomfortable, as if she is looking into my soul. 'Do you remember giving Laura a riding lesson on the day she disappeared?'

'I don't recall,' I answer blankly. Even through the numbness and confusion that clouds my mind, I know this is bad. Real bad. 'I'm sorry. I don't really remember anything about that time. Until you showed me this, I didn't even know that I'd met Laura.'

'Mrs West,' the detective says, enunciating every word as if I am a recalcitrant schoolchild, 'is there someone who can verify where you were the weekend that Laura West disappeared?'

'Mommy? Mommy?' I look towards Alice. The swing has come to a standstill. I get up and push Alice until she is back soaring through the air.

'Sorry, detective,' I say when I return to the patio. 'I'm not feeling well today. What was your question?'

'I asked,' she says in a clear voice, 'whether you can account for your whereabouts the weekend Laura West was murdered. We'd like to eliminate you as a suspect. Or . . .' she leaves the sentence unfinished. I know the implications. The coincidence is too great. Even in my confused state, I can see that.

'It was years ago,' I say in the petulant tone of a child. 'How could I possibly remember where I was six years ago?'

'Mrs West. Julie. I don't mean to be rude, but this is an investigation into the murder of your husband's first wife. It strikes me as strange that you were possibly the last person to see his first wife alive. So we really are going to need details of where you were and who you were with on the day and during the hours in question.'

'I guess it looks bad.' I hate myself for the desperation in my voice.

'Yes. It does,' she agrees.

CHAPTER THIRTY-SEVEN

Mel

I never thought I'd say it but I was pleased Joe had been suspended from school. It brought us closer. And it helped get him fired up again. It had been a long time since I'd seen Joe this enthusiastic about anything.

'Cognitive psychology,' Joe said, making a face over his granola bowl at the breakfast table. He did not expect to spend his last day of suspension from school in a university lecture hall.

'Smile, Joe,' I said. 'You might actually enjoy it.'

We arrived halfway into the lecture through a door in the back of the hall. The auditorium was packed with students, none of whom, from what I could see, had their laptops open or their phones in hand. They all sat in rapt attention as Matthew West paced across the podium with his hands in his pockets as he spoke.

I thought we'd arrived unseen but it soon became clear that our presence had been noted.

'We have a special guest today from our local police department,' Matthew West said. He looked in my direction, which prompted his students to turn their heads to look at us as well. 'Detective Carter might not be happy to hear that, while witnesses might not always lie, they often don't tell the truth either.'

He addressed the room. 'What do I mean by that? A witness will get up on the stand in a court of law. And swear on the holy bible to tell the truth, the whole truth and nothing but the truth. The witness may mean every word of that oath. And then he or she will give false testimony. Why?' He looked at his students. 'Anyone?'

'Because of perception?' A student in the front piped up.

'Jason over here is absolutely correct. People perceive things differently,' he said. 'That's why witnesses give radically different accounts of the exact same event. Not just because each witness saw something different from his or her vantage point, but because of how we process information. We've talked about this before. What else can affect the reliability of a witness? Anyone?'

'Leading questions,' said a girl.

'That's right. Psychologists in a series of experiments conducted as far back as the seventies found that when subjects were shown footage of a car accident, their recollection of what appeared in the footage was affected by the questions they were asked. For example, if the word "smashed" was used in a question then subjects were more likely to recall seeing broken glass among the wreckage, even though in reality there was no broken glass in the footage they viewed.

'Our memories of events are influenced by how we process them afterwards. What others tell us. And what we hear in the media. But there are other factors that play havoc with human memory. What are they? Let's hear from the fifth row.' He pointed at a student slumped down in his seat. 'Tom?'

'Trauma,' said the guy, straightening up.

'Trauma,' repeated Matthew West. 'We've discussed in previous classes how trauma shapes and reshapes our memory.'

He put up a slide of a young man taken in the late eighties, judging by the clothes and hair style.

'It's 1986. The year most of you probably started kindergarten. Adam Logan is an honor student at a Pennsylvania college. He's popular and well regarded, with a high GPA and a great future ahead. He's recently become engaged to his high school sweetheart and is in the process of applying for graduate school. One night, he's driving home to his parents' house for the weekend when the police stop his vehicle.

'The policeman asks him to stand outside his vehicle. Adam Logan doesn't argue. He's a fine upstanding citizen. He does as he's asked. While he is standing there, the policeman determines that Adam Logan fits the description of an assailant given by a woman attacked in that area the previous night.

'The police put Adam Logan into a line-up. The victim immediately points him out as the attacker. She is "absolutely certain that it is him". Her exact words, written in the police report. Adam Logan is arrested and charged.' Professor West puts up a mug shot of Adam Logan with a pale face and bloodshot eyes.

'His bail is denied, as might be expected for a suspect involved in a vicious assault. He has to spend the next few days in police lockup as it's the President's Day weekend. Unfortunately, while he is in lockup, he is beaten up by another inmate and permanently loses the hearing in his right ear. When he finally meets his public defender, he gives irrefutable proof that he could not have been the attacker. The evening of the attack Adam Logan was working as a waiter at a restaurant near his university campus which, as it happens, is located in another state, more than a four-hour drive away. The cops check his alibi and reluctantly admit that he is telling the truth. Charges are dropped and Adam Logan is let out after spending three days in jail. He's left with partial hearing and post-traumatic stress disorder. It puts a big dent in his GPA and ruins his Ivy League graduate school plans.

'So, how did the witness get it so wrong?' Professor West asked the silent rows of students. It was a rhetorical question.

'You know, it was an eye-opener when the attacker was finally caught a month later, during another assault on a victim in the same neighbourhood. The attacker was three inches shorter than Adam Logan. He had blond hair, not dark brown hair. He had a goatee beard, while Adam Logan was clean-shaven. He had half a dozen tattoos. Adam did not have even one. On almost every detail, the victim got it wrong. Yet she was not knowingly making it up.'

Behind him, on the screen, he put up a slide with a photograph of Adam Logan alongside a photograph of the assailant who was ultimately convicted of the crimes. They looked nothing alike.

'The witness identified the attacker as driving a red hatchback. While the attacker's car was red, it was in fact a sedan. Not a hatchback. Why did she get it wrong? Because she herself had once owned a red hatchback and when she saw red cars she was more inclined to perceive them to be hatchbacks.' He put up a slide of the real assailant's vehicle and Adam Logan's hatchback.

'But why of all people did she pick out Adam Logan in the line-up, a man she'd never met in her life? Well, when I looked into this case, I found that Adam Logan resembled the victim's ex-boyfriend; they'd broken up a few months before because he was violent towards her. Adam Logan had the same stocky weightlifter's build as her ex, and similar colouring. Added to that, it turned out the victim hadn't seen the attacker's face properly. The trauma of the assault was so severe that when the police asked her to pick out the suspect, she pointed at Adam Logan, who she associated with violence because he had the same colouring and a vague resemblance to her violent ex-boyfriend.'

He paused to let his words sink in.

'Let's be clear, the witness was not purposely trying to mislead the police. She honestly believed Adam Logan was the man who'd attacked her. She was suffering from trauma and this caused her memory to play tricks on her.

'Do honest witnesses lie?' Professor West asked. 'Witnesses are unreliable for the simple reason that human memory is unreliable.'

He broke off and loudly clapped his hands twice. 'People, a reminder that tomorrow is the deadline for you to email me your interest in attending my summer school class.'

Joe and I stayed in our seats as the students filed out of the lecture hall. When the last stragglers left, I approached Professor West. He was on the podium unplugging his laptop.

'I hope I didn't completely ruin your faith in witness testimony, detective,' he said without looking up.

'Not at all,' I answered. 'We rarely rely just on witnesses these days. We have DNA and other forensics for confirmation.'

'How is your investigation going?' He stopped fiddling with his laptop to look up at me. I saw expectation on his face. Concern.

'It takes time investigating this type of case,' I said. 'Six years is a long time.'

He nodded, almost sympathetically.

'Is there something you need from me today, detective? I'm sure you didn't sit through the class due to an interest in psychology.'

'Actually, the class was fascinating. But you're right. I came to find out if you have Laura's work notes from the period before she disappeared. I understand you were collaborating with her on a research project.'

'I'm surprised you know about it,' he said, without looking at me, as he put his papers in a pile and packed them into his brief-case. 'The study was in the initial phases. We didn't advertise it.'

'May I ask what it was on?' I asked more out of curiosity than anything else.

'Memory, of course,' he said. 'It was my area of interest. Implanting memories, to be specific. We know that people forget things, but can people vividly remember events that didn't happen?'

'Can they?' I asked as I followed him out.

'Unfortunately, when Laura died, I abandoned the research, so I can't answer that question with complete certainty,' he said, turn-ing off the auditorium lights as he spoke. 'What I can tell you is that when you think of memory, think of a Wikipedia page. Memories are constantly shifting, constantly updating and supplanting each other. How we store memories and retrieve them is one of the great mysteries of the human brain.'

He held open the auditorium door to let Joe and me out.

'You're saying that memories can be altered over time?' I asked. 'That they can be manipulated.'

'Memories are more fluid than fixed. That scares people. Because memories are our reality. Our inner truth. Our memories define our identity. But what happens when those memories are false? Yes, detective,' he said. 'In answer to your question, memo-ries can be created just as easily as they can be erased.'

CHAPTER THIRTY-EIGHT

Julie

I lie on my pillow willing myself to open my eyes. No matter how hard I try, I'm unable to comply. Sleep overcomes me like the pull of the tide as I drift into a world of unsettling images; Roxy dead in my arms, blood dripping off the dashboard of a car, trees swaying in a gentle wind at the clearing where Laura's body was buried.

Through a thick cloud of sleep, I register everything around me. And nothing. A telephone rings until its persistent peal is answered. I hear the hum of a whispered conversation on the landing outside our bedroom. I can't make out the words. I'm vaguely aware of the bedroom door opening and a still figure watching me sleep. I struggle to open my eyes. They don't obey.

When I break through waves of sleep to return to the world of the living, I am assaulted by bright rays of sunlight slipping through half-drawn curtains. I hear happy shouts of children riding their bikes on our sloping street as they do most afternoons.

The realisation it is afternoon does what nothing else has done all day: it wakes me up.

'Alice.' I imagine her standing alone outside the school, her eyes filled with tears, as nobody arrives to pick her up. I am filled with panic that she is alone, abandoned at school, even though rationally I know the teachers would have brought her to the office to wait.

I pull my legs out of the bed and stand up slowly to get my balance. While I am looking for clothes to throw on for school pick-up, I hear the slam of a car door in the driveway. Alice's excited voice tells me that she is home. I sink back into bed, relieved.

Alice's chatter drifts into the bedroom moments later. Her soft face presses against me in a deep embrace. She hands me a picture she has drawn at school. It's a picture of a woman in bed; me, judging by the woman's yellow hair. It's the only joyful colour in an otherwise sombre drawing.

'It's to help you get better,' Alice confides.

Matt comes over to the bed and kisses my forehead. His expression is remote. When he realises I'm watching him, it softens into a forced smile.

'You're looking much better today, darling,' he tells me.

'How long have I been like this?' I ask in a husky voice.

'A couple of days,' he says.

I have more questions but I'm afraid of the answers, so I lie in bed silently looking at him. He gently brushes my hair away from my face.

'Come downstairs into the garden, Julie, honey,' he tells me. 'It's a beautiful afternoon. It'll be good for you to get fresh air.'

Matt helps me out of bed and escorts me towards the bathroom. Even though my legs are weak, I put on a brave front and let go of his hand. I hate being helpless.

'I'll shower myself,' I tell him as we reach the bathroom door.

Once I've shut the door and turned on the shower I lower myself onto the marble floor of the cubicle and sit under the stream of water. I am lulled back to sleep by the crackle of spray hitting the tiles.

I jump at a loud knock on the door.

'Julie, are you alright?' It's Matt. He sounds worried.

'Almost done,' I call out, trying to sound in control.

I turn off the water and wrap myself in a towel. Matt has laid out clean clothes for me on the freshly made bed. I dress in jeans and a thigh-length woollen sweater the colour of oatmeal. I tie my hair and apply lip gloss. Matt returns to the bedroom to help me downstairs and into the garden. I curl up on a patio armchair and watch Alice on her swing. The leaves create shadows on her face as she propels herself into the air and then swings back down.

I still remember the day we put up the swing. It was Alice's fourth birthday. Matt straddled the branch like a modern-day Huckleberry Finn to fix the ropes while I stood below instructing him on where to position them. The branch almost buckled under his weight. When he finally came down, I kissed him hard on the lips and told him he'd given me the fright of my life.

Matt's right. It cheers me up to sit in the warmth of the sun, shrouded by the incandescent sky. The ropes groan against the branches as Alice swings backwards and forwards on the white-washed timber seat. She lifts her feet up to propel herself higher into the air. When I feel strong enough, I get up to push her.

'I can do it myself, Mommy.' She admonishes me in that independent tone she's learned from school. I stroll to the back of the garden to check the latch on the rear gate is secure. The forest is exploding with life. Summer is around the corner. I should be pleased the cold spell is over, but it leaves me feeling bewildered.

How did time slip away without me noticing?

'Honey, honey?' It's Matt's voice. I look at him, uncomprehending. His tone is soft and caring. Rather than find that consoling, it confuses me. His solicitousness, his attentiveness, seem out of character after days of coldness. I never know what to expect from him anymore.

'It's my mother's birthday and we're having dinner with her tonight at that new Italian restaurant in town. I'd love for you to join us, but the doctor says you need a few more days of rest at home.'

Matt talks. His lips move. I hear nothing except a loud hum in my ears. When my attention returns back to him, I catch him saying something about bringing back food for me from the restaurant. He asks what I want to order. 'Nothing,' I tell him. 'Nothing.'

And then for no particular reason I burst into tears. He pulls me to him and caresses my hair while whispering in my ear. 'It's not good for Alice to see you like this,' he says.

I stop sobbing. Matt knows that I would do anything for my daughter. She is my life. Without her I am nothing. I walk back to the swing after drying my eyes on my sleeve. Alice looks at me warily.

Later, as Matt and I sit together on the patio, I whisper to him, 'I've been ill. Haven't I?' I want to ask him whether I had a breakdown, like the time I lost the baby, or after Roxy was killed.

'Matt,' I ask again. 'What happened to me?'

'You were found on the road leading to the lake house,' he answers. 'You had an asthma attack. A bad one. You didn't have your asthma spray with you. It seems that when the attack began, you panicked. From what we can figure out, you ran to find someone to help. That only made it worse.'

'Did I call you on the phone? Are you the one who found me?'

'No. Your phone battery was dead. You probably forgot to charge it. A park ranger found you lying on the side of the road.'

As he speaks I have an image of a man with a buzz cut wearing a green ranger's uniform looking down at me. 'Ma'am, ma'am.' His face comes close to me, pinched in concern. My eyes blur until I see nothing.

'The ranger said when he found you your face was drained and your lips were tinged with blue,' Matt says. 'He was there by chance to examine a tree hit by lightning in a storm. It was sheer luck that he was in the vicinity and found you in time.'

As he speaks another memory returns. I am running from the lake house down a tree-lined forest road. My chest burns. I am filled with terror. Something frightened me, but I don't remember what.

'The ranger called an ambulance. When it arrived, the paramedics put you on a nebuliser and oxygen and took you to hospital.'

'Was I in hospital for long?' I have a disjointed recollection of lying on a hospital bed with an oxygen mask over my face while a doctor reassures me. I don't know whether it was from this hospital admission or a previous one.

'You were there for one night. The asthma attack wiped you out,' Matt says. 'And it gave us a terrible fright. The doctor gave you a sedative yesterday and then this morning. That's why you've been sleeping so much.' I have another vague memory of a man with grey hair leaning over me with a syringe.

'I'm sorry about the lake house, Matt,' I say after contemplating what he told me. I don't want him to be mad at me for going there behind his back. 'I was fixing it up so I could bring you and Alice down there in the summer. I was hoping to change your mind about the place.' He walks off without saying a word. I want to tell him that we need a place of our own where we can be together as a family without Laura's memory hovering over us.

Later, I stand by the bedroom windows and watch Matt reversing the car down the driveway as he and Alice drive off to the restaurant to meet Anne. I collapse back into bed.

When I awake, it's dark and the house is ice cold. I have no idea of the time. I stumble downstairs still in my pyjamas to fix myself something to eat. A draught hits me as I enter the dark kitchen. The wind has blown open the French doors in the living area that lead onto the patio. Matt must have forgotten to lock them properly. I step onto the porch to grab the door handle. Alice's swing whines as the ropes chafe against the tree branches in the wind.

'You're not safe, Julie.' That voice calls out to me again as I bolt the door shut and close the drapes. I feel dread in the pit of my stomach. Something happened at the lake house right before I had the asthma attack. Something that frightened me. I don't know what.

I walk on the cold kitchen floor in my bare feet. A creak from upstairs sends an electric current of fear through my body. I stop. Another creak makes my throat tighten. I swallow hard. Someone is with me in the house. Lights flicker in the hall even though I'm sure that I didn't leave any turned on.

I slide my hand along the kitchen counter until I reach the knife block. I silently remove a butcher's knife. A floorboard creaks loudly. It's getting closer. My heart beats wildly. I do the only thing that I can do; still gripping the knife with both hands, I open the pantry door with my elbow and hide inside.

Light flickers under the pantry door. The creaks are coming closer. I hold my breath and stand completely still. Ice-cold fear courses through my veins as I wait for the intruder to find me.

All my senses are focused on what's happening on the other side of the cupboard door. Minutes pass. I hear nothing except my heartbeat. Finally, I muster whatever courage I have left. I leave the pantry with my knife held out and burst into the kitchen. The room is dark and empty.

It feels as if someone is toying with me. Pulling me apart piece by piece.

'You're not safe, Julie,' I tell myself, repeating the warning over and over again as I walk back upstairs holding the knife in front of me. I feel so vulnerable in this house of Laura's, alone most nights with nothing to protect me except a half-blunt kitchen knife. The knife is just for show. My reflexes are dulled by medication. If I truly want to protect myself then I need a gun.

CHAPTER THIRTY-NINE

Mel

Will and I worked out the play in advance. Will would take the lead in the interview, I would hang back. We wanted to keep Matthew West off balance when we hit him with what we had. Matthew West had not yet met Will. My partner was an unknown quantity. We'd use that to our advantage.

West arrived at the police station just before 5 p.m. You could tell he was annoyed. His jaw was tight and he was impatient. We kept him on ice in the downstairs lobby just to get his juices flowing. When he was finally shown upstairs he was antsy as hell.

We'd set it up so that Will was alone in the interview room when West was escorted inside. He'd be expecting to see me. He'd get Will instead.

'That would be enough to throw anyone off balance!' joked Will when we'd planned our strategy over a late morning coffee.

The meeting room looked different from the last time West came in, when it had been bright and sunny with the shades all lifted up. This time it was dark and stuffy. The blinds were down and we'd rearranged the table and chairs so that West sat with his back to the window. We'd turned up the thermostat so the room was a couple of degrees hotter than usual. There was no pitcher of water.

'What was so important that I had to drop everything to come in?' West was asking Will as I arrived in the room. I was carrying a large file that I passed to my partner. That was in the script too. We wanted him to think that Will was in charge of the case and that I, the detective he knew and trusted, had been demoted in the investigation. I gave Matthew West an encouraging smile as I took my seat at the table alongside Will.

'I had to cancel meetings to come here,' West complained, looking to me for support. 'And then I'm kept waiting for almost half an hour.' I looked suitably sympathetic and not a little embarrassed by my partner's lack of tact.

'I'm real sorry, Professor West, to have messed up your afternoon by asking you to assist our investigation into your wife's murder.' Will made no effort to disguise the sarcasm in his voice. Will was unshaven, still tanned from his vacation. He had an arrogant smirk on his face. He spoke slowly with a mocking drawl that obviously grated on West. That, of course, was Will's intention.

'Professor West,' I interjected, feigning discomfort with Will's lack of manners. 'I'm sorry for the inconvenience. It's just that Detective Peters has returned from vacation. When he reviewed the file, he raised a few questions that I didn't cover when we last met. Also, we've since obtained information that we'd like to review with you.'

'We have here,' said Will, picking up the remote control to turn on the television, 'footage of the conference you attended on the weekend your wife disappeared.' I watched Matthew West's face closely as Will told him about the video. If Matthew West was in any way concerned we had video footage that might put his alibi at risk, he gave no indication.

Will played the first thirty seconds of Professor West's speech at the conference on normal speed. He then fast-forwarded the video, slowing it again at the point where Matthew West finished his speech to resounding applause.

'After the speech, you went to your table and listened to the next speaker,' Will said, fast-forwarding again with the remote. 'But here,' he paused the video, 'after forty-three minutes, you left the room.' He played the video in slow motion. It showed Matthew West getting up from his table and walking out of the conference hall.

'So?' said Matthew West. 'I probably went to the men's room. I've already told Detective Carter that I can't account for every minute of those two days in Charlotte, but I was at the conference all weekend. That I know.'

'That's what he told me,' I said to Will, with a fake note of frustration in my voice that suggested he was wasting everyone's time.

'The trouble is,' Will said, 'I've gone over the tapes. We don't see you again at the conference that afternoon. Yes, there were a couple of people who said at the time that they'd seen you at the conference centre later in the day. When the original investigators asked them to give a time estimate, suddenly they weren't so sure.

'You are listed as having attended the dinner that evening, which began at 7 p.m., and indeed you appear in a group photograph taken at the restaurant. We've been advised the photo is usually taken at the end of the evening. So you might have arrived as late as 9.30 p.m and skipped the dinner itself.'

'What's your point?' West interrupted.

'My point is,' said Will, 'there's at least six hours during which your whereabouts are unaccounted for. That gives you enough time to drive home, kill your wife, bury her body, and get back to Charlotte in time for the group photograph after dinner. What we have here, Professor West, is a hole in your alibi.'

'That's ridiculous,' said Matt, getting to his feet. 'I did not kill Laura. I loved her. I did not leave Charlotte that weekend, not until the conference ended at lunchtime on the Sunday.'

'Well then,' said Will. 'We will need you to tell us in detail, and provide corroboration, as to your exact whereabouts on the Saturday afternoon that your wife disappeared.'

Matthew West walked over to the window and pulled a cord to open a blind. He stood silently for a moment, watching the snarl of afternoon traffic in the street below.

'You have to promise me to keep this between us,' he said, turning around abruptly, with his hands in the pockets of his pants.

'We can't make promises,' I said. 'But you have my word that we'll do what we can to maintain confidentiality.' I gave Will a look that said he should step back. It was my turn now.

'I'm not proud of it,' said West, rubbing the salt-and-pepper stubble on his jaw. 'On the weekend that my wife disappeared, I was with another woman back at my hotel room in Charlotte.'

'What time were you with her?' I asked. I was pleased he'd finally confirmed my suspicions.

'She was with me most of Saturday afternoon and in the early evening. I left her at the hotel when I went to the dinner at that French restaurant. We met back at my hotel room at around 10 p.m. And then she and I were together until Sunday morning.'

'So you were having an affair that weekend,' I said. 'And you lied to us to cover it up?'

'Yes,' he responded. He had the decency to look ashamed. 'I've always felt guilty that at the time Laura was murdered, I was with someone else. But equally, I felt obligated to protect the privacy of the other woman.' He looked straight at me. 'That's why I didn't go into detail about my whereabouts that day.'

'We'll need her name.' I pushed over a notepad. 'We're going to have to contact the woman in question to verify your alibi.'

'Her name is Chelsea Marshal,' he said. He wrote down a phone number. 'She's married. To a colleague. For her sake and her husband's sake, I'd appreciate it if you could be discreet.'

'And for your sake,' added Will. West flinched. Will's barb had hit its mark.

A few minutes later, I showed him out. I was conciliatory as I walked him to the elevator. I promised to be discreet when we spoke with Chelsea. At the end of the day, we all wanted the same thing, I told him. We wanted to find Laura's killer.

When I returned to my desk downstairs in the squad room, Will was viewing the video of Matthew West's conference speech again. Will leaned forward in his seat as if he was watching a championship football game.

'Have you watched the whole thing?' he asked.

'Bits of it,' I said. It was dense, mostly technical psychology material, aimed at experts in the field. I'd watched the footage mostly on fast forward. 'Why this sudden interest in psychology, Will?'

'Look at this,' Will said. He spooled through the video and then paused it on a shot of Matthew West on the podium. Behind him was a large screen with slides from his presentation.

'Look at the photograph in the slide behind him on the screen.' Will pointed at a photo of several people in a laboratory.

'This guy here,' he said, touching the face of a young man in the far left of the photograph. 'Do you recognise him?'

I shrugged. Will created a split screen and added another photograph; an old photograph from a driver's licence.

'It's the same guy,' he said. 'Now tell me you if you recognise him.'

'The face is vaguely familiar but I can't think of who it is.'

'That's because it's out of context,' Will said. 'That guy in the photo is Alexander Henderson. When he was young. Before he lost his good looks to drugs.'

'Are you saying this guy in Matthew West's presentation slide is the driver killed in the car accident down at Kellers Way, less than a mile from where we found Laura West's body?'

'That's exactly what I'm saying,' he answered. 'Looks like Alexander Henderson participated in Matthew West's psychology study. And then, six or so years later, he dies in a single-car accident after overdosing on some weird psychedelic drug, on the same stretch of road where West's wife was buried.'

'Jeez,' I said. 'The problem with living in a small town is half the time you don't know if it's coincidence or a smoking gun.'

CHAPTER FORTY

Julie

The hardest part of buying a gun is deciding which one to buy. I spend the morning in a gun shop, weighing deadly cold steel in my hand. The grip is rough in my palm and the stench of gun oil is intoxicating. It makes me feel in control instead of afraid of my own shadow, as I was last night, terrified to be alone in my own house.

I never thought I'd say this but it's exhilarating to squeeze the trigger of a gun, even if it isn't loaded and the barrel is pointed at a faded shop carpet. It makes me feel secure for the first time in a long time, after weeks of feeling helpless and afraid of things that I can't even describe. 'You're not safe, Julie.' The words ring in my head all the time.

It's not just fear that grips me. I've lost control over my marriage. I am sharing my husband with another woman. A woman as young and beautiful as I had been when I caught his eye. A woman who is accomplished and intelligent. And most importantly, a woman who surely, even just at a subliminal level, reminds him of Laura.

I concede that Matt has not been faithful to me, but there has always been a thread of decency running through him that reassured me he would never leave. Just as he would never have left Laura for me. Not if she'd survived.

This time it's different. Young women today don't know their place. Emily is greedy. She won't be content to share. She wants all of him.

'That piece is too heavy on your wrist.' The salesman's voice breaks through my thoughts as I hold the gun in my hand.

He opens a glass cabinet with a key and removes another gun. This one is slimmer, smaller. 'It feels too flimsy,' I tell him, and hand it back.

'Try this one,' says the salesman, handing over a third gun. 'Feel the weight on your wrist.'

He's a big-bellied man in his fifties with a thick moustache and a T-shirt that says 'Free People Bear Arms'.

He uses words that I've never heard outside of movies and TV shows. He calls the guns 'pieces'. He talks about 'clips' and 'compacts' and 'sub-compacts'. For a crazy moment, I think he's talking about ladies' accessories.

He shows me mainly small guns designed to fit in purses. Guns that aren't a dead weight on the wrist. My wrists, he says, are narrow. I need a piece with low recoil. He tells me that for a hundred dollars they'll let me test out some guns and show me the basics of how to shoot.

I hand over the cash and he calls an instructor to take me to the firing range out back. The instructor swaggers into the store with a bulldog expression on his bearded face. His tarnished dog tags rattle around his neck as he escorts me to the range.

'Firearms are like shoes,' he tells me when we're in a shooting booth facing a target. My selection of handguns is set out in a neat row. 'The only way to know which one fits is by trying them on for size.'

He shows me how to grip the weapon with two hands and how to position my feet. 'You need to use your whole arm to act as a shock absorber,' he explains. He pulls down my earmuffs and I fire my first round. The recoil is so unexpected that it unbalances me. The instructor puts out a hand to hold me steady. I fire five more rounds into a paper target down range. When I'm done, the instructor reels the target towards us via a pulley system, to examine the bullet holes.

The first gun makes me shoot too far to the left. He suggests another gun that he thinks will fix that tendency. Eventually, eight pieces of target paper later, I have a shortlist of two guns.

'I'll take the Glock 42,' I tell the salesman back in the store ten minutes later. 'How much is it?'

'It's $640, including taxes. I assume you have your permit?'

'I'm working on it,' I tell him.

'Afraid I can't sell it to you without the permit. How about I put it aside? All you need to do is head over to the sheriff's office and buy a permit. It costs $5. You'll have to wait a few minutes while he runs a check to make sure there are no exclusions against your name.'

'Exclusions?' I ask.

'You know, a criminal record.'

'Oh, well, that should be fine then,' I say. 'I'll be back shortly to collect it. Could you put aside a box of ammunition too?'

An hour later, I'm back with my gun permit and filling out the paperwork for my new Glock. I pay in cash. Clean bills with a snap to them. Straight from the bank.

I put the gun in the inside pocket of my purse with a box of ammunition alongside it. It's not loaded. The safety is on, just like I was taught.

It's strange, because I'd never thought of myself as the type to carry a gun. But I'm scared. More scared than I've ever been in my life.

I pretended to be asleep when Matt came home from the restaurant last night after celebrating his mother's birthday. It got me out of taking my meds. My mind was clear when I woke this morning. I remembered the asthma attack at the lake house. The events of that morning came back to me with startling clarity. I swam laps alongside the jetty. The water was crisp. Refreshing. After a while, I dragged myself onto the jetty and lay on the beams warmed by the sun.

A loose nail in a beam scratched me. It drew blood that ran down my leg in a single trickle of red. I went into the boathouse to get a hammer to knock the nail back into the timber. I opened a rusted paint tin on the shelf, thinking it might store tools. Inside was a notebook with Laura's name written faintly on the inside fold.

The notebook pages were stiff and yellowed, and stuck together. The ink had run from water damage, badly enough that it was impossible to read most of the writing. A few lines were vaguely legible. One of them, written in a hasty scrawl, said, 'I think my husband's lover is trying to kill me.'

From the gun shop I drive straight to Alice's school. I wait on the front lawn with the other mothers until the school bell rings and the kids come running out of the front entrance. My handbag is heavier than usual from the gun. I slip my hand inside to feel its weight.

When we get home, Alice and I go into the garden to water the strawberry shrubs she planted with Matt a few weeks ago. There are no signs of strawberries but she checks on them every day, just in case a berry grew while she was at school.

I'm baking banana muffins for her school lunch tomorrow when the doorbell rings. Through the intercom monitor, I see the detective's familiar face. What does she want now? Doesn't she know she throws our lives into disarray each time she stops by?

I press the button to open the gate and wait by the front door, holding it half open.

'I'm afraid my husband's not home yet,' I tell her. It's just past three. Surely she realises that he works.

'Actually, I wanted to speak with you, Mrs West.'

'Come in,' I say wearily. 'Can I offer you a cup of coffee, detective?' I ask as I return to my baking ingredients set out on the kitchen counter.

'No, thank you,' she says. 'I have to get going in a moment.'

She spreads photos on the counter as if she is dealing cards. They're mostly of me riding horses, or training kids at the ranch. My face is rounder, less angular than it is today. My hair is light brown with blond streaks. It feels as if I am looking at someone else's life unfolding in these faded photographs. I pick up a couple of photos to look at them more clearly. I was happy in those days. I can see it quite clearly on my face.

'That's me,' I tell her. 'Why are you showing these to me?'

'I thought it might jog your memory about the period you taught Laura horseback riding,' she says.

'It doesn't,' I respond curtly. 'I taught many students. Usually children, and occasionally adults trying to overcome phobias.' I crack eggs one at a time into the mixing bowl while she watches.

'Laura West was taking lessons to overcome a fear of horses,' the detective says quietly. 'But you already knew that, didn't you?'

I'm not listening. I'm back in the paddock with Laura, holding her trembling hand as she sits on the horse. I am telling her to calm down, to take a deep breath. I'm telling her that horses know when a rider is nervous. I tickle the horse's face to distract it while Laura pulls herself together. Gradually, the colour returns to her face and the look of terror fades.

I hold the mixing bowl to my chest and beat the mixture with a wooden spoon extra fast until my arm aches and I have to stop.

'How did you meet your husband?' The sudden change of topic surprises me.

'Are you asking out of politeness, to make small talk? Or because of your investigation?' I try to keep my tone light. I want to tell her that maybe she should focus on finding Laura's killer instead of dissecting my marriage. I'm smart enough to hold my tongue.

'A bit of both,' she says lightly, like she's a close friend. She sits on a counter stool and waits for me to talk.

'After Laura died,' I say, 'Matt needed someone to take care of the baby. Alice was less than a year old at the time. I applied and got the job. After a few months, well, we fell in love.'

'How did you find out about the job?'

'I was studying at college, the community college in town. If I remember correctly the career centre on campus contacted me because I'd been looking for child care work.'

'That was the first time you met him?' she asks.

'No,' I say after a pause. 'He taught seminars at my college, but we didn't have any direct contact until he hired me to work as his babysitter.'

'That's strange,' she says, her eyes fixed on my face. 'Because I've spent most of the morning talking to people from your college days. A couple of them told me there was a rumour going around at the time that you and Matthew West were sleeping together months before Laura West died.'

'Well, that's rubbish.' I'm relieved I don't have to meet her eyes as I pour the mixture into the muffin tins. 'I don't know why people make up stories like that.'

'You're a lot younger than him, aren't you?' she asks.

'You make it sound like he's a geriatric,' I respond without looking up.

'It's a big age gap.'

'Matt is twelve years older than me. It's not like he's a sugar daddy or anything.' There's a bitchy note in my voice. I can see that she's noticed it. She misses nothing. She observes my hands as I pour the muffin mixture into each compartment in the tray. It takes everything I have to keep them steady.

'Matt's a good husband,' I say with a smile that I hope doesn't look strained.

'Laura's disappearance must have been hard on him,' she says, again in that conversational tone. I am not your friend, lady, I want to tell her. I bite my tongue.

'To this day, he is devastated,' I say instead. I speak with the utmost honesty.

'He described Laura to me as his soul mate,' the detective tells me. 'It's not easy losing a soul mate.' Her eyes bore into my face to record the slightest reaction to her intrusive question.

I turn pale at her words. My hand trembles and I spill muffin batter on the side of the tray. She's hit me where it hurts most.

'He's a handsome man, your husband. Charismatic. Loads of sex appeal.'

'Yes,' I say helplessly.

'I sat in on his lecture this morning. His female students

practically threw themselves at him afterwards. Does that bother you?'

'I honestly don't give it a second thought.' My indifference rings false even to my own ears.

'Of course you don't,' the detective says. She watches me until I can't hold her gaze any longer. I bend down to slide the muffin pans into the oven.

CHAPTER FORTY-ONE

Mel

I called Helen Williams just before bedtime, asking her to come in for questioning the next day. The call was deliberately timed. I wanted her memories of Laura to rise to the surface as she tossed and turned in bed all night, thinking about our upcoming meeting. I wanted her subconscious to do the work for me, to sift through old memories so she'd be ripe for the picking by the time she came into my interview room.

The next morning Helen arrived five minutes early, wearing fresh lipstick and a wave of heavy perfume that did nothing to mask her trepidation. The moment she walked into the interview room, I knew I'd pressed her buttons just right. She struck me as very different from the rather plain, introverted woman I'd spoken with at her office.

'Thanks for coming in. This shouldn't take too long.'

She swallowed hard from nervousness and nodded slightly.

'I understand that, contrary to what you told me before, you actually helped out on the study that Laura and Matthew West collaborated on?' My tone was icy. 'Ms Williams, homicide detectives don't take kindly to witnesses who lie to us. It wastes our time, and quite frankly raises suspicions about the person doing the lying.'

She looked at her hands like a rebuked schoolgirl. And then, as if remembering she'd come to cooperate, she sat forward in her seat. 'I didn't think it was important. It was a minor study that didn't go past the first phase. Laura wanted her involvement kept confidential and I was trying to respect her wishes.'

'Laura is dead,' I said. 'I don't care what she wanted kept confidential, I need to know everything there is to know about her work and her private life as part of my investigation. Do you understand?'

She nodded.

'Is it true Laura wanted to kick you out of her department shortly before she died?' I asked the question as an aside but I was very interested in her reaction. She looked like she'd just been slapped.

'We'd had an argument,' she said in a nervous voice.

'About what?'

'It's not a subject I feel comfortable discussing.'

'We've gone over this already. I need to know everything.'

She sighed and began speaking so fast it was hard to keep up with her. 'Laura was convinced that I was having an affair with her husband. She said she couldn't have someone working for her who she didn't trust. I told Laura that nothing had happened between us but she wouldn't listen.'

'It turned out to be good for your career when Laura died, didn't it?' I asked, taking the conversation on an abrupt tangent. 'You're now an adjunct professor, heading for tenure from what I hear.'

'I've never thought about it in those terms,' she said stiffly.

'What was Laura and Matthew's study on?' I changed the subject again.

'Their study was on memory.'

I sat forward in my chair. This was going to be like pulling teeth.

'Can you tell me specifically what aspect of memory they were studying?'

'Memory implantation,' she said. 'Whether memories can be planted and then processed by the brain as if they really happened.'

'You're talking about feeding people false memories and making them believe they're real?'

'Yes, that's more or less correct.'

'That sounds like the scary end of psychology,' I remarked.

'It might seem frightening,' she agreed. 'But it has positive applications. If we can plant new memories then we can help people who have suffered from trauma. Soldiers returning from war with post-traumatic stress disorder could be given replacement memories to forget a traumatic incident in the battlefield. By the same token, as you've pointed out, this field is filled with ethical dilemmas.'

'Such as?'

'For example, to do this particular study we had to create false traumatic memories,' she says. 'But that would be unethical because a trauma, even a false trauma, can be harmful. And it's unethical to do anything harmful to research subjects.'

'So how did you get around that problem?'

'Well, our two lead researchers volunteered to have false memories implanted.'

'You mean Matthew and Laura West?'

'Yes,' said Helen, playing nervously with a gold bangle on her wrist. 'Nothing major. The memory Matthew had planted in his mind was of almost drowning as a boy.'

'And Laura?' I asked. She didn't respond. 'What about Laura?' I repeated. 'What was her fear?'

'Equinophobia,' Helen answered eventually. 'A fear of horses. Her implanted memory was that she'd almost been killed in a horseback riding accident when she was a child. It made her terrified of horses.'

'Did she try to overcome her phobia?' I asked. 'By getting riding lessons?'

'I don't know,' she said. 'Laura dropped out of the study. It was very problematic. The study, I mean.'

'In what way?'

'It wasn't possible to do a study that tested the boundaries of memory without implanting highly traumatic memories and, as I said, we weren't ethically able to do that. But by using the researchers as subjects instead, we were injecting bias into the study. No peer-reviewed journal would publish an article with such a flawed methodology. In the end Professor West, Matthew, took the study to a local college and focused on less controversial elements of the same general principle.'

'Such as what?'

'Implanting insignificant memories in subjects.'

'What would be considered an insignificant memory?' I asked.

'Bad memories around food or drink. Getting a subject to believe that when he was a boy he came out in hives after eating raspberry jam. That sort of thing.'

'And what were the results of that study?'

'I don't know exactly,' she said. 'I wasn't involved. But I gathered they had some good data. A person who believed he'd once gotten food poisoning from eating a hard-boiled egg suddenly stopped eating eggs. That sort of thing. The trouble was it couldn't be properly quantified. The sample was too small. And in the end . . .' Her voice trailed off.

'In the end?' I prompted.

'Well, Laura died and Matthew lost interest in the study. From what I heard, he didn't apply for the funding to be renewed. Eventually, he shut it down.'

'Do you know where I might find the documentation from the study? Initial results, a list of subjects?'

She picked up her glass of water and drank it until it was empty. I could see her mind ticking as she thought through her possible answers.

'I don't know what happened to those documents,' she said finally. 'I tried to access them a couple of years ago as a reference point for my own research, but they weren't in the system at either university.'

'The documents disappeared?' I asked. 'Just like that?'

'It believe they did.'

'Is that usual?'

She said nothing. I saw her swallow again. 'It's not usual,' she finally ventured.

'I understand that Professor West's new research interest is unconnected to memory?'

'Yes,' she said. 'He has recently produced important work in the area of impulse control. He's making a name for himself in that field.'

I knew there was more to it than she was letting on. 'But?' I said. 'I can tell there's a "but" somewhere.'

'No,' she said, still unable to meet my eyes. 'There's no but. Impulse control was Laura's area of interest and it's good that someone is continuing her work.'

'Did he plagiarise Laura's research?' I asked.

'I wouldn't go that far,' she said. 'Laura did extensive preparatory work in this area. His work wouldn't exist without Laura's contribution.'

I thanked Helen for her time and showed her out. Picking up the work where his wife left off was hardly a crime. But could it be a motive for murder? Even that seemed far-fetched for a couple almost universally described as deeply in love, even if he couldn't keep his pants zipped up.

Helen Williams, on the other hand, had at least two reasons to want Laura West dead. She'd clearly had a crush on Matthew West, if not a full-blown affair. If that wasn't enough, Laura was trying to get her fired. I could tell Helen still had a soft spot for Matthew West from the way she said his name and the way she refused to say anything negative about him, even though she clearly had reservations about his research.

When the interview was over, I ran a check on the charitable foundation that Matthew West set up in Laura West's memory. Helen Williams had received several generous grants from it over the years. I mulled the implications of her conflicts of interest as I headed out to meet Will for an early lunch.

'Hey Will,' I said, joining him in a red vinyl window booth at a diner two blocks from our office. 'Did Matthew West's alibi check out?'

'It sure did,' he said, biting into a BLT and speaking with his mouth half full. 'Matthew West has very good taste in women. Chelsea Marshal was a stunner. The wife of his best friend, by the way.'

'So she confirms she was with him over the weekend when Laura West was murdered?'

'All afternoon and all night,' he said after swallowing his food. 'She said her husband was abroad at a different conference, in Shanghai. And she spent most of the weekend with Matthew West in Charlotte. She joined him at his hotel after lunch on the Saturday and stayed until breakfast on Sunday. They spent the whole time in

bed except on the Saturday evening when he went to the gala dinner for a couple of hours. Then they resumed their dirty weekend.'

'So,' I said after processing the implications of that information. 'Sounds like Matthew West is a first-class wife cheater, but his
sexual indiscretion probably rules him out as a murder suspect for
the simple reason that it gives him a solid alibi. What else do you
have?'

'Something very interesting,' he said as the waiter brought my
chicken caesar sandwich.

'How interesting?'

'I was working on the Henderson case this morning,' he said.
'I went to his old college to access his student records. Turns out he
paid his way through school by working at a campus burger joint.
So I went over there as well, and you won't believe what I found in
his employee records.'

'What?'

'His ex-girlfriend was none other than Matthew West's second
wife. Julie West.'

'Damn, Will.' I thumped the table. 'You know how I hate
coincidences.'

CHAPTER FORTY-TWO

Julie

I've made a decision. I'm not going to allow Emily to destroy my life. It's because of Emily that my marriage hangs by a thread. It's because of Emily that I may lose Alice. It's because of Emily that everything I have built is teetering on the edge of oblivion.

Now comes the hard part: figuring out how to get her out of our lives. A guilt trip might work. I could tell her what a divorce would do to Alice. I could convince her to back off for the good of the child. Except that might not mean much to Emily. She doesn't strike me as the type to lie awake at night racked by guilt for destroying a family.

Emily looks particularly pleased with herself this morning, nonchalantly swinging her leather satchel as she walks to her lunchtime yoga class. I follow her wearing my university gear, a baseball cap and glasses. She doesn't notice me. I'm wallpaper. I put my hand inside my heavy purse and run my palm over the cold metal barrel of my pistol. Its weight is reassuring, especially when I see the secret smile on that bitch's face. She's thinking about her morning rendezvous with my husband.

Matt left home early, long before I woke up. He makes no effort to cover up his transgressions. He doesn't care what I think anymore, so why should I? Why should I be the one to show an ounce of common decency when nobody else does?

Emily's yoga class goes for fifty minutes. I watch through the window of the yoga studio door until the students move into their first pose. Then I head to the locker room down the corridor. I unlock Emily's locker using the combination code that I wrote in a notebook when I first started my surveillance.

I take out her purse from the metal shelf and remove the key to her apartment. I would have preferred the easier option of using the key she'd given Matt, but I couldn't find it when I snuck into the garage and searched his car again. I don't know where he hides it now.

Copying a key is simple if you plan properly. I found out how to do it from a YouTube video by a smart-ass kid who never quite explains what he does with the keys he copies.

I take Emily's key ring to a shower stall. There I loop a thread through the hole in the top of the key and shove it deep into a block of softened paraffin wax that I bought at an art supply store. I leave the key in there for five minutes to set and then put the paraffin block in a freezer pack that I've brought with me.

It takes forty minutes until it is cold enough for me to remove the key without damaging the indentations in the wax. With just minutes until Emily is due back in the locker room, I snip off the thread, wipe the key clean and put the keyring back in Emily's locker. I walk right past her in the corridor as she comes out of her yoga class.

Step two is even easier. Back at home, I shove epoxy putty into the cavity in the paraffin block created by the key. When it's set,

I break the paraffin block by hitting it with a brick on my patio floor. It cracks to reveal a key made from putty with all the ridges perfectly replicated. A shady locksmith across town uses that to cut me a real key in two minutes flat. It costs me ten bucks and it's worth every cent.

The next morning, Matt leaves early again for yet another morning rendezvous at Emily's house. I hear his car backing out of the driveway not long after dawn. I drift off once he's gone. My sleep is filled with images of the two of them writhing together in her bed. When my alarm goes off, I wake Alice.

After I drop off Alice at school, I head to the university and wait until Emily enters the auditorium for her first lecture of the day. Then I quickly double back to her apartment, which I know is empty because Matt is the one teaching her morning class. I slide my key into her apartment lock and pray under my breath that it works. It opens with a click.

The blinds are half drawn. The apartment is tidy and feminine, just as I'd imagined it. Though there are no photographs of ballet dancers on the wall. The place is filled with Emily's distinctive floral scent that I know so well because Matt brings it home every night.

On the counter are two coffee cups, still warm to the touch when I press the back of my hand against them. Two cereal bowls are in the sink. The bed is not properly made. Not a surprise. Matt always leaves it to me to make the bed. The sheets are rumpled. The quilt is half on, half off the bed. One of the pillows has fallen to the floor. I pick it up with hands clad in disposable gloves. I put the pillows on the mattress, one next to the other. I smooth down the bottom sheet before throwing on the quilt so that it's all nice and neat.

I check the cupboard under the bathroom sink and find a toiletry bag inside. It's black. Masculine. Inside is a toothbrush, male shaver, and the same shaving lotion brand that Matt uses.

In the kitchen pantry is a jar of Matt's favourite coffee and the cereal brand he eats for breakfast. It's as if Matt has another home. Another wife. All that's left is for her to move into our house and for him to kick me out. Alice is still so young, she'd eventually adapt to another mother. With time, she'd forget about me.

I open the drawer of the table in the entrance hall. There is a pile of greeting cards tied together with an elastic band. They're for Emily's birthday in November. Almost five months ago. One of them is unsigned. It's written in black ink, in the distinctive jagged handwriting that Matt uses. Their affair has been going on for months.

Matt has been away a few times at conferences. He doesn't take me along. I've asked often enough. I thought myself enlightened, letting him go on a golfing weekend with the boys to Florida back in February. Now, I question every excuse he has ever given me. Every place he has gone overnight without me. He has been lying to me for months. I've been gullible, and stupid, and incredibly naive.

No, Emily. It stops here. It stops now.

In the kitchen, I take a glass tumbler out of the cupboard and fill it up with water from the faucet. When I'm done drinking, I smash the glass in the sink. I put the broken pieces in a plastic bag, which I tie up and store in my purse to throw out later. I collect the tiny slivers of glass lying in the sink and carry them in the palm of my hand to the bedroom, where I pull off the quilt and scatter the shards on Emily's mattress. Instead of rose petals, the two of them will get what they deserve. I neatly arrange the quilt on top.

On a corner table next to her dresser is a framed photograph
of Emily with her arms around her parents at the Washington
Monument. They obviously love their daughter very much. I almost
feel bad for them.

CHAPTER FORTY-THREE

Mel

The fingerprint report was in a large brown envelope waiting on my desk when I returned to the office. The lab had expedited the job for me.

Julie West's fingerprints were all over the photographs that she'd looked at when I stopped by her house. I'd bagged the photos in the car after the meeting and taken them straight to the lab. It was sheer good luck that she'd handled the photos so thoroughly. I could hardly let good forensic material go to waste. If truth be told, I was hoping she'd get her fingerprints all over those pictures, which is why I'd gone to see her.

Julie was a person of interest because of the rumours I'd heard from her old college classmates that she'd had an affair with Matthew West while he was still married to Laura. She was also one of the last people to see Laura West alive, at the horse ranch. That was motive and opportunity right there.

There was a nervousness about her, a palpable anxiety that she tried to hide during our meetings. I never trust people who can't look me in the eye. Whenever I talked to her, Julie West looked everywhere but at me.

I took the fingerprint report from the envelope and opened it with a certain amount of expectation, the same feeling I have when putting a piece of a jigsaw puzzle in a gap to see if it fits.

'She's clean,' I said to Will after I'd digested the information in the report. 'Julie West is absolutely clean. A model citizen.'

'Yeah, those are the ones I worry about the most,' he said absently. 'Hey, do you want to come with me to the lab? Dennis wants to go over the forensics for the Henderson case.'

'Might as well,' I said. 'After that I have to head over to my kids' school. I promised to help out at Joe and Sammy's baseball club barbecue tonight.'

Dennis was waiting for us by the garage of the forensics building, at the back of the lot. He was chewing gum rapidly.

'Nicotine,' he said in answer as we approached. 'I'm trying to quit again. Better to chew it than smoke it. Right?'

Dennis opened the garage door with a remote control to reveal the damaged silver car I'd last seen weeks before, crushed against a tree at Kellers Way. I got the impression that Dennis knew something we didn't and he was enjoying this moment of superiority.

Under the fluorescent light inside the garage, patches of dry blood were clearly visible on the car upholstery. There were hard crusts of congealed blood on the steering wheel and blood splatter on the driver's window, where Alexander Henderson's head was resting awkwardly when his body was found.

'Let me take you through what happened,' said Dennis. 'The driver hit his head against the side window on impact.' Dennis used a laser pointer to indicate the first point of impact against the side window.

'His head ricocheted and then hit the steering wheel, which is why we have plenty of blood on the window and the steering wheel panel. Here. And here.' Dennis pointed the laser at the locations of blood splatter in the car.

'The blood over there was probably from his nose. The autopsy showed his nasal septum was crushed. We also have blood on the head rest and the seat, possibly from the arm wound after he was cut by a broken whiskey bottle that was loose in the car.' He pointed the laser at dark patches on the fabric of the seat.

'Presumably that's all standard in a car accident of this type?' I asked.

'It is.' Dennis nodded in agreement.

'So why are we here?' asked Will.

'What isn't standard is that we found blood drips here.' Dennis pointed with his gloved finger to the edge of the front passenger seat. 'It means the driver wasn't killed on impact. It suggests Henderson leaned over. Maybe he tried to get out of the car on the passenger side. But he was too injured to climb out, so he fell back into the driver's seat, where he died.' He paused to allow us to take it all in. I still didn't get why this was putting a glint of excitement into Dennis's grey eyes.

'Within the congealed blood over here,' he continued, again pointing to the drops of blood on the front passenger seat, 'we found a partial fingerprint.'

'Which means it was applied after the accident?' I said.

'That's right,' responded Dennis. He pointed to the door. 'We also found a partial bloodied print on the front passenger door handle. It too would have been applied after the accident. Neither print belongs to the driver. Both prints were on top of the bloody surface. That means someone was in the car with the driver after the accident.'

'Are you aware that a cyclist found the body first?' I said. 'I took his statement at the scene. If memory serves, the cyclist said he opened the car door and leaned across the front passenger seat. That might explain the prints you found.'

'I saw that in the report,' said Dennis. 'I asked the cyclist to come in yesterday to run his prints against those from the scene. I can tell you with complete certainty that these partial bloody fingerprints were not from the cyclist.'

'Maybe they were from the cops, the first responders?' Will squatted down so he could get a good look at the location of the prints in the car. They were marked with fluorescent stickers.

'We've ruled out everyone who attended the scene,' said Dennis. 'This morning there were no matching prints on the database. By lunch, the system found a match. So we don't need to guess. I can tell you for sure who was in that car after the accident.'

'Who?' Will and I both asked in unison.

'This is the strange part,' Dennis said. 'The prints belong to Julie West.'

'As in, Matthew West's wife? I brought in her prints last night for analysis.'

'Yup, and good thing you did. The system flagged that Julie West's prints were a match to the bloody prints here in Alexander Henderson's car. We have two partials with about ninety per cent certainty that they are Julie West's. As the prints were formed into Henderson's blood, the logical conclusion is that Julie West was here in the car with him *after* the accident.'

'Do we have other forensics that put her in the car?' asked Will.

'No,' said Dennis. 'There are no hairs, or blood, other than the victim's own. No other prints.'

'What about traces of the drug? What's it called?'

'Scopolamine,' said Dennis. 'We checked all over the car. There are no traces in the car. Mike took another look at Henderson's body and found a fresh needle mark. Henderson was apparently a recovered drug addict. The needle marks on his body were old. All except one. Mike believes the scopolamine was administered by needle.'

'Did you find a syringe in the car?'

'No,' said Dennis. 'We found joints in the car. There were faint traces of cocaine and other drugs in the carpets, heroin included, probably from his past use. But no scopolamine and nothing that he might have used to administer it.'

'Do you think that Julie West injected him with scopolamine after the accident to make sure he died?'

'I suspect the accident was caused because the drug was already in his system,' he said, carefully. 'Maybe she met with him earlier, administered the drug and then tailed his car in her own. When he crashed the car, she climbed out of her vehicle and made sure that he bled out, or blocked his airways to speed things up.'

'Or maybe,' said Will, who delights in playing devil's advocate, 'maybe it was more innocent than that. Maybe Julie West was a passenger in the car and she fled on foot after the accident because she was afraid her husband would find out she was with her ex-boyfriend.'

'It's unlikely,' Dennis responded. 'We would have found more fingerprints if she'd been in the car for any amount of time. Prints on the safety belt, for example. Not to mention traces of her blood. Not to mention traces of her blood. If she'd been in the car when the accident happened then she would have been seriously injured, given the speed at which the vehicle was travelling when it hit the tree. The physical evidence we have indicates only that Julie West was present at the scene of the accident. That's all. It's up to you guys to figure out how she was involved in Henderson's death. And why. Because one thing is for sure, this was no ordinary car accident.'

'What do you think?' said Will, looking at me. 'Should we bring her in for questioning?'

'There's too much we don't know yet.' I shook my head. 'We need to find out more about her relationship with Henderson. Were they in touch recently? And did she have access to scopolamine? Let's not show our hand before we have to.'

'Come on, Mel,' said Will. 'This woman is tied up in the death of two people. She was the last person to see her husband's first wife alive. And now we find out she was at the scene of her exboyfriend's fatal car accident, in which he crashed a car into a tree while loaded with a near-fatal dose of a rare hallucinogen.'

'You don't need to convince me, Will,' I said. 'The trouble is that, as things stand, everything we have with regard to Julie West's involvement in the Henderson case is circumstantial. It would be a hell of a thing to prove murder, given it looks like a car accident. That's reasonable doubt right there.'

'You're right,' Will conceded. 'We're on a stronger footing with the Laura West murder. I'm really starting to like Julie West for that case. She was having an affair with Matthew West. She wanted his wife out of the way. Not to mention his money. So she killed Laura West. A year later she is the second Mrs West, living in a palatial home and never having to work another day in her life. A jury would buy that in a second.'

'Except for the fact there's not a single piece of evidence that puts her at the scene of Laura West's murder, or ties her to the body,' I pointed out.

'It's kind of ironic, isn't it,' Will observed as we walked out of the garage. 'We have Julie West at the scene of Alexander Henderson's suspicious car accident, but we have no motive or definitive means of murder. On the other case, we can pin a motive and opportunity on Julie West for Laura West's murder, but we don't have any forensics to show that she did it.'

'And then there's the question of why she'd want her ex-boyfriend dead after all these years, a boyfriend she had around the time of Laura West's murder. It makes me think there's a connection between the two deaths,' I said.

'Scopolamine is not an easy drug to get hold of. Not in these quantities,' Dennis said. He set the alarm code for the garage and bent down to lock the door. 'It isn't sold on the street as a recreational drug. The killer would have bought it over the internet, maybe through multiple purchases over months to accumulate this quantity. There would be a paper trail.'

He popped a fresh piece of nicotine gum into his mouth.

'You're suggesting there was premeditation in the Henderson death,' I said. We walked down the driveway to our car. 'That Julie West planned Alexander Henderson's murder over a long period of time, hoping to use the scopolamine to kill him in what would look like a standard DUI car accident. If she was that thorough, then Laura West's murder was probably equally well planned.'

'That's exactly what I'm saying,' said Dennis. 'It seems to me that Julie West plans meticulously. If we can find evidence that she planned Laura West's murder then that may be enough to build a case against her with what we already have, even if we never have forensic evidence that ties her to Laura West's body.'

'Or,' I said, 'it might be enough to get her into an interview room and push her into telling us herself.'

CHAPTER FORTY-FOUR

Julie

The first notes of Tchaikovsky fill the studio. The girls stand in a row at the barre, in position for their warm-up routine. Emily walks along the line of miniature ballerinas in pink leotards calling out each step in a lilting voice that rises over the music.

Alice's face is almost comical as she sinks into a grand plié. I rummage in my bag for my phone to photograph her. By the time I find it, the hilarious expression has disappeared. I take a photograph anyway. Alice looks so pretty in her leotard.

'And a one, two, three,' Emily calls out. She is dressed in a dusty pink slip dress she wears over tights. Her hair is pinned at the top of her head. Emily moves gracefully among her students as she straightens their backs and moulds their feet into position, all the while whispering words of encouragement. There are bruises under her eyes from lack of sleep. It's from all the late nights or early mornings she's spent in bed with my husband. She tried to disguise them with concealer but the harsh studio lights are ruthless.

It can't be easy, studying a graduate degree in psychology and teaching ballet, all while having an affair with a married man.

Poor thing, I think to myself. She might have to drop one of her extracurricular activities. I look up to see her lifting her leg into an arabesque and holding it while the girls copy her, with various levels of success.

The reality is that even tired and run-down, Emily is exquisitely beautiful. She stands on her toes with her leg extended under the adoring gaze of the starstruck girls, their faces filled with genuine awe.

As a mother, I appreciate Emily's teaching ability and the connection she has built with my daughter. As the wife of the man she's screwing, I have no sympathy.

Beneath her ethereal smile, Emily's ambitious. Emily is greedy. Emily covets. Emily needs to learn a lesson. I've come to the conclusion that a sprinkle of glass in her bed isn't going to be enough to get my message across.

When dance class finishes, I wait with the other mothers by the studio doors for the girls to come out. Alice is the last to leave the room. Emily remains inside the studio, packing up while an unruly line of kids in karate uniforms wait by the door for their class to begin.

'You were great, honey,' I tell Alice as we walk down the corridor towards reception.

Alice's white button-down jacket is on the coat rack by the entrance. I hand it to her and then kneel down to untie the ribbons of her ballet shoes. I slip them off her feet, wrap the satin ribbon around both shoes and slide them into my handbag. Next to my gun.

I deliberately take my time helping Alice button up her thick coat so that I can synchronise our departure with Emily's. From the corner of my eye I see that she is behind the reception desk, changing her shoes. By the time we're ready to go, Emily is ready too. She leaves the dance school right behind us. Just the way I'd planned.

'Would you like a ride home?' I ask Emily when we're on the street. A gust of wind blows a piece of trash across the sidewalk, right past our legs.

'It's nice of you to offer, but really, I'll be fine,' she answers, watching the trash roll around like a tumbleweed.

'It's no trouble. We go that way anyway,' I respond with a smile. My heart beats fast. I try not to sound too pushy, but I have to get Emily into my car.

'That would be great,' she says after a brief hesitation. She wears a long scarf wrapped around her neck.

When we're in the car, I pass Alice a hot chocolate that I've kept warm for her in a thermos. It's a standard hot chocolate except I've added a liquid antihistamine for children. It will make her sleep. I told the pharmacist we were flying to London for a wedding and I wanted my daughter to sleep on the plane. I don't usually give Alice medicine unnecessarily, but I'm giving her a half dose, less than the recommended amount. Tonight, just tonight, I need Alice out of the way for a short while. I need her to sleep while I do what needs to be done.

Alice sips the hot chocolate as I pull out of the parking spot. The rush hour traffic is thinning as we cross the main intersection and head towards the university district.

'Mom, the hot chocolate tastes weird,' complains Alice from the back.

'It's a new flavour,' I tell her. 'Limited edition. Drink it up and if you still don't like it then I won't buy it again.'

I turn on music. Light jazz. It keeps me relaxed. It keeps Emily unaware. In my rear-view mirror I see that Alice is fast asleep in the back seat, still holding the flask.

I ask Emily about her studies as if I know nothing about her. In reality, I know so many of her secrets. Too many. She says she is studying a masters in psychology.

'Why psychology?' I ask. I signal left. The clicking of the indicator seems to mimic my rapid heartbeat. 'Psychology is very different from ballet.'

'I've always felt that, to be a better dancer, I need to understand the motivations of the various roles that I dance. Like Odile from *Swan Lake*,' she explains. 'Studying psychology has helped me deepen my performances. I've always been fascinated by the internal workings of a person's mind.'

'Funny you should say that,' I say, taking a sharp right a little too quickly so that she is thrust to the side by the turn. 'My husband Matt often says that too. Word for word. He's a psychology professor at the university. Matthew West. Do you know him?'

'Oh,' she says, swallowing. Her face burns. 'You're Professor West's wife. I didn't realise.' She says it clumsily, as if her tongue has gone numb.

'Yes, I am.' I say nothing for a while. I want her to squirm. I can sense the tension in her body as the reality of her predicament hits her. It must be excruciating. Taking a ride with her lover's wife. I can almost hear her counting the seconds until we get to her apartment. I locked the doors when we got into the car. She has no way out except through me.

I drive slowly past a row of houses that are indistinguishable in the dark except for the golden glow of lit-up windows. We head along the main road that leads to the university. Her tension eases as I turn towards the off-campus student apartments. As we approach her street, I speed up and drive past it.

'Oh, I think you missed my street,' she tells me in a nervous voice.

I ignore her and keep driving until I make a sharp turn down the entrance of Kellers Way. It's pitch dark here. The canopy of trees blocks out the faint light from the half moon. I turn on my high beams as I drive slowly down the steep hillside.

'So tell me, Emily,' I say. 'How long have you been sleeping with my husband?'

'I don't know what you're talking about,' she says. Her voice quivers.

'Honey, he's practically moved into your apartment. His clothes are in your closet. He has his own shelf in your bathroom cupboard. My God, you've even bought his favourite breakfast cereal.'

She flinches as if I've hit her. From the corner of my eye, I see her fingers creep towards the door handle until she is surreptitiously trying to open the car door. It holds fast thanks to the central locking. When she realises she is locked in the car, she tries to open the door again. This time desperately.

'Look, Mrs West, Julie.' She turns towards me. 'I don't know why you think I've had an affair with your husband but it's not true. He's my lecturer. Nothing more and nothing less.'

She sounds so sincere. I admire her acting ability. She's a wonderful liar. Convincing. Charming. I might have believed her too if I hadn't seen the evidence with my own eyes.

'If that's the case,' I say, looking ahead of me as I navigate the dark road, 'why was he at your apartment this morning?'

'Professor West wasn't at my apartment,' she says in a pathetic whiny tone that makes me want to smack her.

'Professor West,' I mock her prissy inflections. 'I bet you don't call him that in bed. Don't lie to me, Emily. I've been watching you for weeks. I know everything there is to know about you.'

I turn my SUV off the road and into a thicket of bushes at the bottom of the slope. When we are at a stop, I turn off the engine. There's a ravine around here. It floods sometimes but not at this time of the year. Alice is asleep. I twist around to take the thermos from her sleeping hands and put a heavy blanket over her still figure. I open her passenger window a fraction to let in fresh air.

'You and I, Emily, need to have a long talk.' I release my safety belt. It clicks open. 'I hope you're wearing good walking shoes,' I say as I jump out of the driver's seat.

I walk around to her door.

'Get out,' I order.

'Please,' Emily begs. 'Let's talk in here. It's cold out.'

'Get out.' She doesn't budge. I take the pistol from my purse and point it at her chest. The blood drains from her already pale face.

'Walk,' I tell her.

Emily climbs out reluctantly. She turns towards me with her palms outstretched. Pleading. How long have I wanted to see her begging for forgiveness? I get no pleasure out of it. It's a survival mechanism. She's not really sorry. Emily has no remorse.

'Please don't do this.' Emily sobs. The crunching of dead leaves under our feet is the only sound as we walk deep into the forest.

CHAPTER FORTY-FIVE

Mel

The baseball club barbecue was held near the bleachers of the school's baseball field, where a kids versus parents match was underway. The parents not playing baseball were helping at the drinks table or barbecuing meat on a long gas grill. I had arrived late, following a drawn-out discussion with Will and the district attorney about our next steps, now that Julie West was emerging as the prime suspect in both cases.

Sammy beamed when he saw me standing at the grill in a green apron, holding oversized barbecue tongs. It was the first team barbecue I'd attended in ages. So I was not at all pleased when, ten minutes later, my phone started vibrating like crazy in my pocket. I answered the phone, holding it against my ear with my shoulder while I turned over half-cooked sausages.

It was Dennis, from the lab. I couldn't hear him properly over the sizzling of two hundred sausages and hamburgers on the grill. 'I'll call you back in a second, Dennis,' I told him. I asked someone to take over my section of the grill and scuttled off to an empty bleacher to call him back.

'I'm at my kids' baseball barbecue. What's going on?'

'Sorry,' said Dennis. He didn't sound sorry. He sounded elated. 'An item we found by Laura West's grave was sent to the FBI lab for further analysis, and we just received the results. You're not going to want to wait until tomorrow to hear this.'

I didn't have time to play twenty questions while I still had a pile of sausages and hamburgers to grill. Aside from getting dirty looks from the woman who'd taken over my section of the barbecue, Joe was glaring at me from the field, where he was playing first base. Things between us were better, but delicate. I didn't want to let my kids down by spending the evening on the phone dealing with work.

'I have thirty seconds, Dennis. Spit it out.'

'We found a torn piece of a disposable glove in the soil at the scene,' he said rapidly. 'There was a partial print on the inside of the latex that, incredibly, withstood the ravages of time. But it was too small and too faded for us to do a proper analysis. I sent it to a friend at the FBI lab three weeks ago. He got back to me this evening to say that it's a match.'

'A match for whom?' I put up a finger in Joe's direction so he'd know I'd get off the line in a second. I'd promised the boys not only to take them to the barbecue but to help out and mingle with the other parents. My kids deserved my undivided attention for two lousy hours. There were too many school events and sports meets that I missed.

'The prints are a match for Julie West. My FBI pal assures me there's no doubt. The only problem is that the forensics probably won't stand up in court. The technique they used is new. A defence attorney would drive a truck through it on the stand. But my pal says it's accurate. He swears by it, Mel.' The words tumbled out of Dennis's mouth.

I couldn't blame him for being excited. It was the biggest break in the case. We had motive. We had opportunity. And now, we had evidence Julie West was present at the crime scene.

'Great,' I said, trying not to emulate Dennis's euphoria. There was still a long, tough road ahead until we got an indictment. 'I'll talk with Will about our next move.'

'Hey Mom.' Sammy sat down next to me on the bleacher as I hung up the call. He dipped his head in the way he does when he's disappointed but doesn't want to show it. 'It's all good, Sam.' I squeezed his shoulder. 'Let's go cook some sausages.'

I texted Will while I barbecued the rest of the sausages and six dozen hamburger patties. The kids scoffed them down in five minutes flat.

Will and I decided that we'd head over to the Wests' house straight after the barbecue. I kept quiet until after ice-creams were served and people started making noises about heading home. That's when I told the boys I needed to drop them at home and go to work.

'C'mon Mom,' said Sammy. 'Nobody's leaving yet. Everyone's staying until much later.'

In the end, I arranged for Jason Scott's parents to drop them at home. Our regular sitter would meet them at the house and ensure they went to bed on time because I had no idea when I would be getting back. The Scotts lived at the end of our street so it wasn't out of their way. I'd really hoped to go home to change and wash out the grilled-sausage smoke in my hair before heading to the Wests' house, but I was running late and there wasn't enough time.

'Why do you smell of cooked meat?' Will asked when I picked him up in the police car park.

'Dinner,' I said 'For about sixty hungry baseball players!'

I sprayed myself with a perfume to mask the smell of barbecue when we parked outside Matthew West's house. It did nothing to make me feel less grimy.

'Let's do this,' said Will as we climbed out of the car. It was pitch dark, but someone was home. The driveway gates were wide open and a car was parked outside the garage.

While I'd been barbecuing, Will had convinced the prosecutor at the DA's office that we had enough evidence for an arrest warrant and a search warrant. The plan was that we'd ask Julie West to come willingly back to the station for a discussion but, if she didn't agree, the judge would have the warrants signed by 9 p.m. at the latest, after his weekly squash game. The prosecutor's office was sending an attorney over to the judge's fitness club with the documents drawn up and a black pen at the ready for his signature.

I knocked on the stained glass panel next to the Wests' front door. A light immediately turned on inside, followed by footsteps in the hall. There was a loud click as the bolt opened. Matthew West looked expectant and then disappointed when he saw us.

Under the bright light of the hall chandelier his face was flecked with worry.

'Thank God you're here,' he said, running his hands nervously through his hair. 'Julie and Alice haven't come home. Julie's not picking up her cellphone. Her phone and the car's GPS tracking have been turned off.'

'Were they supposed to be out?' asked Will.

'Yes, Julie said something about trying out a new ballet school.

But they should have been home by now. I have a bad feeling,' he said, swallowing hard, 'that Julie may have taken Alice.'

'Why would she take Alice?' I asked.

'Julie's had anxiety issues. It's become worse since Laura's body was found. She doesn't sleep. She has memory lapses. She's constantly jealous. And she's erratic. One minute she's hyper. An hour later she can barely move.' He checked his watch. 'They're almost an hour late.' He rubbed the back of his neck with his hand as he led us into his study.

'Is Julie getting therapy?' I asked when we were sitting on the expensive leather couch in his dimly lit study. He poured himself a drink with trembling hands.

'Julie wouldn't see a therapist,' he said. 'God knows I tried to get her to see someone. I've been doing everything I can to help her. I'm clinically trained. Our family doctor has been prescribing her medications, but she doesn't always take them. I never thought Julie would lay a finger on Alice. She adores her. But she's been so irrational lately; paranoid at times. I should have never left Julie alone with Alice. I should have seen the signs.' His voice was raw.

'We'll need a complete list of the medications your wife is on and any medical records,' said Will. 'Before you do that, please write down your wife's cellphone number, the licence plate number of her car and her credit card numbers.' Will handed him his notebook. 'We'll run the numbers through our system and trace them if she turns on her phone or uses a credit card.'

'There's something else,' said Matt, as he wrote out his wife's cell number.

'What?'

'After our conversation about insurance I realised that I'd been lax, so I had all our jewellery assessed by my insurer. One of the pieces was a diamond pendant that Julie inherited from her grand-mother. Anyway, I received a letter from the jewellery assessor this afternoon suggesting the diamond in Julie's pendant was the diamond from Laura's engagement ring. Laura was wearing that ring when she disappeared. I immediately contacted the assessor to tell him there was a mistake.'

'What did he say?' asked Will.

'He said he's certain it's the same diamond. I can't believe I'm saying this,' said Matthew, almost to himself. He took a deep breath. 'I think that Julie might have killed Laura.'

CHAPTER FORTY-SIX

Julie

I walk with the barrel of my gun pressed into Emily's back. We stumble into the darkness of the forest with only a thin beam of light from my torch to show us the way.

'Keep walking,' I order. Her shoulders heave as she weeps silently.

Our bodies are pressed together as if we're a single being. I get a whiff of the familiar honeysuckle scent of Emily that's infused my marriage for so long. The scent is different tonight though; it's mixed with fear, and the pungent earthy odour of the forest.

I shove the gun between her shoulder blades. She flinches. I could end this with a gentle squeeze of the trigger. Ever so softly. And it would all be over. The temptation is overwhelming.

We reach a clearing. Emily's tired, barely able to stand. Her legs are trembling violently. From the cold? From fright? I don't know. I care even less.

'Stop here.' She turns to face me, uncertain but compliant.

Emily's pale, fragile face reminds me of a doe the moment after it's shot, when the realisation it's dying clouds its eyes and the pupils flicker in terror at the unknown.

'Please don't hurt me,' Emily whispers. 'I don't want to die.' An owl hoots somewhere in the forest. She jumps in fright.

I almost feel sorry for her as she cowers in fear, shivering uncontrollably. She's pitiful now that she's in my territory, under my control. My senses are at their peak. Adrenalin pumps through me. I'm finally taking back my life. Did Emily really think that I was going to sit back and allow her to destroy it all?

I take off my jacket and throw it to Emily. 'Put it on,' I tell her. 'It'll keep you warm.'

She puts on the jacket with a confused expression. She's not sure how to interpret my gesture.

'Sit down,' I order abruptly. When she fails to respond, I push her down onto a pile of leaves. I sit opposite her, cross-legged like a high-school camper. The forest is my natural habitat. I'm not afraid of the dark or the shadows. My whole life with Matt has been filled with shadows, and deception. His deception. And mine.

'Tell me, Emily.' I hear sobbing. I'm surprised when I realise the sobs are mine.

'Why Matt? Why did you have to go after him?'

'I didn't go after him,' she says. 'There's nothing between us. Please believe me.' Her voice rises in hysteria.

Her words take me back to when I was a student. To Matt's sudden interest in my work. Extra study sessions. Mentoring. His warm breath against my neck as he leaned over to point out a line in a textbook. I felt flattered by his interest. Intoxicated by him.

'Stop blaming everyone but yourself, Emily!' I shout so suddenly that it makes her jump. 'You played a part in this too. It wasn't just him.'

'Please, I swear to you,' she says, tears streaming down her face. 'There's nothing between us. I have a boyfriend, Charlie. We're talking about getting married. I'm not having an affair with Professor West. I swear it.'

'*I'm not having an affair with Professor West,*' I mimic her prissy, entitled voice. 'Enough games, Emily.' I'm composed again. I speak so quietly that she strains to hear me.

'I can prove it,' she says. 'Look at my phone.'

I train my gun on her as she opens her purse and throws me her phone. She tells me the passcode and I unlock the phone.

'Look at the photos from this morning. Last night.' Her voice is laced with desperation.

I scroll through her photo folder. There is a series of shots of Emily with a man, mid-twenties, light brown hair, round silver glasses. Definitely not Matt. The photos document their evening at a restaurant last night, right down to a picture of a dessert plated up in layers of luminous colour.

I scroll to the next set of photos, back at her apartment where there's a selfie of the two of them on the couch, arms around each other. The next photo is of Charlie sleeping bare-chested next to her in bed. I recognise the floral sheets. I check the date of the photo. She's telling the truth. It was taken this morning.

I scroll through her text messages. She's been messaging 'Charlie' all day, flirty messages filled with emojis.

'How long have you been together?' I think back to the times I parked my car outside her apartment at night and watched the silhouette of a man through the drawn, illuminated blinds. I assumed it was Matt.

'We've been together for almost five months, but we've kept it low-key because he wanted to break up with his old girlfriend in person. She's in Seattle. He shares an apartment with roommates, but he spends most nights with me. I swear I'm not having an affair with your husband. He's my professor, and my faculty advisor. I would never do that. Professor West,' she looks suddenly embarrassed, 'he's a lot older than me.'

I turn my head as we both hear rustling in the bushes. It's from squirrels or raccoons scampering up a tree in search of food. 'Please let me go,' she says, following my glance. 'I don't blame you for being upset. I would be angry too if I thought my husband was cheating on me.'

She looks at me expectantly to see if her words have worked. Ever the psychology student.

'Please,' she begs as I remain silent and impassive. 'I'm really scared. I don't want to die.'

I look at us as if I am watching from above. Two women in a forest clearing. Me with a loaded gun pointed at her head. Emily terrified that she is about to die. What has Matthew done to me? What have I become?

'Nobody is going to die,' I tell her. I am not yet sure what to do. Or how I will keep that promise. I know Matt is having an affair with someone. If not Emily then who?

I stand over Emily's huddled frame. I have the power to determine her fate. And my own. I know what I have to do.

'You can go,' I tell her. She looks at me, uncomprehending. 'Go.' I toss her the car keys. They fall onto the ground next to her. 'All I ask in return is that you take care of Alice. Make sure she's safe.'

Emily bends to pick up the keys. She takes a first hesitant step in the direction that I gesture towards with my gun, back to the car. She takes another step and another until she disappears through the trees. I turn in the other direction.

CHAPTER FORTY-SEVEN

Julie

I navigate through the forest as if I was born in this wilderness. The nocturnal hum of animals and night-birds foraging for food rises into a crescendo that eventually drowns out everything, even the police sirens wailing in the distance.

I work my way across the forest using instinct and occasionally the light of the moon when it creeps through the foliage. I jump over logs and run through thick brush. I trip more times than I care to count. My clothes get torn, thorns scratch my skin and draw blood. When a chopper hovers low over the forest, I press myself against the rough bark of an oak tree until the harsh spotlight of the chopper moves in the opposite direction.

I make my way to the edge of the forest and enter familiar territory. I can see into our house from my hiding place in the brush. It looks naked and exposed with the curtains wide open and the rooms lit up. I watch uniformed police rifle through my cupboards and carry boxes from my bedroom to the downstairs hall. A female and a male cop come onto the patio, where they spread a map across the table and hold a heated discussion. They both wear navy bomber jackets with 'Police' written in yellow letters. Even in the dark, I recognise the woman. She's the detective who came to the house to question me. I can't hear what they're saying over the deafening cacophony of cicadas.

I sit with my back against a tree and drift off. When I wake, the house is dark and quiet. I walk in the shadows towards the back gate, which has blown off its hook in the wind. Matt should be more careful. The deer will tear up the flowerbeds by morning.

I collect my spare key from under a pot plant, soundlessly unlock the French doors and slip inside. The house is dark except for a strip of light under Matt's study door. I open it to find him sitting like a statue on the brown leather sofa. He is drinking a double bourbon, neat, with the open bottle on the floor next to him. The flush across his face tells me this is far from his first drink.

'Sit down,' he says unsteadily, tapping his hand on the seat next to him. I obey. I don't know why. Force of habit, I guess.

'The police think you did it,' he slurs.

'Did what?' I ask in a shaky voice.

'Killed Laura.' He says it so matter-of-factly that it makes me flinch.

'Why would they think such a thing, Matt?' I ask as a wave of nausea rushes up my throat. We sit so close that I can smell the stink of alcohol on his breath.

'You're asking the wrong question, Julie.' He talks to me like a grade-school teacher lecturing a failing student. 'The correct question is: why *wouldn't* the police think that?'

Matt pauses to let me contemplate the implications of his words.

'Julie, you had an affair with me while I was married to Laura.

That would give you a pretty good motive to kill Laura. Don't you think? If that's not enough, you were the last person to see Laura alive. And you have no alibi.'

'That's not evidence of murder, Matt,' I defend myself, trying to rationalise the irrational.

'Don't worry about the evidence, my darling,' he says, patting my cheek with his hand. 'There's no shortage of evidence.'

'I didn't kill Laura!' I snap. 'Matt, you must know that.'

'How can you be so sure, Julie?' Matt challenges me. 'Most days you can barely remember your own name.'

I recoil at his cruelty. 'I know that I didn't kill Laura,' I insist.

'Come on, Julie,' says Matt. 'You had everything to do with Laura's murder.'

'That's not true, Matt.'

'Think back, Julie,' he commands. 'Your boyfriend Alex found Laura hiding in the boathouse down by the lake. Alex put her in a chokehold and squeezed her carotid artery until she was dead. You held her feet so she'd stop kicking.'

He lifts my chin so that I look at him as he speaks.

'You cried afterwards, Julie. You'd never killed anyone before. The two of you put Laura's body in the trunk of your car and drove to Kellers Way to bury her. You and Alex struggled to dig your shovels into the hard earth. When you returned to your apartment before dawn to shower, you had to scrub your hands until they bled to get the soil out from under your fingernails.'

'No!' I cut him off, putting my hands over my ears to block out his voice. 'That's not what happened. I *did not* kill Laura. Stop saying that I did. You're confusing me.'

'Julie.' He bends his head to look into my downcast eyes. 'It's time to admit the truth.'

'It's not true,' I protest as tears stream down my face. 'It can't be true. I would never kill someone. You must know it wasn't me, Matt.' I rummage around in my mind for facts to back up my assertion. 'You would never have allowed me near Alice if you'd thought I was capable of murder.'

'Everyone's capable of murder,' he says, 'if there's a good enough reason. Did you, Julie? Did you have a good enough reason?'

I think of everything that I gained from Laura's murder; her husband, her child, her house. They all became mine.

Maybe Matt's right. Maybe I did kill Laura. I lean forward with my head in my hands. I force myself to remember, to break through my muddled mind.

'I was with Alex that night.' I talk slowly as the memories flood back. 'We stayed in. He watched a movie. I studied for a mid-year exam.'

'Your story is hardly convincing, given the police believe you killed Alex as well. Your alibi witness is the very person they think you killed.' He laughs at my discomfort.

'It was you?' I say softly. He is silent as he observes me over the rim of his tumbler. 'You borrowed my car to drive to the conference. You said your car was being fixed. That's why I was stuck at home that weekend. In the middle of the night, you drove my car back to the lake house where Laura was staying, killed her, and buried her in the forest at Kellers Way. Just the way you described it a moment ago to get me to believe that I did it.'

'Surely you can do better than that, Julie,' says Matt. 'Who would believe such a preposterous story? And with no evidence to support it. Not a shred. Plus I have an alibi. I was with another woman that night, a married woman who has no incentive to lie on my behalf. Chelsea's already vouched for me to the police.'

'You drugged Chelsea, Matt. The way you drugged me. Chelsea probably has no idea if you were lying in bed with her that night or not. You fucked with her head as well as the rest of her.'

'No,' he says, examining the amber liquid sloshing around in his glass. 'Chelsea was never susceptible to suggestion. Not like you. You were amazing. I added and subtracted memories from your mind the way I might edit a blog. Your grandmother's pendant, for example. It was the only thing of value that you brought into our marriage. You treasured it. It was embarrassing the way you told anyone who complimented you that it belonged to your beloved grandma who died when you were five.'

'Grandma used to tell me that it had been in our family for generations,' I say stiffly. 'It's all that I have left of her.'

'That's very sweet, Julie. But none of it is true,' says Matt, slinging his arm behind my back as if we're at a cinema on date night. 'Your grandmother was a drunk who'd been reported to child services half a dozen times. I'm surprised the authorities let you stay with her for so long. Julie, I planted those warm nostalgic memories of your grandma, and her diamond pendant. I'm sorry to tell you that your grandmother didn't leave you a damn thing except psychological scars that made you clingy and gave you a fear of abandonment.'

I close my eyes and remember my grandmother giving me a homemade cookie and gently brushing a stray hair off my forehead before sending me into the garden to play. I'd been three or four at the time. Was Matt right? Did this cherished moment never happen?

'Why are you hurting me like this, Matt?' I ask. 'Why are you saying such terrible things?'

'I'm telling you the truth,' he says. 'You should thank me for being so honest. I'll tell you something else. Your grandmother's diamond is identical to the one in Laura's engagement ring. The one that went missing when she died. And when I say identical, I mean it's the exact same stone. That, by the way, Julie, will be one of the most damning pieces of evidence at your murder trial.'

'You deliberately led the police to think that I'm a murderer, Matt?'

'Better you than me, darling,' he whispers into my ear so softly that I wonder if I've imagined it. He rubs his thumb over my wrist. 'Don't hold it against them. The police are only doing their job. They're following the evidence. And the trail leads straight to you, Julie. I made sure of that.'

CHAPTER FORTY-EIGHT

Julie

Matt puts his arm around me slowly and sensuously, pulling us together in an intimate embrace. Confusion and then relief wash over me at his sudden gentleness after all that venom. Maybe Matt was testing me. Maybe it was the drink that made him say all those poisonous, hurtful things.

He slides his arm across my body and rests his hand gently at the nape of my neck. I allow myself to succumb to his heady scent, so achingly familiar after all these years of marriage. My senses are aroused by his soft touch and the warmth of his body pressed against me.

I sigh in relief. Everything will be alright between us. Without warning, Matt wraps his arm around my throat and pulls me to him in a deadly chokehold. I gasp as I struggle for oxygen. I kick my legs. In vain. A wave of black washes over me. Just as I think that I'm about to die, he eases the pressure around my throat and the darkness recedes. I open my eyes and look straight into his. His expression of curiosity reminds me of a child patiently watching to see how long it takes for an insect to die.

'When I killed Laura, I was filled with regret. I was upset that she'd put me in that position in the first place.' His voice is so soft that I have to strain to hear him. 'My emotions are more mixed when it comes to you.'

'Why would you kill Laura?' I ask in a raspy voice that is almost inaudible. 'She was the love of your life.'

'Unfortunately, Laura didn't leave me much choice.' His lips are so close that I feel them rub against my skin as he whispers into my ear. 'Laura and I were collaborating on memory research. Then suddenly she had a change of heart. She didn't want to go as far as I did with implanting false memories of childhood trauma. She said it was unethical.

'I continued the study at the local community college without her, using students enrolled there as test subjects. Simple people who didn't ask too many questions. People like you. Laura found out that I was still working on the research. She threatened to report me to the ethics board. To get me fired. Me, her husband!' he says in outrage. 'That's why she went to the lake house that weekend. She was going to divorce me and file for custody of Alice. I'd have lost everything: my career, my reputation, my daughter. And why? Because Laura thought she was too good to work with me. That my research was beneath her.'

He picks up the half-empty bottle of bourbon on the floor and takes a swig straight from the bottle. He offers me a sip. The gesture seems incongruous in the circumstances.

'Laura thought she was smarter than me. I showed her that she was wrong.'

I run my tongue nervously over my dry lips. 'What about me?' I ask. 'Why are you doing this to me?'

'For the same reason as Laura. I don't have much choice.' He lightly runs his fingers over my neck as he speaks. A knot of fear tightens in my stomach as I brace myself for another assault. 'You were the most exquisitely beautiful woman that I'd ever seen, Julie. My own personal Helen of Troy. There was a time when I had to have you, regardless of the consequences.'

He lowers his head to kiss my neck. I try to wriggle out of his grip but he holds me firm, his arm still around my throat. I strain under the pressure of his body while he runs his lips across my skin.

'We had good times, didn't we Julie? You remember them, don't you? Our honeymoon in Antigua. Our vacations by the beach, collecting shells with Alice, walks along the sand in front of that quaint little beach house on stilts that we used to rent. Those memories were real. Well, most of them were real.' He shrugs. 'And if they weren't, does it really matter? They felt real to you. At the end of the day, that's what counts.'

He shoves me hard against the sofa and tightens his chokehold until the pressure is so great that I feel myself falling into a vortex. He loosens his grip and I am conscious again. I open my eyes to see him watching me with amusement. He's enjoying his game of pushing me to the brink of death and then bringing me back to life.

'I hope you won't think me callous if I tell you that I set up everything so that if Laura's body was ever found, the police would have enough evidence to arrest you. It wasn't personal. I needed to pin it on someone. I thought you'd make the perfect suspect,' says Matt.

'You were the last person to see Laura alive. Except for me, of course. After her horseback riding lesson Laura went to the lake house. I made sure her phone battery was dying and broke her charger. She fell asleep on the couch thanks to sedatives I'd put in the carton of milk in the lake house fridge. I knew she was a creature of habit and would make an afternoon coffee the minute she arrived. The car headlights probably woke her when I reached the lake house after midnight. Eventually I found her in the boat-house, hiding in the rowboat under a canvas cover. Killing her was the easy part. It was getting rid of her body that was difficult. She was still warm when I put her into the trunk of your little Hyundai and drove down to Kellers Way. The ground there was harder to dig up than I'd expected. Winter came early that year. I dropped into the grave a torn piece of a disposable cleaning glove with your fingerprint on it, taken from your kitchen trash.'

'You framed me for Laura's murder from the start?' I whisper.

'It turned out to be unnecessary,' he says. 'I had a stroke of luck when that serial killer, Pitt, confessed to murdering Laura. He thought he'd get money out of it. The case was closed. The coroner even gave me a body burned beyond recognition. I happened to know it was the wrong body, but I buried it anyway and put an Italian marble tombstone on top. Laura would have liked it. I played the grieving widower for a while so the gossips wouldn't talk. And then I married you. I wanted you badly in those days, Julie. You were my obsession. Plus Alice needed a mother, and you were excep-tional in that regard. You have a wonderful way with children, Julie. It's a shame you were never able to have any of your own.'

My face stings as if he's slapped me.

'Marrying you wasn't a terrible sacrifice on my part, Julie.' He lifts up my chin again. 'You were exquisite, flawless in those days. I don't regret our marriage. You shouldn't either.'

'All these years. Everything we shared was based on lies and deceit. And murder,' I say, shaking uncontrollably. 'Our marriage was a sham.'

'Sham is too strong a word. Admittedly, it did get boring after a while. I met someone, of course. Not that silly little student you abducted tonight. The police told me all about that when they brought Alice home. No, I fell in love with someone else. She's smart. Not Laura smart, but smart enough. And very beautiful, though perhaps not as beautiful as you were in those days. She's young, too. We'll have children together. I want more kids. You weren't much help in that regard. I realised a while ago that it was time to move on. There was one thing in the way.'

'Me,' I complete his thought. 'You wanted to get rid of me so you could marry someone else.'

'When a man's first wife is murdered, it's highly suspicious if his second wife dies unnaturally as well. One has to be patient. And when one finally does get around to it, one needs to make it look like something else. An accident, perhaps. That's where your old beau Alex Henderson came in.'

'You sent Alex to kill me?' My voice catches as I recall his car swerving off the road towards me. It was as if the driver was deliberately hunting me down.

'He wasn't the first,' Matt says. 'It turns out that it's very hard to kill you, my sweet wife.'

He proves his point by tightening his grip around my neck again until I'm light-headed. He holds the pressure while he talks, keeping me on the edge of consciousness as he whispers into my ear.

'Alex's predecessor killed poor Roxy before Christmas, when it was supposed to be you who died in the hit-and-run. I felt bad about Roxy. I was fond of that dog. After that, I tracked down Alex. He needed money desperately. Like all reformed addicts it wasn't hard to get him using again, except the syringe I gave him that morning contained a drug that made him highly suggestible.'

I gasp in shock at the realisation the accident happened just the way I remembered. 'Alex warned me as he lay dying that I was in danger and I should get away. I should have listened to him.'

'I suppose even the scopolamine couldn't completely override his sense of decency,' Matt mutters. 'If Alex had survived the crash then he wouldn't have remembered a damn thing. Just like you don't remember anything half the time. Not your fault really. I've tried every psychoactive drug in the book on you. Even the occasional dose of scopolamine to wipe your memory and make you delusional.'

'You tried to kill me twice!' I rasp. I am overwhelmed by the implication of what he's told me. 'First when Roxy was killed and then when Alex tried to run me down in Kellers Way.'

'Three times actually,' says Matt, rubbing his hands on my neck menacingly. I am too afraid to move. 'I'm particularly proud of my third attempt. It was inspired. I took your asthma spray out of your bag the morning you went to the lake house and included a respiratory suppressant in your medication to trigger an asthma attack. I made sure to drain your phone battery that morning too so you wouldn't be able to call for help. If you had an asthma attack then you'd die a straightforward, natural death. Nothing suspicious about it. Just another terrible tragedy for poor Matthew West, who has suffered so much tragedy already.'

He tightens his arm around my neck again. I feel the warmth of his body underneath my own. I struggle to get out of his grip but he has me pinned. I can't move. The pressure on my throat is immense. As darkness engulfs me and my body falls limp, he eases the pressure and I'm back looking into his flawless blue eyes. He's like a cat cruelly playing with a half-dead mouse before he loses interest and goes in for the kill.

'Why?' I ask. 'Why did you want me dead? Why not divorce me?'

'Why?' he asks rhetorically. 'Divorce was never an option. Aside from crippling alimony, who knows what a woman scorned is capable of.'

'I wouldn't have done anything to hurt you, Matt,' I sob. 'I loved you.'

'Our marriage had nothing to do with love,' he scoffed. 'There was sex. The chemistry between us was amazing. But once it ran its course, I didn't want to waste my life staying married to you. You'd lost the vitality that attracted me to you in the first place, the breathtaking beauty. And let's face it, you were never my intellectual equal. Plus you knew too much, Julie, even if you didn't realise it.'

I try to squirm out of his grip but he pulls me back and tightens the pressure around my throat in a silent warning.

'The police were here for most of the night, searching for evidence that I carefully planted. Like the bag of scopolamine that killed Alex. You should have seen the look on the detective's face when he found the ziplock bag filled with powder in your underwear drawer this evening,' he says in a soft, silky voice. 'It was almost as priceless as the look on Laura's face when she realised that she was going to die.'

The paralysis that has gripped me is overtaken by a fierce rage. I turn my head and bite his arm until I taste blood. He groans in pain and loosens his grip. I elbow him hard in the solar plexus. He hisses and bends over in agony. I pull away from him and quickly remove my gun from my purse on the floor. I stand back and point the barrel at his chest with shaky hands.

'I'll tell the police everything I know,' I warn him. 'You'll spend the rest of your life in jail.'

'They'll never believe you,' he whispers through his agony. 'You don't have any evidence to prove it. All the evidence points to you.'

His words make my blood run cold. 'The police think that I'm a saint. It's you they want, Julie. It's you who has a documented history of mental instability. It's you who tried to kidnap and kill one of my students in a jealous rage. There's not a chance in hell they'll believe a word you say.'

I click the safety off my gun and aim at his chest with careful concentration. My arms are outstretched just the way I was taught. I remember the instructor's words. Squeeze the trigger gently and press your hands together as you fire.

'You were right earlier when you said you're not capable of murder,' he tells me. 'More than that, you'd never deprive Alice of her daddy. It would break her little heart.'

I count to three and close my eyes. When I open them Matt is watching me with the same unconcerned expression. I lower the gun. I can barely see through the tears.

'Go,' he orders. 'Get out of here. Tell the police about your terrible, murderous husband and his horrible crimes. Let's see if they believe you.'

I run into the hall and unlatch the front door. I step out onto the porch and walk down the pathway until I'm blinded by a spotlight shining straight into my eyes. There's shouting. I can't hear the words through the hum in my ears.

Within the red-and-blue glare of police car lights, I see the familiar face of the female detective. She's pointing a gun straight at me. I walk towards her with my gun by my side. I want to explain that there's been a terrible mistake. That I never killed Laura. Or Alex. Another spotlight fixes on me. The brightness is agonising. I lift my hand, holding the gun to shield my eyes from the blinding lights.

The detective shouts something. I ignore it. I'm tired of the noise.

A loud bang rings out. Another sharp crack follows. I look down and see my gun by my feet. A red stain spreads on my chest. Blood is such a beautiful colour, I think to myself, as my shirt turns crimson.

CHAPTER FORTY-NINE

Mel

The ticking of a clock high up on the wall echoed through the spartan, windowless interview room. I looked out at a metal door at the end of a long, empty corridor. The door opened with a clang. Julie West walked down the corridor towards me in an orange prison jumpsuit with her hands cuffed in front of her.

A female guard with cropped hair and a humourless face escorted her into the room. I was sitting at the end of a scuffed table. The guard attached Julie's handcuffs to metal loops screwed onto the other end of the table. She stood behind Julie with her legs slightly open and her hands behind her back.

I motioned with my head for the guard to leave. She didn't like it but she grudgingly went out of the room. Julie immediately straightened her shoulders. Her meekness was nothing more than the survival instinct of the incarcerated. I pushed a cup of water towards her.

'Thank you.' Julie picked up the cup with her cuffed hands and bent forward to drink thirstily. When she was finished, she looked at me expectantly. Her face was thin and sallow from too little sun-light in the many months she'd been locked up here. Her eyes were wary, more fearful than defiant.

'I read the transcripts you sent, of your sessions with your psychiatrist,' I told her.

'So you believe me?'

I shrugged. I'd come here out of curiosity. To hear what she had to say. That was all.

'Matt said all the evidence points to me. It was the perfect crime, you see,' she said.

'He's right,' I answered. 'All the evidence does point to you.'

On the drive over here, I had tried to reconfigure the case from her perspective. Since the night I shot Julie, I'd had an uneasy feeling. My gut instinct told me there was something unfinished. It was ridiculous. Even Will said so. The evidence was overwhelming. We'd rarely had such an ironclad case.

'That's exactly what bothers me about it,' I had told Will.

Will said my doubts were residual guilt from almost killing her. I had been the first to reach Julie after I shot her. She was splayed on the slate pathway with blood gushing from her chest. I used the full weight of my body to press down on the wounds to stem the bleeding.

She barely had a pulse when they put her in the ambulance. My hands and forearms were covered with her blood. Will said the shooting was by the book. Nobody could fault me. I wasn't so sure. Perhaps that's what brought me here.

'What is it exactly that you want from me, Julie?' I asked. 'I am not a defence attorney, or a private eye for hire. It's my job to put you behind bars and make sure the jury throws away the key.'

'I know that,' Julie said, looking down at her hands. 'But you wouldn't be here if you didn't believe there was at least some truth to my story. Would you?'

I looked into her bruised sky-blue eyes and said nothing. She was right. I wouldn't have driven all the way across the state to see her if I didn't have doubts about her guilt. I had the same doubts when I slipped into the back pew at the church to watch Matthew West marry his former research assistant, Kate. Her ivory bridal gown barely disguised her pregnancy. He inclined his head towards me as they left the chapel. It wasn't so much a greeting as a cocky salute. It left me with a feeling of disquiet.

'You claim you were with your boyfriend Alex on the night of Laura's murder,' I said to Julie. 'Was there nobody else with you that evening? A friend who dropped by for coffee? Anyone who can vouch for you?'

She shook her head. 'It was just Alex and me. Alex would have confirmed it if he was still alive.'

'Except he isn't alive,' I pointed out. 'Dead men don't make good alibi witnesses.'

That morning, before driving to the prison, I had read a report prepared by the court-appointed psychiatrist after a session he conducted not long after Julie's arrest. 'The patient exhibits delusional and paranoid tendencies that are exacerbated at times of deep emotional stress,' he'd written. The psychiatrist hired by her court-appointed defence attorney had submitted a contradictory report that described her mental health as normal. I wondered which shrink was right.

'What you didn't explain in the correspondence that you sent me is why you stalked Emily.'

'I don't understand it myself,' Julie told me. 'It was a compulsion. Whatever drugs my husband gave me made me manic. Made me fixate on Emily. I don't believe I'd have abducted Emily if Matt hadn't been feeding me pills.'

'Perhaps,' I said. 'But there's no evidence he gave you anything other than your prescription medicine. The medication we found in your bathroom cabinet and next to your bed does not create that type of mania.'

'Matt controlled my medications. He controlled my mood, my memory, even my personality, with all sorts of meds,' Julie said. 'He manipulated me for years.'

'He says that you were the one manipulating him, Julie. He calls you a pathological liar and a sociopath.' I sighed. 'Look, the evidence is against you. Worse, you have no credibility.'

'What do you mean?' She looked hurt.

'You kidnapped Emily at gunpoint and took her into the forest. Whether you meant to talk to her or to kill her is a moot point. To be realistic, I can't see how any attorney could get you off the hook. Let alone convict Matthew for Laura's murder, based only on your testimony and without any corroborating evidence.'

'I'm fine now that I'm off the medication,' Julie said, holding back tears. 'I've remembered things that could help you investigate him. That might incriminate him.'

'And then there's the murder of Laura West itself,' I continued. 'There's overwhelming physical evidence that you were involved. Your fingerprint was found on a torn piece of a disposable glove buried at the crime scene. You claim your husband planted it but there's no way to prove that. Your alibi witness, a former boy-friend who may have been an accomplice in Laura West's murder, was killed in suspicious circumstances. And there's considerable evidence that you may have been the one who killed him. Your husband, the person you claim killed Laura, was two hours' drive away having sex with a married woman. A woman who has since submitted an affidavit confirming his account, despite all the difficulties that may cause with her husband.' I paused to let her digest the overwhelming case against her. 'I'm sorry, there's no evidence that supports your version of events.'

'Yet here you are,' Julie said.

'Yet here I am,' I conceded.

'There's evidence if you look hard enough,' she said quietly.

'What evidence?'

'Matt thought he destroyed all the files on the memory research he did behind Laura's back, but he didn't. Alex kept copies at his aunt's house. The files prove that Matthew manipulated my memory. And that Laura was opposed to his research. That would give him a motive. Wouldn't it?' Julie said hopefully.

'Maybe,' I shrugged. 'I'll look into it.' I didn't want to give her false hope. I shouldn't even have been there. Despite my better judgement, I was there because something about this case had kept me up every night since I put two bullets in Julie West's chest.

'I have a question for you, Julie.'

'Go ahead,' she said.

'Did you kill Laura West?'

'No,' she said in a voice that was more weary then emphatic. Her eyes never left my own. I've spent my adult life looking into the eyes of murderers. When I looked into her anguished face that afternoon I didn't think that Julie West was a killer.

The guard opened the door. 'Time's up,' she bellowed. She removed Julie's handcuffs from the table with a loud metallic rattle.

'Thank you,' Julie said, turning her head in my direction as the guard guided her out of the room.

'For what?' I said. 'I haven't done anything yet.'

'For believing in me,' Julie said.

I was about to tell her that she was being premature. But the guard was already steering her towards her cell like she was a stray sheep being put back in her pen. When they reached the metal door at the end of the corridor, Julie turned to look at me one last time as if there was something else she wanted to tell me. The guard shoved her through the doorway before she could say a word.

She was right about one thing, I thought, as I drove along the state highway back home. If Matthew West did kill his wife then he committed the perfect crime.

Acknowledgements

It would have been impossible to have written this book if it had not been for my family, who gave me the time and space to immerse myself in my writing, and the fortitude to persevere through self-doubt and discouragement. *The Girl in Kellers Way* would almost certainly still be sitting in my desk drawer if not for Sarah Fairhall, who graciously read my manuscript and offered to publish the novel at a time when I was close to giving up. To Johannes Jakob and Ali Watts, I wish to extend my deepest appreciation for the unsung and meticulous work of all great editors and publishers, and for their encouragement and guidance. Thank you to Chloe Davies, Louise Ryan and the rest of the Penguin Random House Australia team for championing my work. While writing this book, I delved into research on memory that was both fascinating and at times unsettling. Of note was the work into the malleability of memory by Dr Elizabeth F. Loftus, who has been a leader in memory research for decades.